VANISHING LOVE

Vanishing Love

A novel
by

JOSEPH REILLY

Adelaide Books
New York / Lisbon
2020

VANISHING LOVE
A novel
By Joseph Reilly

Copyright © by Joseph Reilly
Cover design © 2020 Adelaide Books

Published by Adelaide Books, New York / Lisbon
adelaidebooks.org

Editor-in-Chief
Stevan V. Nikolic

For any information, please address Adelaide Books
at info@adelaidebooks.org
or write to:
Adelaide Books
244 Fifth Ave. Suite D27
New York, NY, 10001

ISBN; 978-1-953510-84-6

Printed in the United States of America

Dedicated to my wife Amanda,

my sister Abby, Dee, and all the strong women who have

influenced me throughout my lifetime.

Contents

Guilt and Bars

MONTHS AGO – Leona shut her light and cashed out the last customer. She wondered what she'd eat during her fifteen minutes. *I had a big lunch with Mateo, maybe I shouldn't. Mom will probably have dinner.* She made her way to the frozen foods aisle and fussed over the microwavable dinners. All she really wanted to do was snuggle with Mateo. *Why can't this kid just be happy? He beats himself up so much even when I clearly let him know that things are fine.* She could feel her phone vibrate. It was a text from him –

"I love you."

Her heart melted. "Awwww I love you too! You said it first!" She texted back.

Leona eyed the chicken and mashed potato dinner through the glass refrigerator door and grabbed one out of the case. Holding the box, she questioned herself on buying it. Deciding, she made her way to the register but stopped midway. A feeling in her gut sat heavy. *He never says it first.* She put the dinner down on a shelf and texted again. "Is everything okay? Haven't heard from you much."

She waited five minutes and then called but it went straight to voicemail. She called two more times but nothing. Now she was sick. *Okay, what's going on?* Leona texted a few more times, called again and waited, but zilch. Her mind debated with her feet and after mere seconds, clutching the phone in her hand she ran passed the time clock and out of the store.

"Leona where are you….." Mike yelled in the distance.

Leona was running but time was walking. Something wasn't right. She thought back to his aunt's words "Matty isn't himself, his depression is there." Leona's hands went clammy. *Maybe I'm just freaking out, maybe he's busy. All these months together and there's never been a time where he couldn't respond.*

Leona dug her index finger into her thumb as the parking lot appeared like a vast never ending wasteland teasing her to her car. She pawed through her bag but for the life of her couldn't find her keys. *C'mon C'mon C'mon.* Her eyes became blurry as the tears finally fell down her face.

She began to cry and shake, tremble and panic like both an earthquake and the people involved with it.

Finally getting the keys out of the bag she dropped them and it took her uneasy hand a good few seconds to pick them up.

Unlocking the door, she got in and turned on the engine. Her tears would not stop as the worst thoughts popped into her head. She started to make sobbing noises as her breath disappeared.

Leona drove as fast as she could, blowing all the lights and crying the entire time. Her legs shook the car, the snot ran down her nose. *Baby please be okay, please be okay, I'll do anything just please be okay. Just answer me, make this all for nothing, and make this be me over reacting.* Her head began to rock back and forth as her eyes stung with tears. The accidents that she almost caused nearly killed her five times over. *Pick up your phone Mateo! Please! Baby Please!*

Finally, she reached his apartment building and booked it out of the car. Her clammy hands pushed through the lobby doors as her spaghetti legs took her up the three flights of stairs.

Once at his door, she knocked and there was no answer. *He said he'd be home early.* She used her shoulder to ram into it, but the wooden brown mass would not budge. "Baby please open up." She cried, hoping that maybe he wasn't in there. Leona took three steps back and ran into the door full force, it still wouldn't budge. She collapsed on the floor crying for a few moments and then gave it another shot, opening it this time. Closing it behind her and searching the place with her eyes, they spotted the bathroom light on.

Sitting up against the tub on the floor was Mateo; pill bottles were opened next to him. His eyes were half open as Leona let out a scream. She kneeled down and to her surprise he gently grabbed her face as she sobbed uncontrollably.

"Please you're okay baby, you're gonna be okay." She fumbled for her phone and dialed 9-1-1. "Hi….Yes….." She couldn't help but cry some more. "My….boyfriend….I think he overdosed."

PRESENT DAY – The fear mocked, but hiding it was still possible. Leona may never find out. It wasn't that which worried him, it was something else; maybe guilt. That had to be it. But fear wasn't completely absent; it stood there every time the guilt took the bench. What if Noelle were to tell her? *She wouldn't,* was the easiest hope. What if Leona were to go through his phone? She wouldn't. What if, someone saw him leave her house? Unlikely. But it was all possible, and instead of worrying about one of Leona's exes Mateo Colon was now thanking his blessings that his neck remained free of love bites.

The difference one night can make he thought. In one hand, he held the weight of his mistake, in the other, he held the shame of enjoying the girls' body; both his hands clutched the steering wheel so tight that he could feel the blisters forming.

Sharp lefts and tight rights, the car drove through Nome City the way he felt, zooming down the street as if the faster he went the quicker Noelle would disappear. There would be no outdriving this, unless he decided to flee. That thought occurred to him already, but executing that would be even worse than Leona never knowing. Or maybe her simply never finding out would be worse. There were many scenarios, but not one settled his stomach.

At the end of his destination she waited, innocent and un-knowing. Every minute with every mile facing her grew harder. But she needed to be picked up and that guilt free mask would have to stand before her un-deserved trust. That's when the weight of his weakness broke him. Not today could he see her, not after what just happened. She would be left, for the better she would; standing there at the mall with bags most likely filled with a few things that she couldn't help but to pick up for him. Letting her wait for a boyfriend who would never show up was better than riding shotgun to one who should be shot in his groin with a real gun.

About seven miles away from town he drove until there were only highways and trees. The goal was to find a bar. Finding one held slim odds as the random exit ramp lead to houses. But finding a diner would only succeed in reminding him of Leona; that fateful day where they met and she reluctantly handed over her number. Reluctance was right, if only she could understand that he's more trouble than he's worth, he knew she should be the one driving miles out of town.

Finding a bar proved to be less fruitful the farther he drove into town. It seemed as distance grew the houses found ways to fit more of themselves onto each block. The frustration towards himself sent his palms against the wheel until they grew red with pain. *I fucked up,* he thought to himself. *I threw everything away like it was nothing.* But as the hatred swam, his eyes laid upon the bittersweet fruits of his labor: 'Anne's pub'.

Finding parking was suspiciously easy, as if the devil himself coordinated the entire trip. The locking of his Mercedes broke the silence of the neighborhood leading Mateo to wonder whether the pub with the door nearly falling off its hinges was still in business. The middle aged woman inspecting a glass beneath the light answered his question.

"Cracks look like dirt, dirty glasses scare away the ones with real money. Don't judge me." The lady blurted out.

"I'm the last person who has the right to judge you." Mateo took a stool.

"With that ride, you could wear a black robe and throw me in a cell. Just don't be cheap with your asking."

"There aren't any windows in here, the hell you know what type of car I drive?"

"That ain't no engine of a Sedan boy. The engines of my customers tell me if I'll be eating steak or chicken at the end of the week, call it analytic hearing."

"Open a tab and start me off with whiskey, straight." Mateo said, looking forward to the Band-Aid of his mistakes.

"I'm out of whiskey, how's some bourbon?"

"That'll do." Mateo watched as the women cracked open the bottle, pouring the brown liquid until the rim had less than an inch beneath it. Something made him remember his phone, shutting it off before taking the first sip. "Is this place always so damn empty?"

The women took a moment. "Is the lack of sound making your problems worse?"

"I don't know what you're talking about it." He took a gulp this time.

"I do it on purpose y'know?" Her obsession with cleaning the glass was the second most fascinating thing aside from whatever it was she was talking about. "I don't have music in this place because tunes make a person feel better. Feelin' better don't need no booze. Problems buy booze."

"You're a smart lady I guess." Mateo tapped his glass and she filled him up.

"Smart, or do I just act on my observations? But you're not a talker so I'll shut up."

"In every movie the bartender starts to ask the guy drinking his problems away what his problems are, you're not gonna do that shit are you?"

"No, I'm not, because talking only makes you angry. Something already did that and something is already enhancing it." She shot a look to his shot glass.

"I don't want to go back there. I messed up."

"We all mess up." The woman took the empty glass from him, lofting into the stained sink.

"I kinda need that." Mateo said.

"Real drunks don't talk about their shit before they're drunk. I'm Anne." The woman leaned up against the sink and extended her hand.

"You're starting to weird me out." He left her hanging. "If you're not going to serve me alcohol then—"

"Go. Be my leaving guest." Anne nodded to the door but Mateo remained in his seat. "You can't leave. Whatever it is you did was that bad huh? Well, you know what I have to do then?"

Mateo put his feet to the floor as Anne's shotgun rose from behind the counter. "The fuck are you doing?!"

Anne ignored his cry and moved from around the counter and to the door. The first shot missed its target, the second echoed, until Mateo realized she was shooting out his tires. Out he ran from the empty pub, by the time he reached her trigger happy hands the fourth tire had been blown.

"Are you out of your mind?!" Mateo yelled while Anne went into the bar. Not a second later was she back on the pavement with a gallon of gasoline.

"I'm going to pour this on your car, now you can stop me and I won't fight it." She gave him a look and took three steps towards his Mercedes. The gas rinsed over the car just as the bourbon had fallen in the glass. Then the match held a flame and next the car was a blaze. Mateo looked on without anything inside his conscious.

"We best be going back inside, this shit may blow." Anne said. "I'll call the fire department."

Mateo stood before the inferno. "Why did you do it?"

"Because, cars are big, and you don't want to be found. Am I wrong?"

Mateo watched the flames engulf his car, no answer left his lips.

Later that night in the kitchen of Anne's home, Mateo ate broccoli and veal cutlets with the barn standing yards from the window. With nothing but a dim light and moon outside, Anne sat across from him at the small table chewing on a piece of left over ham.

"She's going to be hurt that I—"

"Shush, do not mention your life outside this town." Anne interrupted.

"Why are you letting me stay with you? Why am I even here?" Mateo put his fork down, letting the panic rise up instead.

"Shhhh, you'll understand one day. I'm helping you. You can tell me your name now."

"I don't even know you. It's Hector, Hector Rivera."

"Okay Hector, look around, it's just me here. I've spent so many years pulling apart the shit that I've done to people that I may not have people who give a rat's ass about me now, but I sure as hell have some damn wisdom under my belt." Anne put her fork down this time. "That look on your face says a lot more than your mouth. I don't need you questioning me. You're in my house, accepted my invitation, you want to change your ways – you'll let the look on your face continue to do the talking." She picked her fork back up and dug into her ham. "Crazy is what you label it, don't look so much into things and maybe you'll learn a thing or two."

Behind Anne, removing himself from the darkness of the living room now stood a lanky boy with orange hair forcing Mateo to rise to his feet.

"I thought you said you were the only one here."

"Out of the both of you." She bit into her ham again. "I'm the only one who believes they belong here. Bradley have a seat, this is Hector."

The boy slowly pulled a chair and took his time sitting down, never removing his eye contact from Mateo."

"Does he talk?" Mateo asked.

"Only when he trusts you."

"Does he talk to you?"

"He doesn't trust me yet no, but I don't expect him too. Unlike you, I know his story." Anne ran her fingers through Bradley's mop of dirty orange curls. "Anyway boys, eat up. Tomorrow we have a big day."

Mateo did just that, doing everything in his power to forget and not think. But with every swallow of food, Leona was in his thoughts; her laugh, her smile, her anger, her jokes, her love. "I can't do this." Mateo rose.

"You will do this. You will sit down and eat your food." Anne shot from her seat.

"I can still fix things, I can make everything better. I'm taking the cowards way out right now and—"

Anne left her seat and pushed Mateo against the wall with the palm of her hand. Her gaze fell to the floor and her breathing was nearly non-existent until her eyes met his. "Starting over isn't the cowards way out. You're here to learn from your mistakes. The hard part isn't running back to your....." She cut her words off and sat back down.

"What?" Mateo asked.

"I will not stop you from leaving." Anne focused on her food and Bradley nibbled at his.

Mateo found himself at the table once more, forcing an appetite and indulging in the silence of the room. *I'm sorry Leona,* he thought.

Vanished

Leona Price checked the basement twice after calling her cell-phone too many times. The bedroom was empty as well, along with the front and back yards. No one was in the kitchen or the living room; the only other soul to occupy the house was Remy. Soon she would discover the pleading little piece of paper too; one that barely hit the border of being a cold riddle.

Take care of each other.
Please don't mistake this for me not loving you.

And that was the entire note, left on the empty dining room table. The questions continued asking themselves, hoping for answers to arrive before her sister Remy awakes. And after running through the same pattern of checking places that were empty in the house, none did. Instead Leona found herself cleaning the house – too afraid to see if Max and his dirty collar was gone too. Countless times she checked on Remy sleeping, too many times she checked out the window for no reason. It was all too much to comprehend.

Leona combed over yesterday, mentally scanning it to see whether anything stood out from the ordinary. Nothing presented itself, aside from Mateo. The memory sat her down, she waited an hour for him to show up but he never did. Until now it hadn't sunk in, but he was gone too. With every phone call that went straight to his voicemail her nail dug deeper into her thumb. By the end of the hour she had already called his Aunt Rosa. But she was as clueless as Leona. The worst of course entered her psyche, stifling it with a forced positivity that only Mateo could provide her. When Leona's mother picked her up ten minutes passed the sickening hour, her reaction wasn't astray from the norm. Not a single red flag or warning sign left itself to be discovered and at the end of Leona's mental replay she could only stare at all the rejected calls in her phone log, marveling at the situation and its unreal contents.

Outside remained Leona's car and in front to her surprise sat her mother's. The empty front seat of the dented hunk of metal taunted. For a second she had wondered if her mother had been kidnapped; forced to write the note at the angry hands of someone like Hank, her ex- abusive boyfriend. It was enough to bring the tears to her cheeks. The sides of her balled up fists slammed the windowsill with enough force that she stopped herself. The pain wouldn't bring her mother back, wherever she was. The car was the nail in the coffin to confirm that. And like straight out of a movie, the rain met the ground, creating a layer of 'life goes on' between her, the window, and the car. If there was ever a time she needed Mateo the most, now was that time.

"Where's mom?" The words bit Leona's spine and Remy never sounded more innocent.

"We're out of eggs, but there's oatmeal if you want."

"Where's mom?"

Leona's tongue lost the ability to move.

The soft footsteps of her little sister filled the room, Leona shut her eyes with the last of her tears drying up into salty grains. Remy's cold hand turned Leona forward with just enough time for her to clear her face. The outlines from the evaporated moisture must have given it all away because Remy waited to ask again. This time her curiosity knew the answer.

"Mom left, where did she go?"

"I don't know. Nothing but that note was left." Leona pointed to it with a limp hand and Remy grazed it with little care.

"Mistake what? Her leaving?"

"I guess so. I don't know." Leona sat down, slumping in the chair until half her rear-end hung off.

"She was fine yesterday, I don't get it."

Leona didn't want to say *I don't know* again, still, other words took too much energy. "I don't know Remy."

The expression on Remy sat Leona up in her chair, her lack of answers wasn't going to be good enough. No matter how upsetting the situation was, the title of big sister wasn't going anywhere.

"Don't panic, it's going to be okay."

"How?" Remy asked.

"We don't know anything right now, the only thing we can do is remain calm. We'll figure it out. Aunt Betty must know something." As sure sounding as Leona's voice may have been, she didn't believe a word from herself.

"Did you call her yet?"

"No, I'll call her now." Leona slipped into the kitchen but Remy followed. One more minute by herself would have helped to gather a better plan of action as fabricated in its efforts as it may be. Instead spontaneous on the spot faking would need to be employed.

The phone dialed and after half a minute it went to voicemail. The irrational but rational fear that her aunt disappeared too was punching her in the stomach. "She didn't pick up."

"What do we do now? Did mom take Max too?"

"I don't know Remy." Because she didn't want to.

"What do you mean you don't know? You didn't check?"

"I don't want to know."

"Too bad, that's our dog, we raised him not mom." Remy marched off, calling Max's name and searching through the rooms as Leona reluctantly followed. The game was hide and seek with a party that Leona knew had been most likely been gone.

"Remy, please, he's gone too."

But Remy persisted in her efforts, checking everywhere Max would snuggle up into from closets to laundry baskets. After every empty spot her little sister's face lost a bit of light. Once Remy opened the bathroom door a third of the way Max came sprinting out as if he had been playing a prank on them. After Remy began crying through hugs too tight for a dog's health, Leona let herself cry too, but not enough to fall prey to it. There was still a problem at hand. Leona's phone rang.

"Hello?" Leona said. She could hear the nervousness in her own voice.

"Hi dear, what's up?" Her aunt Betty replied.

The range of emotions halted Leona's speech like a traffic jam.

"Did she pick up?" Remy asked.

"Do you know where my mother is?" Leona finally responded.

"No? She's not home? Have you tried calling her?"

Everything left Leona in that moment. Whatever feelings that had been there, ounce of energy, and the imaginary spirit which filled her fled. She handed Remy the phone and took a walk into the dining room where she let her legs collapse herself onto a seat. Like a dreary hangover, Remy's mumbling voice from the kitchen boomed with Max's nails against the hardwood floors. The shock to her system spun like a game-show wheel with Mateo in the middle. Not a text or phone call, nor a goodbye, or explanation. Did they leave together she wondered? Is this all some trick or dream? Reality was pudding and nothing seemed to make sense.

In came Remy who silently handed Leona her phone back. If Leona could have borrowed her sister's posture she would have bought it. "I didn't expect you to be this upset right now." Remy said.

"Mateo disappeared yesterday, I haven't heard from him either."

Remy seemed as though she was expecting him to somehow save the day and was let down by the news. "What do you mean?"

"Just what I said, like mom he's gone. I don't know."

"Stop saying you don't know."

"I don't know though Remy. What did Aunt Betty say?"

"She's on her way over now, said not to throw out the note. Why would mom leave?" Again, Leona only had one answer that Remy wouldn't accept.

"Everything will be okay, I promise."

"Who's gonna pay for the house and stuff?"

Leona stood from her chair, legs as straight as they would allow. "Hold on one second okay?"

"Alright."

In the backyard, Leona shut the screen door and peered back inside at Max and Remy. She dialed Mateo's cell and wished for the naïve best. Why? She had no idea, but one more time calling couldn't hurt.

It rang, and it rang some more. With every ring, she attempted to will the other end to answer but eventually it went straight to voicemail along with her patience.

"Please, why won't you pick up? I need you right now." Leona said to the voicemail. "My mom is gone and I don't know where you are. Please Mateo, I'm alone and don't know what's happening. Please, call me back as soon as you can."

Leona wanted to cry but didn't. She wanted to scream but couldn't. With her breathing becoming shorter with every inhale and the pace of her legs shaking greater by the second, Leona assumed she was hallucinating when she glanced in at her sister punching the diner room wall.

The screen door had never been more difficult to open as Leona nudged the thing open with her shoulder and ran to where her sister created a dent in the wall with knuckles the color of roses. Punch after punch, splatter after splatter; the deadpan eyes of her sister could have lead one to believe she had been possessed.

"What the fuck are you doing?" Leona halted her little sister's fist, painting the inside of her palm like a bloody canvas.

"Everything was fine and she had to go mess it all up. We were fine Leona, for once we were fine."

Nine months had passed since Hank was locked up for assault and Mateo's failed suicide attempt scene. June wasn't even hot yet but her sister was right; everything had remained copasetic. Instead of finding Mateo with a bottle of pills in the bathroom, he had been working extra hours and contemplating attending university while her mother had taken up yoga classes and begun writing in her free time. The curve ball of disappearances almost made Remy's candy-apple like fist justified.

"It doesn't matter, you aren't to hurt yourself." *Still it isn't right. You're not to hurt yourself.* She could hear Mateo's hypocritical voice as clear as day while her sister stared at the drops of blood on the floor. "Come." She took Remy by the wrist and brought her into the kitchen, under the faucet, and ran the cold water over her ripped up knuckles.

"Ow." Remy said following a moan.

"You shouldn't have done it."

"You've never been so mad that you've wanted to—"

"Don't go there, you know the answer to that." Leona dabbed Remy's damp skin with paper towels. With every dab, Remy flinched a bit. Once the blood had lessened Leona went through the cabinets for Band-Aids. "Doesn't matter how mad you get, punching walls isn't going to make thing better. Who's gonna fix that dent now?"

"I don't know, that's the last thing I care about right now."

"We just need to stay calm okay?" Leona eyed her sister rubbing her hand. "Life isn't over. For all we know mom is just having some sort of breakdown or something."

"The note sounded pretty final," Remy went to the window.

"Nothing in life is final." Leona couldn't help but think about her father and Mateo.

"Except death."

"Remy."

"We're not going to be able to stay here." Remy reminded. "If mom doesn't come back."

"Don't think like that."

"She's not going to, I'm sure of it."

Leona poured herself a cup of orange juice to replenish all the moisture she lost through her eyes. "Why do you say that? If you've learned anything by now it should have been to think positive."

"Her car is gone and everything."

Leona wasn't sure if she heard that correctly and moved to the kitchen window, pulling back the curtain and scanning the empty parking spot in disbelief. "What the fuck?" She shoved passed Remy and rounded the wall separating the rooms. Fumbling with opening the front door, her feet brought her to the white gate in about four steps. The motor oil was still wet on the ground.

"Mom?" She muttered and looked around, left and right, front to back with the rain beating down on her astonished body. But the car was gone. "Mom?"

The anxiety returned as Leona brought herself to the parking spot, lending herself to its mystery and unforgiving emptiness.

"Leona?" Remy said from the doorway. "What's wrong?"

"Mom.....Mateo?"

Back to the Barnyard

With all his strength Mateo threw the stacks of hay into the back of Anne's red pick-up truck while she sat in a lawn chair eating ice-cream from a bowl. The sun wasn't all that hot but the work made it feel like the ball of fire was sitting in the barn a few yards away. Until today Mateo hadn't realized that one could get splinters from a hay stack. As he tossed and wrenched he wondered if maybe the proverbial needle in the haystack got its origins from farmers getting splinters. Trivial thoughts as such stole him away from Leona. The constant wondering whether she's okay and acknowledging that she may hate him kept him up last night. That and Bradley's snoring.

"I bought him the nasal strips, but the boy shakes his head at what he don't like." Anne said.

Mateo continued to chuck hay. "Let me ask you somethin...."

"Shoot your question."

"Why did you torch my car? You seemed to know I'd go with you regardless."

"And how many memories did you make in that overpriced engine holder? I could've let you park the thing right in front of my home but how many times would you have looked out that window and second guessed your decision?"

"Valid. I don't get how taking in a wanderer is okay with you though."

"You ever heard the expression those who wander ain't always lost?"

"Yup."

"I only take in those who are lost." Anne stood from her chair once the spoon scrapped the bowl. Her thin frame carried her back to the house. As thin as she was, her muscles ripped in the sun. Mateo found something comforting about the woman. He couldn't put his finger on it.

With nothing but the task set before him, Mateo went back to the trivial wonders; no long-term plans before him he lost his head to what would happen to his apartment, construction job and again, Leona. There was enough money in his bank account to pay the rent for a long-time courtesy of his rich but absent father. His job and Leona was another story. The idea pained him, the only thing to do again was toss himself back into the hay at his feet. But he wasn't strong enough. Physically the work was no problem; mentally Leona wouldn't relent. If Mateo hadn't shut off his phone and relinquished it to Anne, he most likely would have sought her out. Instead he found himself sitting at the end of the pick-up truck feeling needy.

It was an urge that he wasn't quite familiar with, whenever he needed the physical contact or the shoulder to indirectly lean on, it was there; whether it was a random hook-up, Noelle or Leona. But this time the isolation left him in a puddle of desire and what he could only classify as flurries of paranoia. He clutched the chain around his neck, remembering when Leona did the same. That was the thought that broke the camel's back.

Mateo rose and began to pace, debating on whether he should barge into the house and retrieve the phone that would calm all his nerves. For once he wasn't sure on how to react and knew that this time anger wouldn't get him anywhere. There was a hopelessness that laid in between it all, in a way, that was liberating; tearing away all the layers of guilt that blanketed him inside the layers of failure. He clenched his fist and needed to place it against something and as soon as he opened his eyes to direct the energy there stood Bradley.

"How long have you been standing there?" He asked the boy.

But Bradley remained silent, letting his stare do all the talking. Cadaver eyes was what came to Mateo' mind, the black unmoving whites of the boys' peepers made him appear dead and if not for the blinking, Mateo would have heavily considered it.

"If you're not going to speak I don't need the audience. I have enough on my mind."

But the boy continued to stare, standing in place like it was a discipline.

"Why the fuck did this woman take me in? I don't belong here, not even here. I don't belong anywhere man." He shot a look at Bradley who blinked in place. "People keep giving me damn chances, isn't there a fuckin limit on them shits? When do I get punished? When do I get what I fuckin deserve?" Mateo finally slammed his knuckles into the side of the truck, that's when Bradley took off running – away from the house and away from the barn. "Where the fuck are you going?"

Mateo took off after him and as his speed picked up the dust beneath his feet did the same, enveloping himself in a cloud of mustard yellow. The boy was faster than his demeanor had portrayed and his toothpick legs disappeared in their own speed.

"Bradley, I'm sorry relax!" Mateo brought himself back to his training days, envisioning himself punching the speedbag and running across the Nome City Bridge back home. That did the trick, his grip was firmly on the collar of the boy now, yanking him back just enough to get him to stop but not enough to put anymore fear in him. "Stop. I wasn't mad at you or anything." Mateo put minimal distance in between them both incase Bradley decided to book it again.

Bradley never did though, and Mateo found himself taking a quiet walk back with the boy. The sound of their boots took the place of conversation and for once Mateo felt himself being the one in need of talking.

"Why don't you speak? It's unnerving you know that? We all have issues but even the worst of us find the nerve to use our tongue."

Bradley looked at Mateo and then back at the ground, as if the words had done their job and quickly left the boy.

"Did something happen to you? Is that it? Some sort of phobia? You spoke one to many times to your parents and they beat the shit out you? I cheated on a girl once and kept dating girls so maybe you stopped talking a long time ago and you got away with it and now it's all you know?" Mateo had known there wouldn't be answer, but rhetorical questions were better than silence, the barn was only a few yards away now.

When they reached the fence of the property Anne stood on the porch of her with a white dirty apron hanging from her neck.

"And where did you two scurry off to?"

"Bradley wanted to play tag." Mateo shot him a look and the boy didn't lift an eyebrow to refute it.

"Bradley, head back inside, Mateo I need a word with you."

Mateo watched Bradley drag his feet into the house and then noticed a red jeep parked next to the house. Anne shut the door once the footsteps were out of reach of their ears.

"You see that truck over there?"

"Yes. It's not bad lookin." Mateo gave it another once over, Anne's demeanor changed, this time it allowed him to see she had a gentleness inside her.

"That right there is property of a Mr. Swanson: Bradley's father, the sole provider of this land."

"You're Bradley's mother?"

"No."

"Married to—"

"No," She looked into the windows of the door while standing on her toes. Mateo didn't need to and could see the man speaking to his son. "It's a complicated thing, but I need you to act polite no matter how hard that may be, and whatever I say just go along with it."

"Not gonna lie, this is getting weird." Mateo took a mental inventory of where the few of his belongings are in the house in case he needed to leave in a hurry.

"I never said that the shit wouldn't be, but that's not why you're here."

"I'm questioning that reason right now."

"You runnin right? You fucked up wherever you came from, you're not the first lost soul to trek through my bar but you're one of the few who wears remorse. What did you do all morning?"

"Chucked fuckin hay."

"Honest day's work, and an honest day's work leads to an honest damn life, you get that?"

Anne had reminded him of his Aunt Rosa in that moment, forcing his eyes to the ground.

"So what am I supposed to say?" He asked.

"That you're my nephew, coming to visit because you heard I was lonely or something along those lines. Just don't be shady."

"You're going to have to eventually tell me what this is all about if I'm going to force myself to sleep at night here."

"We'll talk when he leaves." Anne spied the inside once more, pursing her lips. "I know Bradley is a bit startling to deal with, the no speaking and all, but he'll open up to you."

"Verbally?"

Anne shook her head. "In his own way, now I hope you like creamed spinach, cause it's on the table, get inside." She swung open the door.

Swanson sat down without a word to Mateo, the silence between him and Bradley made him curious as to whether he was really speaking to the boy at all when creeping through the window just a minute ago. Mateo combed over the man's face. His mustache made him look older, something about his eyes made him confident. The polo tee was wrong on him, a suit was the only imagined appropriate attire for the man. But when his gaze fell upon Anne, it was all happy social. The contrast was as jarring as the man's mannerisms.

"I listened at the door like an idiot for at least a half hour." Mateo listened as Swanson continued his story. To make himself as busy as possible he forced down one of Anne's badly made chicken cutlets. The way Anne fabricated her laughter made Mateo lose a bit of appetite on every chew.

"You're Anne's nephew? How long are you staying?" Swanson asked without a hint of emotion.

"I'm not sure right now." The fact that it had only been a day was the only thing flashing through his mind.

"And how are you getting along with Bradley?"

Mateo looked at the boy who was lost in the plate before him. "He's a great kid."

"Don't bullshit me."

Mateo's eyebrows nearly high fived his hairline. "Pardon?" Anne had tilted her head as if to signal to stay calm.

"His lack of speaking isn't the best attribute to the boy's character, you think I don't know that?" Swanson's eyes left Mateo and landed on Bradley as soon as the thought had been finished. "Look at that, another person has to pretend they're okay with you being a misfit. You're not going to have any friends that way you know that right?"

Something smacked Mateo with rage, a breathless anger swamped him and then the words left him. "Ay, don't talk to him like that."

"Oh and you're gonna shelter him from the truth is that it?" Swanson mocked.

"Mateo," Anne pleaded.

"I never told you my…" *How does she know my name?* He acknowledged the regretful face Anne wore and shifted his attention back to Swanson. "The kid is like ten you can't—"

"And you're like twenty. Don't you dare tell me how to speak to my son. Who the fuck are you anyway? To come in here and insert yourself into a conversation that is none of your business."

"Richard, please…." Anne gently interrupted. "Hector here,"

"Is his fuckin name Mateo or Hector?"

"Hector. Hector is a passionate person, you must forgive his loose lips, sometimes shit doesn't always stay in the toilet." Anne tilted her head again at Mateo.

"I see, well, let me give you a piece of advice boy; there are two types of people in this world: Smart ones and stupid ones. The stupid ones eat too much, save too little, and say the first unrevised piece of shit that pops into their weak minds. The smart ones eat right, are careful with their money and are wise on what to release through their lips. Don't be one of the stupid ones." Swanson looked at Bradley. "That's one thing I can complement the boy on: he never says anything stupid.

Mateo now sat as quiet as Bradley, with probably just as much to say on his mind.

Solitary Ride

Leona chose to drive her car over to Aunt Betty's with wonders of how long she would get to keep it as her own. Remy took the ride with their aunt, the much needed ten minutes of alone time calmed Leona's nerves a bit. Her Aunt Betty had shrouded her lack of answers pertaining to the situation with an excuse of *we'll go to my house and figure this all out.* But Leona knew that she had just been stalling. Her aunt was as oblivious as Remy and herself. Watching the never – before seen bewildering portrait on Betty's face was when it allowed Leona to realize that this hurt her too. It was her sister after all.

The selfishness had always been on her Liz Price but never to this extent. The days where Leona's parents argued because Liz would need to gratify her own sense of accomplishment made stupid sense to Leona now. In a way, the note Liz left behind softened the blow, but when thinking about the personality on the other side of the pen it only made the thing seem like a cry for attention. Back when Liz would indulge herself in her own black clouds Leona never failed to relate towards her now deceased father, victim to a heart attack behind the wheel with Remy in the passenger seat a year ago. Whether that was watching the game in the living room or helping him clean something that was only being cleaned because it was his day off; he could never just lay around. It pained her to think that it was all he was doing now.

Leona waited until Betty was three cars ahead before she made the right turn, letting the wheels spin down the quiet one way and up residential blocks until she reached Hyland Road, Nome City's longest one. She allowed herself to get angry, filling the rage into her clammy hands and clenched jaw. Leona laughed at how she was madder at her mother than Mateo; that immature forgiveness that acted as a coupon for whenever Mateo did her wrong seemed to not have an expiration date. She just wanted him back. Everything with her mother would be without that red spotlight if Mateo were around. *Where are you right now? I need you,* she said silently. Leona counted the hours in her head while watching the speedometer climb, it was now about twenty two hours since Mateo went missing, at seventy-two she would call the police. *Could I do that with my mother too?* A note left with a half-ass goodbye didn't necessarily constitute a missing person nor did it constitute enough reason to leave her be. With enough thought, Leona decided to take it hour by hour; it would be less overwhelming that way.

The last bitter moments of Leona's drive, she kept a clear head, letting the damp streets place her into a temporary solitude. With the lefts and rights of her car making sloppy turns onto the soon to be rush hour swamped streets, little drips and drabs of worries made attempts at her mental faculty. The destination flooded her mind instead: the one place where nothing but a loud quiet flourished. After a turn on Genevieve and another on Loeb she was there.

Inside the cemetery with the windows down, the wheels on gravel was the sole sound to her ears. As usual the emptiness could lead one to believe that the place had been closed for decades. Unusually the tears stepped out before she could lay her eyes on her father's headstone. Something made her park in place, her car adjacent to a burial plot that held a giant shrine in the shape of a standing rectangular dome, cemented to the ground by concrete. Without the flowers at the foot of its entrance and the handmade signs stuck to it with masking tape, the giant tribute would have looked cold and heartless; instead it looked as if an oversized giant had been decorated reluctantly. Reluctance was what she sought now because at least it would bring her to what she came for rather sitting in place out of fear to feel more pain than she already had.

I don't think I can do this today, she said to herself. *I can't. Where the fuck is Mateo? Where the fuck is my mother? Why is this happening?* Leona checked her phone but it remained empty. The indifferent screen filled with colorful apps made her feel like she was lost in Vegas without a family or friends. *Once I see him I'll feel better, I'll feel stronger. This is all just in my head.* She gathered an exhale, one that ended prematurely. Anxiety never failed to take her. She turned the engine on and pulled her car away from the monument, driving down the curvy roads and tiny hills. Leona took comfort in the greenery and the softness to the dirt; a little escape in the middle of a morbid place. At that point she couldn't tell whether the panic in her chest had fled or sat resting. When she reached a few yards from her father the exhale finally allowed itself to happen.

Parked a few feet from his headstone Leona left her car and stood before the one spot in the world where she could let herself be free.

"So, mom's gone. So is my boyfriend. Back to back days they just seemed to up and leave. I can't say that I'm okay. I guess for Remy I have to be but—"

It was then that the vehicle made a k-turn in her line of sight. Up on the hill, the dirt sped from underneath the rear tires and without a sign of stopping made its final turn back onto the main road of the cemetery. *Mom's car, maybe not, why else would it make a turn like that?* Leona went over it her head as fast as the Chevy Impala left the horizon.

With no more thoughts, Leona scanned her palm for the right key and hopped in her car, igniting the engine as fast as she could. Once the door slammed, the car was in motion. If Leona could get the dented piece of metal back into her line of vision, in her mind there would be no losing her.

It didn't take long to gain up to where Leona could see the car again; like a racecar driver, it masterfully maneuvered up the small roads and around the tight bends. Leona wasn't as skilled, but as she watched the car pull it all off, it didn't necessarily appear that the driver was fleeing, which lead her to wonder that maybe it wasn't her mother. Maybe she was just seeing what she wanted to see in an attempt to cope with a terrible situation. By the time she reached that conclusion Leona and the mystery car were on the regular streets with regular traffic.

Leona drove to match the speed of the vehicle, by the skin her teeth she missed the license plate number and could not get to the side of the car where her mother had left a dent that only her driving could accomplish. Thinking about that, Leona silently debated on whether the skills of the driver could ever be her mother. Quickly that changed to trying to see the plate again, she was close, very close now, just a few more yards, and Leona turned her head to the left noticing the oncoming traffic. *Am I in an intersection? Don't I have the—*

My Name

Mateo stood behind Anne, leaning on the wall with his arms folded as she washed the dishes.

"If you're going to just stand there at least sing a tune or something, the staring is cute on Bradley, you not so much." Anne said.

"I want to know how the fuck you know my name. I told you it was—"

"Hector, yeah." Anne turned around. "And you think I'm not going to verify that? Your brain assumes that I'm just going to take your word given the fact that you're upstairs sleeping two doors down from me?"

"Whether you know my name or not I'm still a stranger in your house, what does it matter?"

"Boy you have a lot to learn in this life." Anne went back to her dishes leaving Mateo to stand in his confusion.

"About trusting people to not go snooping through my—"

"People who don't trust can't be trusted."

"I trust you enough to stay here right? With no damn plans of a future, how is that not trust?"

The dish either slammed on purpose or on accident, either way Anne had left it in the sink with the water running to give

Mateo a face to let him know she meant business, the type of business only an elder has.

"Did you trust me enough to give me your name?"

"I was…"

"That's rhetorical, and if I hear you talk about how you don't know why you're here or how you're scared of where the future will take you, you can leave. My mother didn't give me ears to listen to you complain."

"What about you going through my shit, I'm supposed to be okay with…"

"As long as you're in my house, you're lucky I'm not patting you down."

Mateo wondered if part of her would enjoy that, her shoulders de-tensed and she took a few steps back, dropping the dish rag onto the table.

"I get that this whole thing is strange, but I know what I'm doing." Anne said.

"Well you have to get that I dropped everything, and I'm here, and I'm….I don't know."

"Scared?"

Mateo couldn't tell whether he was relieved at the word or angry. "I don't know."

"That's fine. Go check on Bradley for me would you?" Anne picked up the rag and went back to the dishes, her lack of asking him to elaborate on his feelings left him with an incompleteness pinched with satisfaction.

"Why did you let Swanson talk to Bradley like that?"

"I'm not getting into that." She turned the faucet a little more to make the water louder.

"It's going to mess him up, everything that man says. At that age Bradley is nothing but a sponge."

The sound of water left the kitchen. "You don't know a thing about Bradley. Understand?" Anne said. "Not a damn thing. This conversation is over." The water resumed and Mateo removed himself.

Right outside the door to Bradley's room Mateo could hear the clambering of plastic on plastic; the door stood decorated with hand drawn pictures of colorful caterpillars. Mateo nudged it open, Bradley sat on the floor playing with an array of cars and action figures. The room itself astonished Mateo with how many different toys lined the walls. When Bradley noticed Mateo his play halted.

"You don't have to stop, I'm just here to check on you."

The boy remained stoic, lifting himself up from Indian position to the bed.

"You didn't have to get up either. You don't have to be…. whatever it is, you're with me man, I'm not out to get you."

Nothing left the boy's lips.

"Okay fine. I won't push." After a moment of more nothing, frustration mounted Mateo. Part of him had expected just a little bit of Bradley to budge on that. It was ironic, Mateo thought – the boy's loud orange hair was a far cry from the quiet that he expelled. "Can I ask you a question?" He waited. "Why don't you say anything when your dad speaks to you like that?"

As Mateo had expected there was no response, just a yarn from Bradley and now the pattering of rain on the window. He took a second to give Bradley's room one more look around, feeling oddly nostalgic when comparing it to the one from his childhood. As soon as Mateo headed for the door the lightning outside made Bradley jump. A slight grunt and pointing at the window came from the boy as he crawled beneath his blankets.

"Are you scared of thunder and stuff?" Mateo asked receiving a refreshing nod out of the boy. "You want me to sit with you until you fall asleep?"

Bradley didn't say anything, just a brief stare and tightening of the grips on his blanket. Mateo took that as a yes and sat at the end of Bradley's bed, once he turned over Mateo knew he had made the right decision.

When Mateo awoke on the floor in his own sweat with his head rested on the edge of Bradley's bed, he saw that the time was two in the morning, He had slept there for six hours. The rain was still pouring heavy with no sign of letting up. Instead of standing right away he sat before Bradley's cars and action figures and let his eyes get lost over them. It seemed like just yesterday where everything was simple and his only worry was how many hours he'd have alone with his imagination; the times where the only things to worry about was his mother and having to leave for school. For whatever reason, Mateo peered around the room for a book bag but saw not one. Quietly he rose to his feet and began to sift through a few of Bradley's things, but there was no book bag. Why it bothered him so much he didn't know, but he did know that it was fishy.

The next morning Mateo sat across from Bradley at the kitchen table while Anne let bacon sizzling on the stove.

"I'm glad you two are getting along. People say a lot of smack about language barriers, and you two found a way to make it work with one of you being mute, now that's progress I say." Anne laughed until it turned it a cough. "Bradley... do me ...a favor and get me my cough drops from my bedroom."

Bradley did just that and once his heels had disappeared from the room Mateo took the opportunity. "Does Bradley go to school?"

Anne was either stalling or legitimately waiting for the cough drops before risking her throat. "No, his father has a tutor come here during the school year."

Mateo disagreed but kept it to himself, not knowing exactly how to leave the topic where it stood.

"Why? You gonna jump down my neck on that one too?" Anne removed the eggs from the fridge and Mateo watched her crack six over a giant metal bowl.

"Even if I say shit, it doesn't matter."

"Not yet it don't. I'm letting you know now, you got a phone call." Anne turned herself to the stove.

"I'm sure I've gotten plenty, why does one stand out more than the other?" For whatever reason his heart sped up.

"It was from North Nome Hospital."

"What was it about?" Mateo rose.

"Mateo…"

"Tell me, what the fuck was it about?"

It seemed as though she was forcing herself to face him, like someone standing up to a bully. Her body language made it clear that she wasn't going to fill him in on what was going on, if she even knew. But his concern outweighed his patience.

"I didn't call to find out." She said.

"Okay then where's my fuckin phone?" Mateo brushed passed her with no idea where to look first. His mind moved like his feet: in circles.

"You call to find out and you aren't welcome here."

"How can you say that? This could be important, why even tell me…"

"This is nothing but something to take you off your path."

"What the fuck does that mean? I don't have time for this. That could be…" He stopped himself.

"Relax." Anne stood.

"No!"

"Do you want to go back to them the way you were or do want to go back them feeling like a good person?"

Mateo for the life of him couldn't keep a straight thought. That's when Bradley returned with the cough drops. The innocence of the boy's face calmed him down, remembering when he dashed from the barn at the sight of Mateo' anger.

"Thank you Bradley." Anne looked at Mateo. "I promise you, it will all turn out okay, no matter what happens on the other side. I've yet to stray anyone down the wrong rode, just trust me."

"I do." He couldn't believe the words had happened.

"Then what's your last name?" She asked.

"Don't you already know?"

"I only needed the first to see whether you trusted me before, I need the last to see if you trust me now."

Bradley watched as Mateo pondered. The boy who at first rattled Mateo's last nerve now seemed to be the deciding factor towards whether Mateo gave into the entire situation or held onto the little bit of skepticism and fear that lingered.

"Colon. My last name is Colon."

Nurse

Patrick Price had always driven on the streets of Nome like he had made them himself. This time was no exception. Next to him Leona sat with the sound of a library while her father kept one elbow on the open window and one hand at two. She could remember being nineteen, but it felt as though she were Remy's age of eleven. Where was Remy she wondered?

"How many times did I tell you to look both ways?" He asked his daughter.

"If I could remember then it wasn't enough."

"You remember me saying that but look where we are now."

Around the car stood nothing but blurry streets in a moving picture. Leona had no control of what took her attention, one minute Mateo flashed by the window, the next it was her ex-boyfriend Michael, or her mother.

"I'm sorry dad."

"Being emotional behind the wheel, you might as well have buckled in drunk. What would Remy have done if this had been more serious?"

What he had been referring to she couldn't grasp. "What's happening? I thought you were…"

"Memories outlive life Leona. You get your temper from me."

Her every fiber picked up their weapons to refute that, but he kept speaking.

"I'm very happy that you choose to remember me in a positive light, but often it's the things you choose not to remember that leave you angry and resentful."

"Dad, every time you got mad it was normal. I don't feel that way." *Isn't he alive? Why am I speaking in past tense?*

"You will with your mother, and there are those who feel that way with me. Just ask the one who sat in that seat before you."

Leona bolted her head to the left, outside the window sped a car. The blurry streets were clear and unmoving.

"Dad we have to move!" The oncoming car sped its wheels in place, not moving forward. "Dad!"

But Patrick was clutching his chest, gasping for air. With each of his sounds she felt herself the one in need of oxygen, until it was impossible to breathe at all. Just like him she was dying.

Leona's eyes opened to her Aunt Betty sitting on the chair beside her reading a magazine, at first the tube down her throat made her want to wet the bed. Her hands felt too heavy to move, her eyes were the only means to reach Betty's attention. But they weren't doing the trick. Betty kept her nose to the magazine. Leona wondered if she died and this was some condition of the afterlife.

"She's awake!" Remy screamed on the way in. Betty's face darted from her pages, her rear end from the seat.

"Oh thank heavens, oh my god." The tears fell from Betty's eyes. Remy now rested her head at Leona's feet in a half hug. The nurse, a skinny framed black male with earrings so sparkly they were the only things Leona focused on, came into the room wearing a smirk.

"I told you girls she would wake up. When I saw her face I knew she was a fighter."

"Is she going to be okay? This is good right?" Her nervous aunt asked.

The nurse straightened up his back after doing various things that Leona could not watch from her peripheral, "I think she's going to be just fine, we'll keep her here for a while to make sure I'm right though. Let me go get the doctor." Cult leader was the level of persuasive comfort the nurse gave Leona, almost leading her to be sad when he removed himself.

Remy stood next to the bed with the body language of a hug addict going through withdrawal. But she held restraint, obviously not knowing whether an embrace would hurt Leona.

I'm... okay Remy, I'm just sore, She wanted to tell her.

After some time, the doctor removed the tube and ran tests that Leona was too tired to internalize. Instead she focused on working her vocal chords.

"How... many bones are...broken?"

"Just your leg, the right one. Other than that your bones are intact. With the shape your car is in, you had us thinking the worst." Her aunt exclaimed with words made of Jell-o. "Do you remember it?"

"No."

That was the moment where Leona realized her mother wasn't there, reminding her of the situation. "You still haven't found our mother?"

"Oh don't bother yourself with that right now." Betty fluffed Leona's pillows that didn't need fluffing. "You were just in a car accident. You mustn't focus on negatives."

Saying it lead Leona to do just that. "Whose fault was the accident?" She had already felt the answer.

"The driver told police that you ran the red. A few witnesses said the same thing. May I ask just what you were thinking?"

Remy had begun to show discomfort at the helm of her own presence in the room, sending her eyes to the floor like a scorned soldier.

"I told you, I don't remember anything. All I remember is following you back to your house. That's it." The accident was tearing at her body in different places. Getting agitated only made it worse.

"The street you were on had nothing to with me. You stopped following me after a bit." Her aunt said.

"I don't have answers, I'm sorry."

"You went to the cemetery." Remy spilled out.

"What, when?" Leona asked.

"When you stopped following Aunt Betty yesterday. I think you went to the cemetery."

Leona sent a search team in her mind to try and drum up whether Remy was right or not, but nothing came forward. "What makes you say I did?"

"The side street you went down, it's the way to the cemetery."

Now Leona knew how Mateo felt most times when always changing the subject. "I don't know if that's true but I'd rather not speak of it. How would you know how to get to the cemetery?"

Rolling up proclaiming that the answer should have been obvious were Remy's eyes followed by a cold shrug.

"You're just not going to answer that? You've only been to the cemetery once so like—"

"You don't know that –"

"Girls please. Leona you shouldn't be straining your voice or your nerves."

Back in came the doctor, a lumberjack looking older man whose white coat seemed a few sizes too small. Leona sat up as much as she could to the gravitational pull of the nurse with the earrings.

"No no please, stay laying Ms. Price; your back isn't terrible but could use the rest. Surprisingly though…"

With Aunt Betty intently listening, a finger to her lips, Leona tuned out the doctor's long monotone briefing. When it was over, she asked Betty for a condensed version and then rested her eyes. She must have fallen asleep because when they opened, there stood the nurse and no one else, placing a tray of food next to her dizzy head.

"I don't know if its cause hospital beds are comfortable or pain makes a person sleepy." He said, earnings nearly lighting up the room.

"Maybe a little bit of both." The Salisbury steak's sour gravy aroma turned her stomach. "I won't even eat that if my mother cooks it, a hospital doesn't stand a chance. Get it away." Leona said.

The nurse held reluctance with the tips of his fingers gripping the tray as to signal she would eat it, his demeanor did all the opposite. "When was the last time you ate?" He asked.

"Why do I feel as though you know the answer to that already?"

He laughed. In return she accomplished something she didn't realize she was trying to accomplish. "What will it take for me to get you to eat this?"

"Were you the one who cleaned me?" She had wondered that earlier, the first time that he indirectly stole her from the reality of a hospital bed and a missing mother and a boyfriend.

"Changing the subject ain't gonna make this steak disappear."

"It's not the nurse's job to make sure the food hits the stomach." Leona noticed his eyes this time, putting her speech on auto pilot while other curiosities filled her. "You never answered my question."

"As a nurse it's my job to make sure the patient is taken care of, food falls into that category and so does bathing." Finally his eyes held a hint of bashfulness.

"So you saw me naked?"

"Yes, it's part of the job. All the female nurses were assigned already."

"Why does that make you uncomfortable?" Leona asked, not knowing if *uncomfortable* was the right word for it.

"I don't usually speak with the patients about that type of stuff. Nome City hospitals don't like that, but they're fine with a male nurse washing a female patient."

"Well, it's silly to pretend that it didn't happen, like the elephant in the room. I'm sure other hospitals allow it."

"I just choose to avoid it." His fingers left the tray. His legs moved him to the door.

"Why?" Pause. "Can you not leave yet?"

"Because most patients I bath don't wake up." He shut the door. "I can't stay long. I have other patients to check on."

"Here I thought I was special." Leona made sure the sarcasm was blatant.

"You're scared and that's ight,"

"Where did that come from?"

"Cause I can tell, I don't know – usually people who just got out of a car wreck are more focused on the car wreck. You have other sh…stuff—"

"You can curse."

"Other shit on your mind. It'll be okay though."

"Both my mother and boyfriend disappeared back to back days without any explanation."

The nurse wasn't taken back, or he hid it very well. "People who disappear don't deserve sympathy."

"I just—"

"I have other patients," He interrupted. "You needa eat that steak." The nurse took himself back to the door.

"Did I say something wrong?"

"Nah."

The metal door meeting the metal frame said otherwise.

Trust

Bradley's arms rattled with every attempt to hoist his chin at least a centimeter above the bar, but a foot remained in between the rusty thing and the very top of his head. To his credit his arms bent this time, to his legs' credit, they were taking a beating every time his fingers left the steel, landing on the ground like sticks of spaghetti. His eagerness to complete a pull-up was the only eagerness Mateo saw on the boy. Jealousy seemed to make its first appearance as well once Bradley stood as audience to Mateo completing fifty of what he couldn't do one of. But his willingness to get better only lessened that. Unlike Mateo, the boy seemed to lack pride, or was it confidence?

"Believe it not I was just like you when I started out, I couldn't get my head above the bar for the life of me. When I saw other guys doing hundreds of them I still thought it was impossible. But it's not. You grip," Mateo leaped onto the bar. "You try to use your biceps." He rose a little. "And then you pull-up." His head went above the bar fifteen times and then his feet met the hay covered ground. "Try again."

Bradley stood under the bar and raised both his hands in the air. Mateo grabbed him by the waist and brought him to where he could grip the thing. This time when Bradley made the attempt, Mateo helped him by pushing his feet up. The sun slapped Bradley in the face so he kept his eyes closed. His arms strained, the back muscles tensed, and he tried his hardest.

The car in the distance coming to a halt a few yards from the barn is what broke Bradley's focus. Mateo had expected it, Bradley's father, adjusting his collar on the way inside the house. For a moment it looked as if Bradley were going to get his chin over the bar, instead the hay scurried in the air from his falling feet.

"You almost got it this time." Mateo said, patting the boy on his shoulder.

But Bradley kicked at the hay, leading him to shut his eyes again in an effort to hush his frustration. Mateo kept himself still, watching the boy figure out a way to keep his demons at bay. If Mateo hadn't grown up with his own, it would have been hard to believe that such a young boy could bottle up so many little devils.

"There's the pride that I didn't think you had. Or are you pissed off?"

Bradley grabbed his t-shirt from the dilapidated tractor and yanked it over his head, punching his arms through each hole. Nothing but silence now filled the barn. In the corner gym equipment sat, raising Mateo' curiosity.

"Fine, you don't gotta talk about it. Why does Anne have all this stuff here anyway? I've never seen her workout t…although, it explains the tone of her muscles."

Bradley gave a shrug and plopped himself down on the tractor tire which rested on its side off the tractor. Guzzling from his water bottle he cut his eyes to Swanson's car.

"I don't like him either, but he's not my dad; he's yours, and I know what shits like to have a parent who treats you like you were a mistake." Mateo remembered being a kid, the arguments between his drunken mother and his aunt fueled the memory.

"I don't fucking hit him, how dare you? Why don't you get off your fucking high horse for one minute."

"Just take him home before it gets dark out. I'm tired of worrying whether or not you two will get back safe."

The water bottle nipped one of Mateo ribs, Bradley was off the tire and gave Mateo a rough shove. Mateo didn't move though, Bradley turned his back.

"You can get mad. I used to."

Bradley turned back around not exactly knowing what to do with himself.

"I used to scream into the mirror, punch things that didn't need punching; I used to be angry all the time, still am a little bit."

After a running start Bradley jumped onto the bar and hung there for a moment, his arms shook, his legs swayed. The pain on his face gave him a glow that outshined the sun.

"The anger doesn't do anything. It just makes you tired. Being tired stops you from being crazy." Mateo watched as the boy struggled for a few seconds and then hit the ground, this time his legs lost balance on contact bringing him to his back.

Mateo walked over to Bradley and extended a hand. The boy ignored and pushed himself up.

"Mateo.....Bradley.....Come to the house." Anne yelled.

"I hope you heard what I said, cause I know a little about this shit." Mateo placed his sights on Swanson's car, a shiny Jeep that appeared just as arrogant as its driver. While he walked, Mateo took the lightest steps he possibly could to listen whether or not Bradley was walking behind him. After maybe five steps, his ears picked up the little feet against the hay.

When they both approached the door Mateo made sure to be the first one to enter. Inside Swanson spoke on his cellphone while Anne sat at the table over a magazine.

"You boys are welcome to watermelon, I just cut the thing up. Bradley your father wanted to speak with you." She nodded her head to the man speaking condemningly on the phone.

Mateo stood the giant bowl with evenly cut watermelon slices, the juices sat atop them like beads of sweat. Before he took a wedge, the dirt sprinkled all over his arms lead him to wash his hands under the faucet. Once he turned it off, clapping flesh filled the room. Mateo turned to see Swanson standing over Bradley who clutched the side of his face. The cellphone was on the floor beside him.

Instinct controlled Mateo by his fists. After one step Anne had her shoulder at the bottom of his chest. She was restraining him before he could even make a move. The only thing he could think to do was catch the expression she wore; please don't, it seemed to plead. But why? He wondered. *Why is she allowing this to happen?* Anne shuffled him back out through the door, shutting it behind them both.

"That's fucking child abuse! Are you fuckin shitting me?!" Mateo stood in place yet his body felt as if it were pacing. Anne now wore that stone look, it tolerated no argument, it lacked sincerity and compassion; it was one Mateo grew up wearing himself. "Speak bitch!"

"You watch your tongue with me boy."

"Why?!"

"Bradley deserved that."

"I didn't just hear you say that."

"Everything that boy gets, he deserves. Do not get yourself involved. No matter how much it hurts to watch, you will not get involved. I ain't peg you for completely brainless, I peg you for somebody whose got enough wits in em to listen to an old lady when she asks you to do something."

Somehow and someway, Mateo found the wherewith all to continue to speak without yelling, as much as it pained him to have a civil conversation, Anne was good with putting down firm rules that held fear at to the idea of breaking them.

"I just watched a kid get his face knocked off, I know you expect me to drop my past, but standing idly by while that happens would bring shame to the ones who raised me."

"He's not your responsibility."

"It doesn't matter, you don't let that happen to a kid, you especially. I don't understand how you can let that happen, and I'm supposed to trust you?"

"By now, you should know I have a logic to everything I do.

Her casual tone summoned the worse part of his rage to the tip of his tongue.

"You mind explaining that logic to me?"

"In due time, you're not supposed to trust me, but I'm asking it for it."

Mateo removed himself from the porch, with each step down more and more contempt clouded him. "I can't watch it though, can't. If this shit has to happen." His own words hit his ears through a megaphone. "No, what am I saying, this isn't how people work. This whole situation, I don't get it."

Anne took herself from the porch as well, grabbing him by the shoulders. "Just because who haven't seen the world work in a certain way, don't mean it don't. What's weird to you, is normal for me. What's weird at first, usually gets normal for everyone. Let it get normal."

The door hit the side front of the house upon opening. "Anne, I need a word with you, away from your….family." Swanson said in the doorway like a false god.

"Remember my words Mateo, and it'll all be easier." She gave him a wink and followed the commands of Swanson.

Mateo took a moment for himself, a moment that was shortly interrupted by a zombie like Bradley passing Mateo as if he weren't standing there and bringing himself to the barn.

The boy walked with the calmness of the clouds in the sky and the speed of a weather vane. Mateo followed at a slower pace and when Bradley entered into the barn, Mateo could see him get a running start to the pull-up bar. In one jump he missed, on the second his hands caught the thing. Again he struggled, he strained. The veins in his biceps blared through his orange skin. By the time his face changed from orange to red Mateo was before him.

"C'mon man, you can do this. Just pull.....push your body up.....give it all you can."

Bradley's fingers were coming loose with every strain.

"Don't let go, your father hates you."

His fingers got a better grip.

"You're a failure as a son…That's why your mom left…. that's why everyone hates you. That's why every fucking morning you wake up feeling like you don't deserve to live… ..C'mon you stupid fucking idiot, pull yourself up!"

And he almost did, but hit the ground and landed on his rear end. The first thing he didn't wasn't grab his back in pain, or let the frustration take him; instead he shot a look at Mateo who had tears streaming down his face.

Bradley stood, that Carmichael face was back, lending itself to Mateo just like on day one. Although this time there was more life to it, a little more compassion than usual. Mateo on the other hand felt sorry that the boy had to see his in the state that it was. But it didn't seem to faze him at all. Bradley walked up to Mateo and patted him on the back, then he exited the barn and sauntered back up the trail. It was then that Mateo realized they had something in common.

An Old Face

Every time Leona awoke, the teal ceiling screamed to her gown dressed body that it was being cradled by a hospital bed. So far the only thing she could recall learning was that most reminders aren't good ones nor are they welcome. The rustling of what sounded like fabric in a chair took her away from her inner monologue and brought her eyes to the empty seats next to her. No, it wasn't coming from there, it was passed her feet somewhere. Unlike the days before, her neck was sore on the turn, it somehow supported her neck enough to see the girl with her oil black hair.

It was Noelle.

"What're you doing here?" Leona's sleep lagged hands pulled at the sheets on her bed, her back prepared itself to rise if needed.

"You're awake, I didn't know whether I should have—"

"Can you answer my question?"

"My friend is a nurse here in the hospital, his patient, you, came up in conversation, so when I heard you were in the hospital I came to see if you were okay."

"Why?"

Noelle had a twitch to her mouth which portrayed nothing but nothing. Either it was there to be patronizing or there to be sincere. Which one Leona could not decipher.

"I feel bad." Noelle said.

"About what?"

"When I tried to get in between you and Mateo some time ago. It still bothers me."

"You liked him." The air felt warm in her lungs. "But nothing really happened so it's fine. I'm over it."

"How is he?"

The little twitch was gone Leona noticed. The way the girl's cheeks lost their color read something beyond being curious, like she wanted answers.

Does she know that he's missing? What is this girl up to? He's fine, everything's good."

Noelle responded with a manufactured sincerity which in turn got on Leona's last nerve.

"What are you up to?" Leona asked. "I can read it on your face, you're bullshitting me. What do you know?" *Fuck I shouldn't have asked that.*

"What do you mean what do I know? Has something happened?" There was the twitch again.

"No. I don't know. Nothing else would bring you here. Not after what I did to you. I know.... you're bullshitting me."

"What is it that you know? Because I'm not at liberty to say what I know until you say what you know."

That's when she knew they were on the same page, if anything Noelle maybe a few pages ahead. "Where is he then?" Leona asked, the weakness in her voice came from a lack of pride not pain this time.

"What do you mean?"

"I'm lost right now, honestly you have no business knowing anything about him and I want to know what you know. Now."

"He che—"

The door swung open and a heavy set brunette nurse pushed in a tray on wheels, what sat atop it looked to be

Pricewise on rye bread. The one bread of all them that Leona wouldn't mind vomiting over.

"Sweetheart you shouldn't be sitting up." The nurse said to Leona, then shooting a glance to Noelle. "Oh howdy, I didn't even see you there."

"Hi." Noelle said.

"My back feels fine, when will I be allowed to leave this place?" Leona lied about her back, as bad as the idea was she almost missed being at Waymart.

"As soon as the doctor clears you honey. These Pricewise are going to disappear unlike the last batch right?"

"I told you the last time, I don't like rye bread."

The nurse ignored her, strapping the blood pressure sleeve over her bicep letting the thing inflate until her hand lost some feeling.

"Well, your blood pressure is still a little high, the doctor won't like that, might run some tests."

"No more tests, I've had enough. I really want to go home" Although she didn't quite know where that was at the moment.

"And you will, once the hospital feels that you're well enough to do so."

"The other nurse...." Leona's eyes went to Noelle and back without her permission. "What happened to him?"

Pause. "The hospital changes us around from time to time."

"Did he request to not have me as patient?"

"I just go where they tell me sweetheart, I'm a women with little answers when it comes to how this place works. The body on the other hand..." The nurse pulled Leona's attention back to the Pricewiches with a motherly stare. "I know how that works just fine and I also know it needs food to keep going. But I'll let him know you miss his service."

Leona reluctantly picked up a half of what looked to be bologna, turkey and cheese in between the dreaded bread. Before the nurse could make her exit Leona made sure to ask.

"What's his name by the way?"

"Trevor." The nurse said, shutting the door to bring Leona back to her situation with Noelle.

"I don't know you well—"

"You don't know me at all."

"But if I were to guess, you like that nurse... who also happens to be my friend."

"He's a nice person. Nothing more. What were you going to say about Mateo before the nurse came in?"

"Nothing, I thought I had seen him somewhere but I was wrong. I don't know what you know."

"And why did you phrase that like you want to know?"

Noelle left her seat and walked to the window where a vase of plastic flowers greeted the sunlight.

"Umm....I don't have a lot of friends.... and no siblings or anything. When we would talk at Waymart, maybe I was delusional but you had a certain sincerity to you. I know about your dad, we've both had troubled pasts with boyfriends. And we both have a common interest in Mateo. I respect your relationship with him, I do. I don't know, I guess I just wanted a friend." Noelle looked over her shoulder at where Leona brought herself back down in a laying position.

"What you did with telling Mateo about Michael, the Pelpage pictures, how am I supposed to let that go and just be friends with you?"

"I was jealous that's all. Obviously nothing could come in between you and Mateo." The twitch had returned. "I learned from you about moving on." Noelle took a seat in the chairs next to Leona's bed. "Just give me a chance."

"I don't know what you want, you can't manufacture a friendship."

"Can I ask you something?"

Leona finally understood why that question always bothered Mateo so much. "Sure."

"Usually, you'd flinch at me mentioning Mateo, and I honestly didn't think you'd give me the time of day. What's changed? Did you two break up?"

"He hadn't been around."

"Where is he?" Noelle asked as if she had known Leona would say that.

"Again, it almost feels like you know something I don't." Leona sat back up as much as it pained her to do so.

"No, why would I? Don't you trust him? If I knew anything then that'd mean he was with me."

Noelle was right, but something felt wrong. "It just seems a little fuckin coincidental that you show up a few days after he goes missing." Leona put her left leg on the floor first. That was when she noticed Noelle's discomfort in the concept of Leona walking and that her thong probably made an appearance when moving her good leg.

"Uhh, are sure walking on the cast—"

"Hand me my crutches and clothes." She nodded to the corner where it all lay, there wasn't an ounce of will on Noelle. "Seriously, I'm getting the fuck out of here."

"And going where?" Trevor said on his way in. "You're not cleared to leave.

"I have to find my boyfriend. I have to find my mother. My sister is, I don't even know. I have to go."

"No. The indestructible smile was absent, Trevor appeared a foot taller when angry. "It can wait. What's the point in helping these people if you're in the shape of a pretzel? Get back on the bed."

The pride in Leona screamed to disobey, the girl in her felt guilt for being attracted and the rational her, as scarce as she was, agreed. "You can't tell me what to do."

"He can't, but I can. So get back into your bed and stop with the angry shoulders." The room around Leona melted into oblivion as Lauren's voice saved her from the weight on her shoulders. Before Leona could even acknowledge the glee, the warm tears drenched her cheeks, calling out the ones from Lauren's eyes as well.

"Can you walk over here and give me a hug? I'm kinda... well." Leona nodded to her cast and Lauren embraced her.

"Uh, I think I'll get going now." Noelle took her bag from the chair. "Think about what I said Leona." She took her leave from the room and Lauren traded her hug for a skeptical mask.

"What the heck was she doing here?" Lauren asked.

"Being creepy."

"She's not a bad person." Trevor added. "Jus a lil misunderstood." He wrote something on his clipboard while Lauren exchanged her skeptical look for one asking *how would he know?*

"You're friends with her? Or so she said."

"Yup, for a few years."

"Wait, can we save this lovely questioning for another time, I'm here and you have a lot to fill me in on." Lauren said to Leona.

"She's right girl, from what you told me, the friend who comes barging into the hospital deserves to know. Don't stress yourself over Noelle, I said she wasn't a bad person. Doesn't mean she deserves your time. If you get your ass back into your bed I'll see what I can do bout getting the doctor to release you."

"Before Leona could drum up a response the shine of his earrings were through the door.

Lauren took a seat after helping Leona get back into the bed. "I honestly never thought that your bare ass would be in front of my face."

"My aunt couldn't find me a pair of granny panties from home."

"Do you even own any?"

"I think once I started dating Mateo I inadvertently got rid of them all. I accidently flashed Noelle before, this thong is see through." she laughed,

"Too much info Leona. So fill me in."

From her mother leaving down to her conversation with Noelle, Leona poured her problems in Lauren's ears. Afterwards, the weight of the world wasn't so heavy, the walls weren't as suffocating and the isolation let go.

"I don't think looking for them will solve anything."

"I still need to put out a search for Mateo though, it's not like him to just up and leave."

"It's sketchy Leona, grown men just don't go missing. I'd hate to say it but he left, he had to."

"Maybe he just hasn't returned my calls. Maybe he broke up with me."

Pause. Lauren pondered. "I guess if he were to vanish on his own he'd let you know some way. It's hard to believe someone in his shape and size getting kidnapped or something."

"I don't want to think about it, but he could have gotten into an accident like me or whatever. Anything could have happened, I refuse to think that he just disappeared."

"Not to be insensitive." Lauren played with her hair. "But shouldn't you be more distraught over your mom—"

"Fuck that bitch."

"Leona—"

"No, seriously fuck that bitch."

"That's anger speaking."

"What am I supposed to do, be sad about it? Hope for her to come back? Chase her? People who leave don't deserve any of that."

"And so Mateo is—"

"A different circumstance. He didn't leave a note saying he was leaving."

"Fair enough."

Later that night, before Leona was to go to sleep, Trevor came in to check on her. Quieter than usual, it gave her a reason to start conversation.

"Of all the nights spent on this cheap mattress, I don't think I've seen you tired before."

"A lot of quiet patients today, they don't got a lot of family to fill the room with noise and take you out your mental. The more time I got to spend in my head thinking about how the person I'm serving Salisbury steak is terminally ill, the more drained I get."

"I'm sorry."

"It's just part of the job." He fussed with the curtains on the window, Leona knew they didn't need any sort of adjusting, he just wanted to be there with her, or so she hoped."

"I'm sure your girlfriend is proud of how dedicated you are."

"Don't have one."

Leona wondered how obvious her veiled curiosity was and why it was there in the first place.

"Sorry, I just assumed."

"Patients don't usually ask me this stuff."

"You're interesting, and I get a different vibe from you. Like, I don't know if this is inappropriate but I'd like to keep in touch after I get out of here." If Mateo were around to hear that, the room would have been turned upside down. Half of her enjoyed knowing that, the other half worried it would be taken the wrong way; the romantic way.

"What do you mean?"

"Like friends, if I can take anything away from this situation it's that I met you."

His body stiffened. "Why, I ain't nothing special. I change bed pans for a living."

"You kept my head above water, you know those people you serve steak to might be quiet but I'm sure they ache whenever you leave that room just like me."

"You ache when I leave?"

"No, I mean yeah, like... not...." She knew she had instantly turned to a tomato. "I have a boyfriend."

"I know, that's why you achin' caught me by surprise."

Pause. Trevor closed the door and took a seat next to her. She had wished for the television to be on in that moment, to give her at least a place to rest her eyes somewhere during lulls like these.

"Look girl, the only reason you feelin' me right now is cause your man hurt you. That shits normal, if he was around you wouldn't pay me any mind." He rose, and the outline of his manhood caught her eye

"You're right. Thank you for not taking advantage of me or whatever."

"You're welcome." He made for the door.

"Can I ask you something though?" Leona asked.

"Sure."

"Why did you switch places with that other nurse?"

"Because if I know I'm gonna have feelings for someone I push them away, or in this case give them to somebody else." The door shut, for once the darkness was comforting.

Starting Over

The frame of the giant hunk of metal rested on the dirt like a burn victim.

"I thought the purpose of torching the thing was to forget, right now all I fuckin see is the life I destroyed." Mateo said to Anne as she stood next to him before his charred Mercedes.

"Rebuilding is another way of starting over."

All Mateo' thoughts did was replay the intimate moments between him and Leona in what used to be his backseat. The magical place where they first kissed; the vehicle that gave him hope towards not dying alone. The selfishness that plagued him interrupted by a realization.

"You expect me to rebuild a Mercedes from scratch? The thing is—"

"You say it like fixing muscle cars don't happen every day, boy I grew up in the country—a man who don't know how to fix his baby—"

"I know how to work on cars."

"So then why the bitchin' an the hollerin'?"

An answer never come forth.

"Man builds buildings because they're confident enough to think that those shits will hold up forever; authors write books to leave something that will outlast them. Why do you think people give up?"

Anne's stare lead him to believe her question had not been rhetorical.

"Everyone has a reason for giving up."

"A lot of folk assume the majority of quitters quit cause the shit is too damn hard. Most if not all the of time they just feel like the end result either ain't worth the effort or just won't happen. And why do you think that is?"

"Laziness?"

"Such a man's answer, No, because they don't got the confidence in themselves and have a hard time trusting anything, from people, to concrete, to their own words on paper."

The motives behind why he cheated presented themselves as a theory all while they ripped away at his conscious. He had never analyzed why he cheated before, and it pained him to consider that in Leona, Mateo still had trust issues– even after all she has withstood.

"Silence says more about a man than he can say with his mouth. I guess I hit a nerve." Anne surveyed the black crispy piece of steel sitting on the dirt. The wrinkles in her forehead revealed her excitement. "I'm eager to see if you can pull this off. What was the last thing you actually committed yourself to?"

Leona, he thought, "I can't recall."

Pause. "What's up there?" Her eyes turned to gun barrels. "What?"

"Your eyes went up and to the left, the tell-tale sign of a lie. So if you ain't lying–tell me what took your attention then?"

"The last thing I committed to, I couldn't hold the commitment."

Anne's gaze fell back to the car, circling around the thing like it were a newly discovered fossil. "Okay."

It bothered him when she did that. "Why don't you ever dig deeper? You scratch the fuckin surface of the conversation and then bounce right before you get to the meat and bones."

"Scratching is all you need sometimes. I've got a few supplies in the barn to get you started on your project here–but we'll need to hit some outside places to fix the whole thing. I'll be the one to fetch it, you supply the list."

Mateo pondered on where to start first, half listening to what she had said.

"And hey, while you do this, remember not only will you be driving it, it's gonna outlast you and there will be other asses in that seat who have to trust you got the wits to build something that lasts."

"Yeah." He watched the meaty calves of the women during her stride back to the house, leaving him with nothing but a mangled foundation and insecure hands.

Later that night Mateo sat on the ground next to all the wires and hood from his crippled old car. It had taken him five hours to disconnect the thin cables from the engine and remove them like a doctor taking out veins. Switching the engine out tomorrow would prove to be the hardest–not because it was the hardest but because the roars it used to produce would make Leona smile and fall back in the seat. Mateo understood the lesson Anne was trying to teach; fixing the car and driving his way back to Leona was what he dreamed about though. Every second invested in the dream was a fairy-tale, 70% of his gut believed that when he did go back to Nome city, Leona would want nothing to do with him. There was the regret.

Regret was easy during down time. Recklessness, selfishness, uncertainty and all their family members taunted. Unlike the wires from his ride, changing was harder than he presumed it to be–overlooking the effects of a life change that's supposed to be the right thing to do, only seemed to carry sacrifice. This is what he learned about change and progress: Pain is the game and its results are not certain.

This choice had to be better than the mess behind him, miles away where his manhood left trails in spots with the power to shatter Leona's heart. *All she ever did was throw a rug over my problems,* he thought to himself, *no girl should take that kind of abuse. This is for the best, even if she breaks up with me. Leona will find someone better–someone to treat her right.*

Like a ghost with the ability to appear out of thin air, Bradley stood before him. With the red sky holding the descending sun, that blank face of his produced a demonic like mind-reading look about him. Whether it was fear or genuine humor, Mateo laughed.

"Sometimes I think you're just a kid who died on this weird ass farm and you're haunting me until I kill myself." Mateo stood from the dusty ground with dirt coating his legs. Bradley uttered silence. "My bad about chick flicking out the other day, you shouldn't have seen that. I don't do well with thoughts on my own."

Bradley took a walk over to the pile of wires: a mess of tangled colors and frayed ends. He picked them up from the ground observing, and then at the exposed hood of the wreck.

"Are you familiar with cars?" Mateo asked, "Tomorrow I'm taking the engine out and seeing if it can be repaired," He twisted at the coolant cover and pulled out the dipstick, surprised to see wet oil on it. "Not everything can be fixed though, no matter how strong an engine used to be, one day that shit is just going to die– like everything else."

There was a sincerity this time combing over Bradley, he must have sensed what was coming: a river of emotions.

"I don't try to break shit, I don't. That shit just happens. When my life is going well, I can't get comfortable. Comfortable aches." Pause. "Whatever man, I'm not gonna vent again to you. My mother would do the same shit to me when I was a little younger than your age. Every fuckin night there would be something else. I don't want to be like that. You're smart for always keeping your mouth shut."

Bradley's sincerity left him, traded for offence.

"What? You're offended by that? You're the one who chooses to stay tight lipped," Mateo gathered his tools from the ground as the last of the sun left the sky leaving in it's path an ocean blue. "If you spoke maybe I'd understand you better–fuck now I sound like... why the fuck does shit have to be so hard?" He kicked at the front of the crispy metal. "I always fuck shit up. She didn't deserve me leaving, I shouldn't have cheated. I was fuckin scared–if I had a backup I didn't feel as vulnerable," Once Mateo eyed Bradley's bemused stare the words halted. "What I just said, stays between you and I." And then he remembered that the boy only spoke in silence, it made him laugh again, the insanity dripping off of Mateo must have been beyond creepy.

Bradley walked up to the fence, a dilapidated artwork of hanging word and nail. His body formed a perfect rectangle only interrupted by breathing. Curiosity brought Mateo to his side.

"Yeah, stare at a swing–because that doesn't make you look like an adolescent serial killer at all." Mateo said.

The swing was nothing but a plank of wood strung to a tree branch almost half a football field away. Mateo couldn't decide which gave him more chills, it or Bradley.

"I never noticed that there until now, the thing looks like a death trap."

Bradley pointed in its direction and then at his chest.

"I don't understand." Mateo said.

Bradley took his leave like a robot being summoned back to its master. But Mateo stayed behind and marveled at the instrument. The solitary nature of the swing and the tree held his attention like a painting in a museum. He had to get closer to it, there wasn't anything better to be doing anyway.

Up the small hill over branches and weeds, Mateo reached the lone tree. At close distance the little wood seat was fastened a lot sturdier than it appeared from up the hill. Right in the middle, in-between the bottom of the massive oak and the branch that held the rope was a carving– *Karen*, it read. Mateo ran his fingers over the ridges of the letters, worn out from years of weather and age. Who was Karen? He wondered. The singularity of the name provoked questions yet also seemed insignificant. With his brain he picked up the name and held it for later.

The swing swayed in the warm breeze, almost calling Mateo' ass to its surface. When the fabric of his jeans met the smooth plank, again, the sturdiness had been underestimated; suporting his weight like it were made of steel cables. Against the dark sky with the windows acting as its only means of presence was the house. From a far it was comforting, giving the field a warm yellow glow as if a happy family with the stench of baked pies filled its walls. Bradley was a child who probably never saw the likes of such a family and Anne carries her self like she were the man of þe house growing up. The misfits that they are proved relatable to Mateo, almost laughable. *I could be with my girlfriend right now, instead I'm in the country while on a swing.*

Against his own sanity he began to laugh aloud. It came from the gut in a juvenile release. The absurdity of the whole situation finally began to tickle him. That was until he remembered Leona's face, his aunt's face and the matter that one of them could be the hospital. His ass left the swing, like Bradley he brought himself to the house, this way it wouldn't just be him and mental scenarios.

When his foot entered through the door frame, the kitchen light lit the interior and like a moth to a flame Mateo sauntered to it. At the table sat Bradley and serving him in snowball sized spoonsful of mashed potatoes was Anne.

"Well call me scared crow, you don't look like somebody bit off all your toes." Anne said.

"I guess working on the car wasn't such a bad idea." Mateo took the seat across from Bradley, filling the void in the room with glances of the dainty oven mints hanging over the sink next to the dangling oversized cooking utensils.

"See, it don't kill you to listen to old Anne Ritter. I know the value of hard work."

"Who's Karen? I saw her name carved onto the tree."

Anne dropped her serving spoon into the gravy, little droplets of brown sprinkled the plastic table cloth.

"What tree?" Anne asked as Bradley extended his arm over the table and pointed a finger so straight that it nearly curved upwards. Opposite his point was the window, and outside that window mocked the tree. "We don't speak of–"

Bradley rose from his seat, flinging the table to its side, spilling the gravy, overturning the bowl of mashed potatoes and sending what looked to be rips into the lower parts of the sink. The wooden table shed its table cloth and had grazed Anne in the shoulder sending her to the floor. With one football punt Bradley connected his boot with her bewildered face.

"BRADLEY what the fuck!" Mateo took him by the arm, nearly slipping in Anne's fresh puddle of blood, but was met with both Bradley's hands until Mateo had his back to Bradley, locked in an arm wrench. With a shove, Bradley released and sprinted from his room and out of the house. Mateo turned to Anne–she writhes on the now cherry red floor tiles, hands to her nose.

"Go after him!" Anne screamed.

"You're–"

"Get my baby–Go!"

Without an ounce of hesitation Mateo booked it, leaping through the door and over the five steps leading up to the house. The dust exploded beneath his feet, spraying into his face to the sounds of boots on dirt. He scanned the horizon for any movement, nothing to the right–nothing in front of him– but to the left was that skinny frame with legs disappearing in their speed. A few yards from the swing Bradley was.

It took Mateo half a minute to meet with the boy. Screams, tears, more screams came fresh from the boys' lungs, clutching at the grass beneath his pointy knees, batting at the bottom of the tree, the shrieks were as if he were being eaten alive.

"Stop!" Mateo was crying too, connecting with whatever it was that this usually silent kid was feeling. Instead of uttering another word, Mateo listened and dissected the forms of Bradley's screams. And for reasons unknown to Mateo that's when the anger replaced his tears, the protector filled him, the savior inside himself puffed out his wings because– Bradley was screaming *mom*.

I'm Here For Her

Aunt Betty never shied away from pouring her guests a beverage, especially when that guest was family. Leona loved that about the woman; from hot tea to coffee, a visit to Aunt Betty hadn't begun unless her index finger was securely wrapped around a small handle, steaming liquids spurting out the other end. This time is it was boiled water, her thin veined hand gently lowering the green tea packet into Leona's mug.

"Where's Remy?" Leona asked, stirring the tea bag up and down.

"She's upstairs with Emma."

"Emma…our cousin from Texas? Why is she here?" Leona never disliked the girl but always had an issue when it came to understanding her. With divorced parents and a little sister who passed away from brain cancer, the girl didn't fall under normal. An anti-social mood, the occasional gothic lipstick, for a sixteen year-old she had all the issues of an average one and then some. "Does she still have that creepy porcelain doll collection?"

"It's the summer dear, and like you and Remy she hasn't had an easy-go as of late. You know how her mother gets."

Leona could only remember Aunt Priscilla from birthday parties, nagging about losing the lotto and how the cake didn't have enough liquor in it. If Leona was Emma she would have probably wished for her mother to leave a note and vanish.

"I don't have any problems with the girl, I was just curious if she still had the murdering dolls."

"You know she's touchy about them."

Leona only knew because during a sleepover at the girls' house one time, Leona popped one of the heads off and strung it above the girls' bunk bed, leaving the rest of the night to be filled with cries so loud the neighbors had called the police. Remy had been probably too young to remember, to this day it still made Leona laugh.

Aunt Betty circled the rim of her mug, the ticking of the owl shaped clock on the wall told Leona what subject it was time for.

"You can talk about my mom, I'm not going to start crying or something."

"I know dear, I didn't want to be insensitive being that it's your first day home from the hospital. I'm sure the cast is bothersome enough."

Leona had spent the night at Lauren's, drinking tequila and playing Monopoly. She hadn't thought about the pain or the accident much until now.

"Just speak like you're informing one of your clients that they're going bankrupt." The analogy was good, given that Betty was a financial consultant.

"Okee doke, to start, your mother paid off the mortgage and your car insurance."

"What about my tuition? Did she leave any money for that?"

Betty frowned, "I'm afraid not my dear—this was left on my steps a few days ago though." She handed Leona an envelope, inside was a money order for three grand and a note that read *Tell Leona to use this for food and put into her savings for a rainy day, I'm sorry it's not more.* "Are you okay?

Betty must have noticed the moisture circling her eyelids. "At least the house is paid off, and I guess the insurance will cover the damages to my car."

"If not I'll pay for the damages. You need to be able to get to and from work when your leg gets better."

Leona had forgotten that she wouldn't be able to work. "I'm going to ask my boss if I can go back to work anyway and do something where I'm sitting down. I can't just stay home with Remy the whole summer."

Betty made the same face as when the abused animal commercials come on television. "With everything that's happened—

"What?" Leona was mad now.

"She's been getting along well with Emma, and if you're going to be working—"

"You want her to stay here for the summer?"

"If your mom doesn't return—"

"More than the summer?" Now it was a flood of tears that forced her eyes shut, stinging as if she were sprayed with mace.

"Oh dear," Betty stood and rounded the table, hugging Leona's top half. "I'm not doing this to hurt you, I just don't want Remy in that house right now–you know how much everything will hurt her. There won't be a minute that goes by where she won't think of your mother, she's far too young to carry that weight."

"You don't think she'll still think about her over here?" Leona cried through her words, like a soldier asking questions.

"I do, but it won't be as bad, and your uncle Charles and I can be there for her."

"I'm going to miss her."

"You're to come over as often as you like. My house is yours."

"It's going to suck being in that house all by myself, it was bad enough when Remy was at school and mom was out shopping."

"Look at the Brightside, now you can stay with Mateo guilt-free." The raw positivity on Betty's face made Leona want to lie that he was still around.

"Guess what." Leona took a sip of her tea, the warmth coating her lips and falling under her tongue."

"What?"

"A day before mom left, Mateo up and vanished too—except he didn't leave a note."

"Are you being serious Leona?"

"That isn't something I'd dream of making up."

Leona saw the cross between anger and grief swarm across her aunt. Anger never came easy on the woman, always giving her this constipated look about her like it got stuck on its way out.

"Again, my house is yours. May I ask how you plan on handling Mateo?"

"I was going to put a search out for him…but I don't know right now."

"If you give me his information I can deal with the police if you'd like?"

Leona was taken back. "Really? You wouldn't mind?"

"Not at all, you have enough on your plate."

"What's your stance on it?"

"I see the good in people, don't make him out to be the villain just yet."

"I still haven't."

"Everyone has a reason for doing what they do. From what you've told me in the past, he's a complicated person, I'm sure nothing serious happened to him."

"What's mom's excuse? She's a Rubik's cube?" Remy entered the room, stopping before the fridge opening it and bending over with no reason just like her big sister had grown to do on habit. She slammed it shut and gave Leona a huge hug, kissing the top-side of her forehead. It almost made her feel as warm as when Mateo would do it. "How's your leg?" Remy said in almost a whisper.

"It only hurts when I think about it, the cast cuts off most of the throbbing." The healing bone began to hurt as she spoke it about it.

"That's good." Remy sniffled, followed it was a thorough cough which sounded like t hurt."

"Sick?"

"She's been showing flu symptoms ever since…this all happened." The words tip-toed from Betty's mouth.

"I'm fine."

"You look like a ghost," Leona exclaimed, "Your face is as pale as my back."

"It wouldn't hurt to eat more than two fork-fulls of dinner every night—tell your sister how you haven't been eating."

The revelation bothered Leona; Remy tended to not eat when she was happy or occupied, when stressed or upset she'd eat like a horse.

"You need to eat—"

"I have been."

"Technically yes, substantially no." Betty said.

"Look at you, the *about to keel over* look isn't a good one on you." Leona said.

"Life is like bad food—it'll make you want to keel over sometimes." Like a heckler at show, the little quote halted the conversation. Without turning around Leona recognized the voice,

Emma. "Don't stop talking just because I entered a room, you're going to remind me of my parents.

"We were speaking about how Remy refuses to eat."

Emma took a banana from the counter and removed the skin entirely, biting into the fruit the same color as Remy's face. "I wouldn't want to either if my sister crashed her car into a ditch."

"See." Remy said.

"It wasn't a ditch—hello to you to by the way."

"Sorry where are my manners, good morning." Emma took a giant bite of her banana, leaving one quarter between her black painted nails."

Was there a funeral at the nail salon? Leona wanted to say.

"Are you both going to have issues getting along?" Betty asked.

"I'm fine," Both Leona and Emma said at once, their eyes met shortly after. Emma had heavy dark eyeliner around her eyes. Her lips were a beautiful pink, a shame that most of the time they were hidden beneath a layer of heavy black lipstick. Her skin color would have most likely been the palest in the room if it weren't for Remy.

"Your sister is good company, I'm glad she's here. I'm sorry about your mother. I never liked the woman." Emma said with infliction that held no remorse.

"That's nice, but I figure Remy can stay with me on the weekends when I'm not working." Leona said.

"I don't want to go back to that house. I want to stay here." When Remy's lips shut, Leona felt a pain in her neck.

"Oh okay, I'll come over here I guess."

"Sure." Remy said.

"Girls, we don't need to outline a schedule of when we'll see each other. Things are bound to change from day to day."

Betty sipped her tea, pinky extended. "I don't want this to turn into a cust—"Betty halted quickly.

"A custody battle? Go ahead say it, it's okay I've learned to bury my emotions." Emma said, never moving a muscle in her face.

The word *bury* was a dagger in Leona for whatever reason. "Why do you have to act like a punk rock band, don't take things so personally." Leona said.

"What about what I just said was personal?"

"Girls please—"

Remy stood from the table and left the kitchen giving back the silence of the room that had been there when Emma first got there.

"This isn't going to be easy," Betty said. "On any of us, but we must make lemonade from this. If not for us—for Remy."

Both Leona and Emma gave the table a long stare.

"Well I'm here for her." Emma said, churning Leona's stomach like butter.

Trevor

Through the thin cheap wood of the door, animated voices from the television seeped through, distracting him from that beautiful girl who left Nome Hospital. The pink spot between her legs coated with a light stubble made his hand grip tighter, go a little faster, stealing his breath all while making sure that gold painted doorknob was still next to the door frame.

Trevor would never see her again, only in his fantasy. He would never know what it's like for his lips to meet hers, the taste between her thighs or the sounds she'd make during love making. He could count his blessings for having the chance to see how perfect her secrets were, how pink and small her nipples were. But he'd never get to go as far as feeling any of it. He decorated the toilet seat with his lust and then wiped it away with a piece of toilet paper, shaking his manhood a few times before pulling up his basketball shorts. He felt better—still sad, but better.

Closing the door behind him as if to leave his longing in there, he shut the television off and made for the kitchen. Pleasuring himself always made him hungry.

"I was watching that!" Robin yelled from her bedroom. His little sister amazed him with how she could watch something when not even being in the same room or paying the slightest bit of attention to it.

"No you weren't." Trevor opened the fridge and found left-over pizza, clad in some plastic wrap from the night before. He bit into it cold.

"Do you have work tonight? Robin asked, now standing before him blowing at her freshly done nails.

"Yeah, at four."

"Grandma was coughing in the bathroom again."

Trevor did his best to not move a muscle in his face. "Has she been taking her medication?"

"I heard her bottles rattling this morning so I guess."

Their grandmother at seventy-eight years old, Julie, mostly laid in her bed. Julie's ailments were now all due to old age, and no matter how much effort she exerted into cleaning the bath-room sink—her blood always remained. Some doctors said it was the early stages of liver failure, others said its due to tumors, a minority said it'll pass. Either way the Bailey grandkids know that their grandmother doesn't have much time, and with her social-security check being half their income, they knew their time was limited as well.

"She might just have another cold or something." Trevor said.

"That's why the sink looks like strawberry shortcake right?"

"Shut up."

"I'm sixteen, not eight, and I'm not blind."

"Yeah I know," Trevor finished off the crust of his pizza, turning his back to Robin while pouring a glass of water.

"Okay, so what are we going to do about this T?"

Trevor lacked an answer, in its place annoyance stood. By now he knew what was going to happen and had numbed him-self to the outcome. Julie had touted the phrase *what happens will happen* as long as he was able to comprehend speech, even when his parents left decided that raising him and his sister wasn't worth the effort, leaving them both with Julie a week after his eighteenth birthday. Today he was twenty-two.

"I'll talk to her." Trevor said.

"What's that gonna do?"

Trevor's patience started to run thin. "Robin,"

"No, the fuck is that gonna do Trevor? Make her stop spitting up blood? Stop her from getting older? When she dies how are we going to pay rent?"

"We'll figure it out." He said in his softest voice, this way when he heard himself speak he knew he was still in control of himself.

"That's what you always say, yet, she still sounds like she's fucking dying."

"I need you to think positively."

"I see through you, you don't have to be Mr. Strong, you know we fucked." Her eyes waited for his to collapse under pressure, to see what her older brother was really made of. But he was wise to her game.

"Here," He turned on the television. "Watch your shows."

The sound of Robin sucking her teeth was louder than the television's volume. She didn't watch it though, storming back to her room where she would most likely spend the rest of her day. Despite being well a tuned to a vast social life, depression had clearly taken her as of late.

"Yo, can you do something other than lock yourself away for the rest of the day." Trevor asked.

"There's nothing else to do." She never turned around, her rear-end giving a bounce after her halt.

"You know after you apply to jobs, it wouldn't hurt to go there and ask about your applications."

"So I can work at Waymart or someshit? That'll only bring in like a hundred a week. That won't save us when she dies."

Trevor watched her walk into her room, the door shut giving him nothing but stickers from her childhood and a Barney poster—a childhood stripped away despite his efforts to save it.

He always knocked before entering Grandma Julie's room, each time her response grew fainter and fainter. On some days though, she would give one filled with slightly bit more energy, extending some hope that maybe she was getting better. Today was not one of those days.

"Hey," Trevor entered, Julie laid on her side listening to news radio, her flowery nightgown stopped at the knee where he had gotten used to seeing her veins say hello. "Did you take your medicine today?"

"Dear, you know as well as I, they might as well be candy at this point."

"You're having a bad day."

"I'm having a realistic day," The clarity in driving her sentences made Trevor hope that maybe it was a sign that all wasn't as bad as they assumed. He wanted to refute what she said but the blood in the sing shot that idea in the face.

"Robin, I know she's upset."

"I don't know how to help her."

"Do what you're doing now."

"It doesn't seem like it's enough."

"Nothing ever does, until it does."

Trevor ran his eyes over the patches of hair which remained from what used to be a giant afro. The pictures from her youth would lead one to believe that they were two different people—maybe they were.

"I don't want you to die." He felt like crying.

"There's no shame in it, it's better than spitting up blood every morning."

The fact that she had admitted it confirmed she was giving up.

"Can you not talk like that?"

"I always used to tell your mother that, such foul language on that one. When she left with your father, to wherever they went, the drugs never bothered me half as much as the cussing, I hoped wherever they went they learned to respect the language."

"How can you not be mad at them?"

"Don't get mad at ignorance, you'll save ninety-percent of your anger for better things." She closed her eyes as if to single she was too tired to continue the conversation. Trevor had nothing left to say anyway.

At the hospital Trevor washed his hands in the sink, the longer he took the more time he got away from the sadness of the building. After Robin's angst and his grandmother's lack of hope, this shift would be like spoiled icing on spoiled cake. After Leona leaving there was nothing to look forward to. At least when she were held up on that mattress on the third floor, there was someone who showed an interest in him, although that might have just been his own lust playing tricks on him.

"Bailey you ready yet? We have a body that needs transporting."

And your fuckin hands are broken? Trevor wanted to say but knew against it. He craned his head to the illuminated door way, the rest of the room was a blue-dark. "You're not a nurse anymore Phillip?" Sarcasm on Trevor sounded sincere, and he knew this about himself.

"I have to tend to the Coughlin girl." Phillip had the excuse ready.

"What room is it?"

"224, Rosa Alvarez, she had no family there, shit was hella sad bro."

"Go to Coughlin,"

When Trevor met the corpse the breathing tube had already been removed, and the woman's skin was an off yellow.

"I hate throwing out the dead's possessions." The doctor said palming what looked to be the woman's earrings, it was a Doctor named Hampton, Trevor hadn't noticed him walk in.

"I heard she didn't have any family."

"Everyone has a family," Hampton responded, "But blood can drip away." Hampton placed the earrings into a Pricewich bag and dropped them into the large pocket in front of his white doctor's jacket. Trevor remained still while Hampton wrote on a clipboard. "Alright you can conceal."

Trevor closed the door behind himself and placed a white sheet over Rosa, from toes to head. Then adjusted the bed to lower her body and make the bed appear as if it were empty. Hampton got the door and Trevor wheeled the body away from where her last breath took place. He couldn't help but think about his grandmother. Remaining numb was easy when; the fragility of life a reminder that the day he was preparing for would be inevitable, not just the worst case scenario. Without Julie, even with Robin, loneliness wasn't a strong enough word to describe his dread.

The body and Trevor rode the elevator. He contemplated on quitting in that moment; the peril of having to deal with the morbid on a daily basis acted as his personal hell. But then he realized outside of that hell was just another hell—a dying grandmother, the responsibility his little sister, and little to no future plans. A lack of hope hurt just as bad as anything else, the morbid concealed in the bed before him almost seemed like the lucky one.

Once the elevators opened, Harriett, the medical examiner stood over her clipboard at her work station next to a vanilla- pale Carmichael.

"Other folk go into the stock-rooms to get frozen dinners, lucky-you, getting to put away the dead." She said, eyes never leaving the clipboard.

"Yup, I'm sure winning the lotto feels just like this shit."

It was a half grin that graced her face, it made Trevor feel proud. He couldn't hold it against her for lacking a sense of humor. The second one finds the courage to laugh down in the cold lowest level—another body comes wheeling in. Harriet finally shot him a look.

"Usually those pearly whites force me to put on sunglasses, why do you look down?"

"My grandmother is gonna be in here soon." He wheeled his corpse to the corner where Harriet removed the sheet.

"Death always feels closer than it is Trevor."

"Yeah."

"Sometimes you just have to accept things and do your best. It'll get better."

Upstairs Trevor was stopped by three different nurses, one doctor and a patient who was a regular; a victim to her Alzheimer's with a routine of forgetting her room.

"Hey Trev, when you're done with Luciano's room, Dr. McMillian wants to see you." A receptionist on her way back to the desk said to him. That's when his phone rang—it was Robin.

"Hey, Grandma's been throwing up, can you bring Pepto on your way home and air freshener, the bathroom stinks of vomit."

Trevor prepared his vocal chords to not give away his grief. "Yeah, no problem."

"You good?"

"Yup."

"Alright, I'll see you when you get home."

"Okay."

After hanging up, Robin's youthful voice penetrated his chest. The things she had to see, the things she must be feeling, he was failing to protect her from it all—failing as an older brother.

Trevor found a small janitor's closet on the third floor, no one had seen him enter; the door had a lock on it as well. Inside he tugged the string, illuminating the cramped space with a lightbulb a foot from his head. That's when he began to cry, sobbing into his hands as quietly as he could. By the first minute the top of his fingers were drenched with tears and every now and again he let out a guttural sound, too hard to cry silently.

Trevor Bailey remained in the closet for what had to be a half-hour. He straightened his face, dried it with a paper towel and unlocked the door. Out he came, bumping into Kim: another nurse.

"There are gloves in Hampton's office if you need them." She said.

Trevor smiled, "Thanks."

Coping

As usual Hanky wiped down the counter off in the corner, the sound of the television remained on mute while he watched the thing as if he were the only one that could hear it. *Ralph's Diner* would have been just the thing to take Leona's mind off of everything—if it weren't the place where she had met Mateo. From the booth with the rips in the seat to the French toast on the menu, everything brought her boy into her psyche. Of course, the usually light rock that played softly in the back ground of the fifty-year old diner was replaced today with nothing but love songs, something Lauren tried to joke about but failed while she ate her Panini.

"I forgot what it was like to do this." Lauren said, lettuce falling onto the plate.

"I didn't, I missed it."

"You keep looking at the door—he's not going to walk in."

Leona tried to not let it show with the muscles in her face. "I know that, I wasn't looking for him."

"Liar."

Leona picked the hardened cheese off the plate from her cheesesteak, leaving silence on the table.

"We could have eaten somewhere else, it's not like diners are in the title of our book or something."

"No, its fine, I'd rather not run from things."

"Okay but you don't have to face this stuff right away, it's okay to distract yourself."

"It's hard to distract yourself from what's missing."

"What's missing doesn't deserve your thoughts right now." There was anger in Lauren's tone.

"I miss him."

"You don't know how you're going to pay for school, don't you think that should be weighing on your mind a little bit more Leona?"

She was right, but right wasn't easy. "I know, I'm too... like sad to care about that right now."

Lauren pursed her lips together so hard they looked like they might explode. "Maybe if you started caring about what matters you'll forget you're sad, it worked with me."

"When did you have to do that?" Leona couldn't remember her ever being sad.

"After I broke up with Jack."

In that moment Leona realized why people's jaws hit the floor when they're shocked—disbelief fills their mouth. "When did you break up with Jack?"

"About a month ago."

It was hard to believe, they had been together for two years and Jack Taylor was the one she had once mentioned giving her virginity to. Now it was all gone, as if it never happened.

"Why? I don't understand, and why am I finding out about this just now?"

Lauren took a moment, biting into her Panini like it were her first bite. "I don't know, the spark was gone. I kept thinking about giving it up to him and it didn't feel like. It felt like we were forcing the relationship."

"Okay, I guess that makes sense, you still didn't tell me for a month though."

"I was numb after it, spent most of my time reading and avoiding my own thoughts. I was kinda glad you got into all this trouble, gives me something else to focus on."

"Well I'm glad my suffering has brought you comfort." Leona laughed.

"You know what I mean."

After they both finished up in the diner, Lauren drove herself and Leona to the mall, where they bought a few pairs of clothes and then they went to see a movie. Getting around in the cast wasn't as bad as Leona had presumed although it still proved to be cumbersome; people in the mall sucked their teeth at how slow she would walk, and getting up in the theatre lead Leona to hold her bladder until the movie ended.

"I don't know what these people expect you to do, stay home until the cast comes off?" Lauren had said in the mall.

"I don't care, it is what it is."

"How's your car coming along?"

"My aunt got an estimate and it should be out of the shop in a few weeks."

"That's good, what about work?"

"Once I can drive, my boss said I could assist the book keeper for a few hours a day."

"That should probably cover food and stuff for you."

"Yeah." The conversation had an obvious pity to it, once thing Lauren wasn't good at doing was making a bad situation seem less pathetic. The more that she would try to illuminate the bright-side, the darker the situation seemed to feel.

But Lauren had accomplished her goal of the day which was taking Leona's mind off of her problems. It was the car ride from the movie theatre that proved to be the most distressing.

Knowing that the empty house awaited her, with no Remy sleeping on the couch and no mother to make dinner. No one would be coming home, there would be no breakfast tomorrow morning—not even a text or call from Mateo. It was petrifying.

They arrived before the little white fence, her mother's car absent, invoking a rage and curiosity that she had hoped to avoid. Lauren must have sensed it.

"Are you going to be okay?" Lauren asked, fiddling with her hair.

"Yeah, I'll be fine."

"I could stay over if you'd like."

"I can't run from this, the ones who run from hell get shot in the back."

"Wow– that was absurdly morbid."

"Sorry, you know I like to face shit head on."

"Pride goeth before the fall."

"I guess. I'll text you."

Despite a number of claims that she could do it by herself, Lauren helped Leona from the car to the door, it made Leona reconsider her offer of staying over but her pride had refuted the idea.

Once the door was shut behind her, the dread sunk in. The quietness of the two story house was like death and a life that was no more. The small hope that maybe her mother would one day come back doused the flames of hopelessness, but only for a short time. They always came back, followed by worries of what will she do about school—and her future. The only way she would combat that was with pride again; the pride that she would just fight, figure it out as she goes and hope for the best. Until that feeling subsided and the whole pattern of thought began from the beginning once more.

At first she tried her best to clean. The sun was setting out the windows, sending a reddish beam through the glass and against the dining room cabinets. That acted as her time limit, and once the sun had vanished she made dinner: microwavable chicken strips along with microwavable steamed vegetables.

Does this thing even work? Leona thought to herself before heating up the food for ten minutes. But it did, and she found herself eating at the empty dining room table despite crying in between spoonful's. The first few bites weren't that emotion in-ducing, it was when she spied the empty chairs along with the sound of Max eating his food in the kitchen that sent her chest to produce tears. It took her forty-five minutes to finish, by the end her make-up was little streaks of blue and black down her cheeks.

Leona let Max go into the yard, once she opened that back door flurries of fear filled her; the idea of someone breaking in and killing her became all too real. She was home alone, with no-one to protect her. She hadn't thought about it until now. *Who would want to kill?* Michael was the only one that popped into her mind.

She was able to calm herself down, losing herself through television. But after an hour of that she still got lost in thoughts. The sight of her phone resting on the living table gave her an idea, like a tool to save her from her own misery, although, she was going to be playing with fire.

Leona sat with the television off and only the reading light on in the corner. The amount of light filling the house reminded her of the night where Hank had struck her mother and tried to do the same with her. A monster of a man he was, leaving Liz to sit in her depression and self-loathing with a bloody lip to show for it all. Maybe the warning signs to her vanishing had been there all along, maybe there was something Leona could have done to prevent it all. Max's head lifted from his slumber, the doorbell rang. Leona's heart raced as soon as it did. She left the couch and placed a stray hair behind her ear, taking her time to the door in her favorite red-shirt and purple-plaid pajama pants. When she opened the door it was the one she had summoned: Noelle.

"Hi." Noelle said while walking through the doorway.

"Hey," Leona couldn't believe what she had allowed herself to do. "Thanks for coming."

"I can't say that I'm not shocked, rewind to a few months ago where I was screaming in a bagel shop as your sister—"

"I know, things change for the crazy. Can I get you anything to drink?"

"No, I'm okay, but thank you."

It took a few moments for the awkward to subside. Noelle sat on the couch across from the television while Leona took the couch adjacent to it, the one that her and Mateo would have sex on while her mother was grocery shopping.

"I'm guessing you called me here for a reason other than just hanging out?" Noelle said, catching Leona by surprise.

"Would I be wrong for doing that? I mean, sometimes friendships are born through small favors. You were the one who originally approached me, and I'm sure it wasn't just for the reasons you laid before me in the hospital."

"You think that I want Mateo? That I would be so insane as to just ask you for him or something?" The heavily mascaraed eyes squinted in displeasure, her massive cleavage sparkled in the light so much that it almost seemed like she were wearing greasy glitter.

"I don't know, I just find it weird that he goes missing and you appear."

"What are you implying?" She asked as if she already knew the answer, Leona had nothing.

"I don't know. I honestly don't."

"That's good then," She crossed a leg, her boots high black boots looked new, or at least well taken care of. "Maybe you'll trust me. But can I ask why you called me here tonight? I feel like I already know but I'm still not sure."

"Trevor."

"Yeps, I was right. You want his number. But if you're still holding out hopes for Mateo, why would you want to even have Trevor in your life, you clearly want to fuck him."

"I do not." Leona could feel her face getting red.

"Have you ever fucked a black guy? Their dicks are—"

"Noelle, we're not cool like that."

Noelle laughed though, sending her eyes to the floor. "But my question."

"I don't feel for him that way, I just know he's a good person and I could use more friends right now."

"What if he liked you?"

Again, her face went tomato. "I would still see him as a friend."

"Pretty heavy amount of trouble you went through to get his number tonight though, wouldn't you say?"

"It's hard to not think you're up to something when you're instigating me to get with this kid."

"I'm just saying, Mateo isn't around, he left you. Why should you—"

"Shut up…" The regret filled Leona like a faucet breaking over a sink. "Sorry, I didn't mean that, I just don't feel that way. I'm not mad at him. Getting with Trevor would be cheating. I don't cheat."

Noelle held back a smile, "What if Mateo cheated on you? Would you cheat back?"

"Mateo wouldn't cheat on me. He has no reason to."

"You didn't answer me."

Leona could feel herself getting upset. "I would not cheat back I would leave him." There was something about the way Noelle accepted her answer that didn't sit well with her. "Why?"

"Just curious, I never really got to know your convictions or anything like that, it's good to know. You're a good person."

"Are you going to give me Trevor's number or not?"

"Yes, do you have to be so hostile with me? I've been nothing but honest with you."

"And massively suspicious."

"Who called who tonight?"

"Touche'."

Noelle kept to her word and forked over Trevor Bailey's phone number and oddly enough they began to watch television together even going as far as laughing together. It made Leona feel less alone for the time being, Noelle did seem to genuinely like spending the time together. When Leona went to make popcorn and Noelle stayed on the couch, she had returned with the kernels all popped and the house smelling of butter to see Noelle with her feet up and her shoes off, that was when she decided to ask.

"You could stay over tonight if you'd like?"

"Yeah, that would be cool. You're best friend won't get jealous right?" She laughed.

"Mateo would likely get more jealous." Leona placed a bowl on the living room table and poured some popcorn for Noelle.

"What's your friend's name by the way?"

"Lauren, she probably will be weary of you off the bat."

"That's understandable."

Leona copied Noelle in pulling her feet on the couch, the misery that had filled her before seemed more like small fry now, she was as alone as her mind lead her to believe. There was Betty, Remy Lauren, and now Noelle and hopefully Trevor. The road at the moment didn't look so treacherous. Hopefully it would stay that way.

The Text Message

Lauren Torres took off her bra and fixed her pony-tail. After shutting off her light the room took in an ocean blue mixed in with a little bit of white from the moon. It felt good to be back in her old room, even after a year in her dorm the four walls had still felt alien. She missed the sound of the train passing by every hour, the pictures from all the places she traveled hanging on her full length mirror. It was a sad thought knowing that one day she would have to leave it all for good.

Lauren tussled and turned in her bed, she was tired but not tired enough. Her mind raced, the blanket became too hot and then too cold. Her legs wanted to keep moving, her back hurt when she laid in one spot for too long. And then there was the laptop, covered in stickers and plugged in while sitting quietly on her desk. It was what she used to communicate with Leona, but more importantly Jack.

Every night they'd skype, until they started losing things to talk about. He seemed to grow tired of the conversation, no matter how much work Lauren had put into it. Questions about his Pelpage internship, about his day, his family, television shows, how he was feeling—she tried so hard. But in the end, she knew what he wanted, what he grew bored with waiting to get—sex. It wasn't fair to him.

After five minutes of thinking about Jack, Lauren threw a t-shirt over the laptop and turned to her side. But still, there was no combating her restlessness. Tomorrow she would go with her father to a car show up town, her father loved the car show every year. She had wanted to get sleep to be able to enjoy it with him, it wasn't happening. So she made her way downstairs, her breasts meeting a breeze up-under her shirt, it almost made her want to laugh from the tickle.

In the kitchen she found a slice of cold chicken and threw it in the microwave for two minutes. While waiting she felt like a fat-ass, remembering her mother saying never to eat greasy food before bed. But Lauren didn't care, it made her feel better. She ate the drumstick on the way back upstairs wrapped in a paper-towel with a glass of water in her other hand. As soon as she got back into her room and laid back down, her phone vibrated, it was a text from Leona. Just from the first line alone she could tell that the rest was going to make the night even worse.

Listen, I may be drunk, but I mean every word of this. I hate u and ur a shitty friend. I don't want u in my life NEmore, u understand? The way u bitch n moan about everything, like shut the fuck up. I'm tired of it. I have my own shit to deal with. I've faked liking you for a while now and I can't NEmore. Don't text me, delete my number, I want nothing to do with u. seriously, this isn't just the alcohol talking. We're better off apart. If I text u tomorrow or whatever, just know, this is how I feel. I hate you and thanks for not fucking being here when I needed u the most bitch.

Is she being serious right now? She asked herself. *What did I do?*

She left the bed and paced for a bit, not knowing whether she should text back or not. She had to, and after asking if it had been a serious text or not, she received no answer. The phone went to voice-mail as soon as she called. That's when the panic set in, was this the end of her friendship with Leona? It couldn't be. It didn't make sense, but then there was nothing to dispute it.

I didn't do anything though, this is sketchy. Where did this come from? She was quiet today, do I really complain about stuff like that? All our years of friendship and she's going to throw it away through text?

One more time she sent a text, but nothing. One more time she placed a phone call and it went to voicemail.

Lauren put her face into the pillow to hush the screams and not wake her parents. When she lifted it up, even in the dark-blue light she could see the puddle in the center of the pillow. She couldn't believe her eyes or what was happening. If the world hadn't crumbled down around her–it had now.

Pride goeth before the fall, she thought. Whether it was Leona being prideful in her anger it didn't matter, Lauren's own pride to fix the friendship kicked into gear. She wiped her face with her Sugenta State College t-shirt and threw the drenched fabric to the bed, throwing on a sweatshirt and sneakers.

When she would sneak out to see Jack past midnight, she would hush the way she shut the front door to not wake her father and her car door would be closed as gingerly as pos-sible—not tonight. Pulling out of the spot like she were off to save someone she sped down the empty streets to confront her best-friend, or former best-friend, the answer was going to be at the end of the trip.

It was an answer that she wasn't expecting—the strange purple Lincoln parked in front of the white fence. *Does she have someone over?*

Lauren shut the door to her car, this time it was louder than when she had shut it leaving. Inches from the front gate, her heart made like the drum in a punk-rock band. The fence creaked on opening, the front door opened so quickly that it made not one noise, but the one who opened it made sure to close it slowly. She recognized the girl—someone she never dreamed of seeing exiting out through Leona's blood-red door, Noelle.

"She doesn't want to see you. If she did she would not have sent me." Noelle said, her eyes had the cut of a cats.

"What is the meaning of this? You don't think I see the sketchiness to it, where's my friend?"

"You might want to put that into past tense. I've never seen someone so annoyed with someone else—so fed up with their *goody goody I'm better than you attitude."*

"What are you talking about?" Lauren felt like throwing up.

"Leona told me everything, vented, and you know what, we have something in common: neither of us are perfect like you. She's tired of feeling like your pile of shit to make you feel better about yourself."

"I'm not stupid." She hoped that maybe this was some ploy, or a prank of some sort. "I'd like to speak with her."

"That's not happening sweetheart." Noelle looked behind herself and took a few steps from the door. "How are you blind to yourself? The way you act...you had to make everything about you didn't you?"

"What are you—"

"Everything that Leona's going through, and you had to turn it around and cry over your own spilled milk, your poor boyfriend and how devastated you were to break up with him." She laughed. "You breaking up with him–somehow you found a way to whine over something you did yourself."

How would she know about that? Why is she over at Leona's house? Is it all true?

"Well? Are you just going to stand there looking stupid? Either say something or go."

"Why won't she come out and see me? Why can't she say any of this to my face?"

For once, Noelle looked sincere. "Leona could stand to see the face that I'm staring at right now, so confused, so caught off guard. From what she told me, I'm really surprised that you didn't see this coming." Noelle turned around and made back for the door. "I'm kinda sorry that it had to happen this way, but at least now you'll hate me a little bit more than you do Leona." Over the shoulder she smiled and the door closed, leaving Lauren standing stupidly by the fence.

Once in her car, she wanted to cry but couldn't. Maybe it was disbelief, maybe a little bit of anger. Either way, she was going to leave Leona alone until she reached out to her. *I don't care, when she wants to come back to our friendship, I'll be here. She's just going through things that's all.*

It was the most comforting lie, not the easiest to believe, but definitely the most comfortable.

My Babies Back

Betty was bent over the clerk's counter while Remy and Emma sat next to Leona, staring at the television that hung from the ceiling over the vending machine. Leona looked around at all the auto parts, the accessories and everything else that still, reminded her of Mateo. She wished that she could keep herself occupied but upon wakening her phone had stopped working, as if the thing had been dipped in water or something. *Mateo loved cars,* she thought. Picking up her own should have been a joyous occasion, instead it made her feel alone yet again.

"People spend so much money on things they spend less time in than sleeping." Emma said, with her usual monotone, 'I hate the world' type of inflection.

"What about the people who live out of their cars? Mom and I saw a guy like that once." Remy said, with the opposite inflection.

"I suppose you have a point."

Leona cringed every time Remy brought up their mother, she seemed to have no qualm with doing so, as if the woman was at no fault at all. It was difficult to get mad at Remy though, instead Leona suffered in silence, changing the subject at every chance she got.

"Maybe something a little bit more uplifting could be spoken about, hobos living out of cars is too much to take in at nine in the morning."

"When's the proper time to speak of such sadness then? If we don't now we'll just procrastinate it—societies good at that when it comes to poverty." Emma said.

"Are you always like this?"

"I think it's honest," Remy said. "Everybody else sugar coats everything."

"Sugar coating only leads to cavities." Emma made sure to get it.

"Well I'm glad you two are the best of friends now." Leona grabbed her crutches and pulled herself from the seat, attempts to not get severely pissed off in jealousy over her little sister's new found friendship were made, but it still made her angry.

"You seem mad." Emma said to Leona's back.

"No, *just* peachy." When Leona made it over to Betty, she had just finished signing all the paperwork, her leg was throbbing.

"So I get my car back? Where is it?"

"You're going to have to spend on gas you realize." Betty held more behind the question, like there was some concern ready to spurt from her mouth, something that she had been festering on.

"Yeah, I know. What? You look like you're going to deliver me more bad news, am I not getting it back?"

"It's not that, I was just thinking on the drive over here, you have the gas money, your phone Hank, food, the electricity, heat, water—how are you going to afford all of this Leona, sure the house is paid for but—"

Leona hadn't thought about all of that. "I'll pick up more hours at Waymart, it's no big deal."

"You're making minimum wage."

"I won't be home to make any of those Hanks outrageous, I'll get a second job or something."

"And what about school?"

Is she fucking kidding me with that one? "I don't know how I'm going to pay for it, so I'm not going back."

"That's not an option dear, you have to go to school."

The idea exhausted her. "To be honest, I have no motivation for that right now and this isn't the place to talk about this." The clerk behind the counter raised his eyes from his cellphone, they almost connected with his bushy red eyebrows.

"I'm sorry, dear. It's just a concern of mine. I need you to go to school."

"Aunt Betty—"

"No, please, it's the one thing that you can control. You won't make the financial aid deadline for the fall, your uncle and I can pay for the fall semester while you apply for it."

Leona couldn't tell where her disbelief landed on more: the fact that the conversation was still going on or that her aunt would really pay for a semester of college for her.

"You don't have to, I can take a semester off."

"No, I'm glad we spoke about this and got it settled. It was really bothering me." Betty snatched the keys from the counter and hung them before Leona, realizing then that she had no way of taking them being that the crutches occupied her hands. Instead, she placed the keys in Leona's pocket. "Are you going to be able to drive?"

"Yeah, I'll be fine."

Betty glanced over to where the girls were sitting. "Why don't you take them to get breakfast, they could both use a time away from reality."

"Emma already lives in a different universe filled with dead unicorns and sick puppies."

"Stop it, she's your cousin." Betty swatted her shoulder. "Here," She took out a fifty-dollar Hank. "Take them to IHOP or somewhere, make sure Remy eats."

It felt beyond good to be behind the wheel again, despite Leona's accident. After the first few blocks she had forgotten that she was even wearing a cast. She wished that she could forget the darkened eyes that caught her every time she checked her rearview mirror. Emma's unhappy stone face seated in the back made her wonder just what Remy saw in the girl, what if anything did they have in common?

At IHOP they all ate quietly. Remy ordered blueberry pancakes with bacon and drenched the pile of batter in syrup. Emma ate her scrambled eggs in nibbles while Leona ordered a sampler, guzzling down her orange juice in between her shovels.

"I don't get why mom never liked this place." Remy said, giving Leona and innocent set of eyes.

"How long are you staying with Aunt Betty?" Leona asked Emma, ignoring Remy's comment.

"I don't know, from what I was told, until the end of the summer."

The conversation ceased after that, the awkward silence filled the table with the only interruption being the waiter, a young girl with jet-black hair who seemed to sense the unpleasantness between the three of them.

"Are you two quiet because I'm here? You both are starting to remind me of my parents." Emma said.

"I didn't think we were being quiet at all," Leona lied. "How do you like this neighborhood and stuff?" She asked Emma.

"Why won't you speak to me about mom? Just because she's gone doesn't mean she doesn't exist anymore...or that the past isn't still there." Remy said, slowing down the bacon to Leona's mouth.

"Because I don't want to speak about her."

"Why?"

Leona glanced at Emma as if to make her disappear. "Because there's no reason to. To be honest I don't know how you find it so easy to do so." That was when Leona remembered her little sister was just that—little.

"Because she's our mom."

"I don't get how you can—"

"Don't get mad." Emma said. "Maybe if you stopped pretending that it doesn't hurt you there would be something to talk about at this table and something to talk about with your little sister."

There was a red IHOP sign across the restaurant, it hung on the wall and looked as if it might give off a slight buzzing noise if one were to get close enough to it, the burning red glow it gave off—matched Leona's anger.

"Shut up, I didn't ask you for your opinion, okay?

"Don't speak to her like that," Remy said, "She's been acting more like a big sister that you have as of late."

There was a flurry of things that Leona wanted to respond with, angry things that she would soon regret if said. But nothing left her lips, she continued to eat her food and the rest of the time at IHOP was spent in silence.

Back at Home Leona struggled to get through the door and find a way to close it without losing her crutch. But she did, hurling the car keys to the dining room table along with the mail. *The bitch still gets more mail than me and she doesn't even fucking live here.* That was when Leona's mind jumped back to the day of the crash, the hospital, Trevor and then his dick. She wondered about it, she wondered about him. Shaking the thoughts away she brought herself to the couch where she laid down, it was now only noon.

Leona made herself feel better by bringing her thoughts to Mateo, using her hand to alleviate the stress, underneath her now was a small puddle. On any other day she would have worried about someone seeing it, but today she knew there would no one. She pulled up her thong and hopped to the kitchen, pouring herself a glass water. She guzzled the thing down and held herself up with the kitchen table, staring at the counter where her mother once cooked every night. Feet away from her was where her father would sneak up behind her mother and wrap his arm around her, kissing her neck. All of that now was gone, dead was the better word.

Leona threw the glass at the counter where the thing shattered into a million little specs of glass. Once it all sprinkled to the floor Leona let out a guttural scream, pulling at her curls with both hands. When she let go of the table she fell to the floor, nearly hitting her head on the way down. The tiles were cold against her thighs, yet she laid there, motionless, with the same face that Emma wears year-round.

I miss Mateo, I miss Mom, I Dad, I miss the old life, why can't anything stay the same?

Leona laid on the floor for a good twenty minutes until she sat up, her leg ached in a mess of tight cast that seemed like it were filled with needles. Trevor entered her mind again, the way he would fluff her pillows and make sure that she was okay. It was fairly obvious that it was all his job, but some of it felt sincere. *The little time that we spoke had to be sincere right? I shouldn't be thinking of him in this way.*

She picked herself up once Max licked her face. *Dog food, another expense,she*e thought. At the couch she went to use her phone and remembered the thing was busted. *Fuck, I can't even call Lauren.*

And then she saw it, like it were written on a piece of paper made from a thinly cut piece of gold—Trevor's number, etched in blue ink by Noelle. It sat crumpled on the living room table, a diamond in the rough. Without a second's hesitation she dragged herself to the house phone and dialed, not knowing whether her hand was shaking from weakness or nerves, the latter one seemed like the answer.

"Hello?"

Hello Nurse

He sat in the passenger seat, quietly. From the very corner of her eyes she watched his hands as they didn't quite know what to do with themselves. It was somewhat awkward: the last time they had been together she was in nothing but a gown, at the mercy of his instructions. Seeing Trevor out of his scrubs, in a t-shirt and cargo jeans wasn't what she was expecting, stupidly she had expected him to still be in scrubs.

"So you take the bus every day?" She asked, not knowing whether she sounded judgmental.

"Yup, can't afford a car right now."

"Even on a nurse's salary?"

"I'm only part-time."

After the conversation took control of itself, they went to a get her a new cellphone. She was beside herself on the matter that they couldn't transfer her contacts.

"At least you have my number in there." Trevor joked as they left the store where most of the cellphone sales reps were covered in acne and almost seemed as surprised as Leona that they were employed there; she couldn't tell whether Trevor was flirting with her or not.

"I would have at least liked to have my best friend's and boyfriend's number in here."

As they walked to her car, Leona stubbornly refusing his help, the silence grew tense, and then he asked the question she hoped he wouldn't have pondered.

"If you have a boyfriend what is it that you want out of me?"

If she had known she would have still probably not have told him. "I don't know."

"There had to be some reason for you calling me to run errands with you today."

I want to suck your dick, Leona tripped on that thought and Trevor caught her before she could hit the concrete. A passerby also stopped to help and Leona could sense Trevor's apprehension.

"You got her?" The stranger asked.

"Yeah thank you." Trevor helped straighten her up. "You good?"

"Yes, stupid sidewalk."

In her car they sat, she started the engine and made a reference to the stupidity back in the cell-phone store. But Trevor remained quiet. That caused her to stay quiet as well.

"You never did answer my question."

"I did."

"Okay, then, how do you not know?"

"After our talk in the hospital, I just didn't want you out of my life."

"And that's it?"

All five of Leona's senses picked up his disappointment, which in turn made her not want to disappoint him.

"I want to—" *Fuck you, and suck your dick and I want you, and that's fucking wrong, it's so fucking wrong.* "Just see what happens, if we can be friends or—"

"Or what?"

"I don't know, can't we just go with the flow, why does everything have to be planned out?"

"Yeah we can, but can I ask you something?"

There it was, reminding Leona how annoying she must have been to Mateo every time she prefaced a question with a question. "Yeah of course."

"Are you attracted to me?"

"Yeah. But that's as far as things are going to go—I have a boyfriend and… fuck I shouldn't have even said that."

"Your boyfriends not here right now."

That made her blood boil. "I don't want to talk about this anymore, nothing is going to happen between us and I just want you as a friend."

"Okay."

"Are you mad?"

"Nah, I have no reason to be."

Leona drove to her home, it was the only place she could think to take him given the fact that she had already eaten out today. Inside they watched television in the living room, on separate couches, Trevor sat on the far one. She could tell he was still uncomfortable. Every time that she felt the urge to jump on him she reminded herself that the only reason for her attraction was because she was depressed and Mateo wasn't around.

"Do you want anything to eat or drink?" She asked him and he never looked away from the television.

"Nah, I'm good."

"Do you still want to be here? You look uncomfortable."

"Because what if your boyfriend were to find out that we were together—"

"We're just friends, I'm allowed to have friends."

She could tell that answer wasn't to his liking.

"Alright."

"If you have more on your mind you can say it, you're allowed to speak freely."

"I don't have anything else to say."

"Are you gonna relax more?"

"Yeah."

For an hour they watched television, they spoke here and there but nothing major. He remained reserved, and she assumed that it was because she had friend zoned him. Part of his trust had fell by the wayside, his guard has enveloped him and she didn't like that.

"Like, I said I was attracted to you. But it can't go further because I'm not a cheater, and I'm not in my right frame of mind."

As if the conversation had never taken a break, Trevor had his response cocked and loaded. "If you're not then why keep me around? If I'm only harming you, if I'm a bad influence then why keep me you know?" He was sitting up from his previous slouch, inching off the couch as if to get up and leave.

"Because I like you, why can't it just be—"

"That doesn't make any sense, you're not listening. You're just keeping me around to Band-Aid yourself while he's gone, so you feel less lonely. Fuck that." He left the couch and Leona left hers.

"No, that's not it." She stood in front of him, holding herself up. "I like you, and whether Mateo was here or not, I'd still have you as a friend."

"That wouldn't work."

"Why? I don't listen Mateo, he's not my boss."

"No it's not that."

"Then what?"

"I like you, I want to fuck you, I want—"

Leona's lips shut him up. He kissed her right back immediately. His lips were big, fast and aggressive. Trevor's hand grabbed her face and she grabbed his. They kissed for a good minute and then she pulled away.

"I know, it's wrong and I should go."

"I'm sorry," Leona said.

"You don't have to be." He took a step—and she held him by the wrist.

"No, I'm sorry if you had other plans."

Trevor looked at her and the lip she was biting. "What do you—"

Leona grabbed in between his legs, it was already getting hard, bigger than she expected, bigger than Mateo, and that made her smile. She looked him at him to see his expression, as bewildered as she had hoped it to be, and then she pulled him down onto the couch on top of her.

"I thought—"

"Shut up," Leona responded. "Have you ever fucked a girl with a broken leg?"

"Nah,"

"Have you ever fucked a white girl?"

"Nah,"

"Really?" She was genuinely surprised, biting at the side of his ear right above his earring.

"Yeah, really, you'd be my first."

"So would you."

That was the last thing spoken, and then she woke up.

Leona picked her head from the now sticky pillow and glanced at Trevor who still sat slouched on the sofa occupied with his phone. She could feel the sweat coating her body from the nap. She wondered if he could smell her from where he was. Then she remembered her dream and knew that the redness in her face wasn't only from being hot.

"How long was I out?"

"Like an hour." Trevor laughed. The way he inched up and put his phone in his pocket seemed as though he wanted to leave.

"You want me to drive you home?"

"Yeah, I have to cook dinner for my little sister."

Leona found that adorable. "I didn't know you had one." She rubbed her eyes, feeling the little specs of sleep on her fingertips. "Why doesn't your mom make dinner?"

He remained quiet.

"I'm sorry, I don't know your situation."

"I'll get my shoes." He left the couch.

When they were a block away from his house Leona felt the urge to speak, to say anything, because him leaving left things unpredictable and if Mateo wasn't going to be around she wanted as many people to interact with as possible.

"Am I going to see you again?" She asked.

"Why wouldn't you?"

"I don't know, you're not mad about before?"

"I was, but not anymore. I'd rather not speak about that."

"Okay."

Leona watched him walk to his building until she felt weird for doing so, driving away and losing the breath in her chest. Going home and facing that empty house again, although inevitable gave her anxiety. Which lead her to wonder how she would get Lauren's number. She could go on Pelpage and message her, but that would eliminate the excuse to occupy herself from the loneliness. So she drove to Lauren's house.

On the way there driving was a chore, her life at the moment was bleak. From having a relatively happy setup at home and having a boyfriend who was just getting accustomed to acting like a human-being to having nothing but an empty house—hurt. Leona remembered those nights, the ones where she would feel delirious, tempted by pain and sadness. Mateo had come to her rescue on those nights, now it was left up to herself: an inescapable burden that oddly, she didn't feel self-pity for.

Lauren's house had a red roof, the same red that covered Leona's house door. The lawn was always so well kept thanks to Lauren's mother. From tulips to daffodils, even sunflowers, it was a difficult task to not smile when laying eyes upon the property. Leona got out of her car and brought herself through the gate. Arriving without notice, no matter how many times she had done so in the past still gave her the sense that she was walking onto a stage and doing something awkward. She rang the doorbell.

Lauren opened it after a minute wait, her face held contempt, her body language was unsure of itself. And then the door shut in Leona's face.

The fuck was that? Leona rang the doorbell once more, waiting while fighting the urge to ring again, knock and tap her foot impatiently. The door opened, Lauren stood before once more, tears in her eyes.

"What's the matter?" Leona put a hand to the door to make sure she couldn't close it on her again.

"Are you serious right now?" Lauren asked, blatantly trying to control the levels in her voice—this made Leona want to cry too for some reason.

"Yes, why do you look like you want to cry, what's wrong?"

Lauren took a moment, went through her cellphone and then handed it to Leona.

"What is this?"

"Are you like…messing with me or something…because it's not funny." Lauren let out a child-like noise, like a cry that hadn't grown up yet.

"I didn't send this…that's not me…even when I'm drunk I don't spell like that, I would never say anything to you like this."

"I drove to your house the night you sent it." Lauren walked from the doorway and closed the door behind her.

"Noelle came out and said you didn't want to see me—why was she there? I had asked to sleep over that night."

"I, she came over so I could get Trevor's number. And then we like connected a bit and since I was lonely I said she could sleep over. That had to be her who sent the text, I would never. I didn't even know that you had come over, I swear on my father's grave."

Lauren cleared her face a bit, still seemingly unsure maybe a little bit confused. And then she hugged Leona, crying into her shoulder and saying way too many things at once for Leona's ears to keep pace with.

"Shhhh, everything's okay. I'm here and our friendship is intact I promise."

"How did she know about me and Jack?"

"When we were talking I had brought it up, I guess that my trust was misplaced."

"You think she sent that text?"

"It would explain why she told you to leave and why my phone was broken the next day." Leona had it in her hands and Lauren grabbed her by the wrist to eye the thing. "That's why I came over: to get your phone number."

Now there was anger festering across Lauren's face, for a second Leona hoped it wasn't growing to be hurled at Leona. "Okay so do you believe me now that this girl is bad news? Like I'm mad because this shouldn't have happened. You're weak right now and she took advantage of you…and me."

"How was I supposed to know she was going to do that?"

"Um, when she tried to break you and Mateo up?"

Leona realized that if she wasn't going to calm down then the argument would grow larger, Lauren had a right to be angry. "Okay, you're right."

"Thank you. I'm assuming you'll cut ties with the girl?"

"I want to hear what she has to say about the whole thing."

Lauren walked away, straight back to the door.

"What?" Leona asked.

"I'm not talking to you while that girl is in your life, do whatever you want."

"I just want to see what stupid excuse she—"

The door shut. Lauren was out of sight. Leona knew she had put her foot in her mouth and still—never got Lauren's phone number. That pissed her off the most.

Waymart

Leona tried her best to not look like a complete cripple while bringing herself to Mike's podium, the manager who was luckily understanding enough to find her another position to keep money flowing in, fitting enough she would be the store's bookkeeper.

"Stop thanking me as if I'm some selfless hero, Margaret is on paternity leave, you lucked out is all." Mike said, using his finger to read off his clipboard.

"Still, you could have picked anyone to cover."

"Do you not know how this store operates? It was either hire someone new or put the workload onto me. Believe me, I'm glad you wobbled in here." He looked at her. "No offence."

"None taken."

"Now I wasn't able to finagle time to train you but here's a to-do list that's to be completed every day. Instructions on what programs to use and how to use them are listed there. Obviously if you have any questions you can annoy me with them throughout the day. Punch in."

Leona took the list from him and grabbed her crutch, before she began walking she had to make sure that she wasn't hallucinating.

"Why does it say I'm working eight hours on here?"

"You wanted full-time right?"

"Yeah, but I didn't think I'd actually get it…my pay is thirteen an hour now?"

"I heard about—your situation so I spoke to Gerry." Gerry was the store manager, a frail man who walked like his back had been broken in as many places as his old age. "He said to give you the full-time and if you're good, he'll keep you and Margaret as dual bookkeepers.

Leona couldn't believe it. Although the idea of spending forty hours a week in a book with numbers was now on the horizon, now she had money. The internal celebration dimmed when she looked up from the paper and spotted Michael collecting his carts from around the store. After thanking Mike too many times, Leona made an about face, punched in and began to head to the back room areas where the lockers sat holding her smock. Even Waymart reminded her of Mateo.

Midway up the cereal aisle while lost in her own depression it landed in her ears.

"Yo."

For whatever reason, she wasn't mad. "What?"

"I heard what happened to you, I'm sorry."

"It's fine, nothing I can't handle." *My best friend being mad at me, not so much.*

"You're a strong chick, sorry for bothering you and shit."

Leona could hear the creaky wheels of the carts rolling, the pit in her stomach jumped up and down like it were on a trampoline, and then her eyes rose the floor. "Dav—"

"Leona." The old familiar voice rescued her from what could have been a moment of weakness. "Don't even think about it." Phil said, sounding as strong as ever.

"Think about what?" She turned to face him, the thin hairs coating his forehead and still tickled each other in the store's manufactured air.

"You were going to call the pot smoker over; stress is never reason to bring on company." He brought himself over to her, extending a light hug. Before letting go he stabbed her with words. "I'm sorry about your mother."

Shock filled her. "How do you know about that?"

"The woman would shop here once if not twice a week, when I didn't see her and heard about you I asked around."

"Does anyone else know?"

"Just Mike, and Mike wouldn't tell a secret if he were being branded like a cow."

Leona wondered if Phil was one that needed the thanking instead of Mike for the hours.

"How are you holding up?" Phil asked.

Leona would have left tears on the colorful floor tiles sprinkled with pickle ads if it weren't for the families and strangers walking around and doing their shopping.

"To be honest, terrible. Before all this happened I never thought about living by myself and on top of my boyfriend leaving along with my mother, the giant house with nothing but my dog is driving me mad."

"Where did your boyfriend go?"

"Oh, yeah, so he vanished the day before my mother. He was supposed to pick me up from the mall and never did, I stood there for two hours."

The old man's face turned lava red, his mouth tightened to the point where if Leona hadn't seen it open before she would have believed it was glued shut. He didn't say anything for a while and then did a motion as if he had just remembered where he was. "Your boyfriend, what's his name?"

"Mateo. Are you okay?"

"His last name."

"Colon. You don't seem okay…"

"I'll find your boyfriend, I promise."

"Whoa, how are you going to go about this? Phil, what's the matter, I've never seen you mad."

"I don't care for men who don't follow through on their commitments, a man's commitment is a man's identity. If you don't care enough to follow through on your word, something that only requires trust, then you don't deserve respect in any of your endeavors—I'm sorry, I just feel strongly about this."

"It's okay," His mini-speech nearly made her want to start a rally of some sort. "You really think you can find him?"

"Yes, or at least I'll do my best."

"I feel like it'd be inconveniencing you tho—"

"Who's the one that offered Leona? With my daughters away at college and my wife consumed with whatever it is she does nowadays, I could use the hobby."

Leona laughed at that. "Okay, I can't tell you how much it means to me."

Phil pondered, taking his time to construct whatever it was he was about to say. "You know though, you may not get the answers you're looking for, sometimes digging turns up things that should stay buried—for our own sakes."

"You're very wise Phil, if this were a movie you'd be the cliché' old wise man, but I've dealt with enough in my life already, having no closure is far worse than knowing the truth."

After that, Leona took her leave and got ready for work. Once she sat down in the bookkeeper's booth the cozy size of it made her realize that on a regular day she would have felt cramped and claustrophobic; today it was welcomed, drenched in numbers to steal her away from the dark clouds that hovered outside of the walls.

The first few hours proved productive, going down the checklist and making sure that the cashier's numbers and the store's revenue was in order. After lunch, and after a half hour to herself with just her thoughts, she went back wishing that the next four hours wouldn't go quickly. Every conversation felt like her last as that looming empty house waited for her. That's when she decided that she would confront Noelle after work. It was an emotionally more exciting idea than having dinner at Aunt Betty's.

When the clock hit seven she punched out, taking her time unlike in the past where she'd rush out of the store and into Mateo' car. On the way to her own she spotted Michael in the parking lot in the distance, smoking a cigarette; just because he was familiar, the sight of him nostalgic, she could feel herself wanting to drift over, but didn't. Leona found a bit of self-awareness instead, it was like a speed-bump to her thoughts, but that also came with a dose of reality; seeing things as they are made her wish that she had been stupid. Stupid people always saw the Brightside.

On the way to Noelle's she realized that she didn't have her address. That made her feel like one of the stupid people. She pulled the car over to the side of the road, turned down the radio which had been making the car vibrate from electric guitars and fast drums, and then shut off the engine. She was angry—at herself.

I have no one to turn to. She laughed to the silence of the car. For a moment she watched the ones whiz by out the window. Daydreaming brought on more guilt though, as if she were wasting her life some more. She drove. To where, she wasn't sure.

About seven miles away from town she drove until there were only highways and trees. Her goal now was to find a bar and finding one seemed to have slim odds as the random exit ramp lead to only houses. There was always settling for a diner but finding one would only succeed in reminding her of Mateo; that day where they met and she reluctantly handed over her number. Reluctance wasn't right, it was the best thing she had ever done because despite everything—she still loved him.

So she drove, passing house after house in an effort to enjoy the seclusion and embrace the loneliness and isolation that now haunted her existence. She was almost sad when she came upon the little pub smack in the middle of two empty spaces that looked as if houses could fit into them. There was one parking spot available, right in front of *Anne's pub*, as if the place had known she was coming.

Leona had only ever drank once and that was with Lauren. It had been on a rainy night when she slept over at Cole's house, her father always had three forties of something in the house, that night they had chosen tequila while Cole's parents slept away unbeknownst. It didn't hurt going down as everyone had warned her, it hurt afterwards, and then in the chest. Before she had realized, that uncomforting sting had been replaced with a spinning head, which was fun. As little as Leona could remember, Lauren didn't get drunk, she got quiet, more serious than usual, which for once put Leona in the lightweight's division from her friend.

As soon as Leona's car door shut closed she remembered that her ID read nineteen years of age, propping herself up on the side of her car while pulling out her crutches. *What the hell I was I thinking?* One half of her wanted to see if she could get away with slipping under the legal age radar while the other half couldn't believe that she had over-looked yet another significant sore thumb.

"You ain't telling me you drove here for the first time with a broken leg to get drunk? In the middle of the week on top of that."

The lady was thin yet chiseled, the tank-top she wore used to be white now almost matching the coal black sports-bra she wore underneath. Her nose had looked to be broken and a black and blue gash lined her left eye, Leona did her best not to stare.

"I didn't plan on coming here, just saw it driving by. Are you the owner?" Leona spoke with nerves, the woman reminded her of her mother when she had discovered that Leona had done wrong.

"I am, what're doing driving with a broken leg? You like slowed reflexes and temptin your death?" The woman was hanging up little interconnected flags along the windows of the pub, she had only looked back at Leona once. The rest of the time she spoke to the rusted walls.

"I manage. Why do you decorated when the walls are rusted?"

The lady looked to have broken a smile, it was hard to tell from behind. "Come inside, get off your foot."

Leona followed the lady into the dimly lit pub, there were no other occupants. From the shelves to the glasses, the interior was clean, well-organized and a complete contradiction from the exterior. There were signed pictures of Frank Sinatra, Elvis Presley, Johnny Cash and a few other people who Leona didn't recognize.

"A girl who minds her surroundings, that's like what hunting is for a man, a good skill to have." The lady placed a clean glass up on one of the shelves behind the counter.

"A lot of famous people have been here huh?" Leona asked.

"Yes, and not all of them come here to drink. I'm Anne by the way."

"I'm Leona." She watched as Anne now cleaned a glass with a rag the same color as her tank-top. "Can I order a drink?"

"You're underage sweetheart, and I wouldn't want you crashing your parent's car."

Luckily the place was dim enough where Leona knew the red in her face wasn't all that visible. "If you knew that why'd you ask me to come in?"

Anne smirked and placed the glass on the shelf with the other glass. "The makeup on your cheek, the driving by, the broken leg, I don't turn down people who are having a rough go, like I said not everyone comes in here to drink."

"I'm having a fine *go*."

"Who was that lie for, me or yourself? I would have given you a drink, you've probably drunken before."

"I have. Why don't you then?"

"Answer my question."

"Which one? About the lie? The lie was for you."

"And that's why you don't get a drink."

Leona was confused, riddles had always made her angry yet her father had always prefaced questions like it were Jeopardy. The thought calmed her nerves. "Because I lied to you?"

"You have people who depend on you don't ya?" Anne took down what looked to be a bottle of bourbon after moving the stack of papers that had rested atop the thing. She poured herself a glass of the dark liquid.

"I used to, they all moved on or vanished or got pissed at me....I shouldn't be talking about this to a bartended that I just met."

"Why? Is there some law or etiquette against it? People vanish and move on for a reason, most of the time it's just cause you guided them enough to fly away. Don't mean they don't fly back."

"You're basically saying that I was used by everyone."

"Interesting!" Anne took herself another shot.

"What is?"

"What you just put in my mouth, is that how you feel? That you were used? Well honey, that's a fact of life. People use people, when you can accept that you'll be better off."

The door let in a cool breeze, rustling the papers on the table. "You have a very pessimistic outlook on life, I've never used anyone."

"Ever had a boyfriend?"

Leona noticed the top piece of paper on the pile, it was a credit card slip. The name stole her from the room. "Mateo Colon, that's my boyfriend." She pointed to the slip, nearly snatching it before Anne could pull the stack away. "That's his signature, he was here," The tears filled her eyes.

"I got a lot of people who come through here sweetheart,"

"No, that's his signature." The chicken scratch had a giant C holding the rest of the name, scrunched up as if the name had been in a head on collision with another name.

"Maybe he was here."

"Can I see the date?"

Anne lost emotion in her face, Leona knew she shouldn't be asking her for a customer's information but it didn't matter.

"That's before my accident, right when he vanished." Leona shot her eyes at Anne who still remained unattached from everything.

"I remember that kid actually, he was all butt—hurt because his aunt died. Wouldn't speak, just drank his sorrows away. You must be the Leona he mentioned."

Leona wanted to ball her eyes out, scream at the top of her lungs, run in every direction, but she kept the wails in the tip of her throat, the tears were coating her eyes. "He mentioned me? What did he say?"

"That he needed you, but didn't know how to be weak, emotional, He was scared of letting you down." Anne looked as if she were tearing, but maybe that was the liquor. "Were you two close?"

"We had been dating for a year, I was there when—" Leona shot a look to the floor.

"When what?"

"When he tried to kill himself."

Anne's glass hit the floor and shattered. "Was there any reason as to why... Were you two having issues or something?" She took a broom from the corner, as if the breaking glass had been common occurrence.

Leona couldn't think straight anymore. "Do you know where he went, what his plans were? He loved his aunt so much, she raised him. I'm Afraid he might hurt himself if he hadn't already done so."

"Give him time, all men return when they're ready."

"What if he doesn't? He's stubborn like that."

"Again, did you guys have any issues?"

"No, not that I know of, he was supposed to pick me up at the mall the day he vanished. I waited around for two hours."

"I see."

Leona wondered about the woman, there was comfort in her assurance yet it carried an immensely depressing notion, everything she said could be wrong—he may never come back.

"How can you be so sure that he'll come back to me?" Leona asked, wishing that whatever the woman's answer, it would be fact.

Anne took a second from sweeping, and lit the room up with her eyes. The wrinkles in her face all but disappeared.

"I can't say that he will. I don't know him. If he truly loves you, he will." She went back to sweeping. "The people back where you came from, they're there now right? Now I'm no philosopher but if you can't find the boy, then you might as well go back and focus on the ones who are there."

It wasn't the answer that Leona had wanted. She had rather been lied to.

"You have no more business in this bar, I'd suggest you leave."

And that Leona did.

Everything Bagel

Leona parked a block from the little deli. The last time she had set foot in the closet sized shop she had been with Remy and Lauren; the day they put the fear of God into Noelle Santiago. This time Leona didn't know what to expect, the girl had asked to meet as soon as possible, paying no mind to the matter that a very unfortunate conversation would have to take place where the girl received her bread and butter. Was she being accommodating because she knew that she fucked up? Was there going to be an argument? Or was Leona walking herself into some kind of am-bush. She wondered with every step and every click of her crutch against the pavement. As much as she wanted to find out, her pace kept slow, sopping in the morning sounds of birds yelling at each other and the warm chilly air drifting this way and that.

When she met the glass door, Noelle was the only living soul on the other side, unstacking boxes, and taking out what looked to be bags of potato chips, stuffing them into the racks. The work almost made her seem less of a bitch. Then there was a slight hesitation, Leona didn't know what to say, and by the time she had acknowledged her non-existent movement Noelle had noticed too. So she opened the door with a blank mind and decided speaking from the gut would be the best option.

"Hey, surprised you actually came." Noelle said.

"What you did was heinous. Lauren's my best friend, and now she's pissed off at me, you broke my phone, I don't have my boyfriend's number, luckily Trevor texted me—"

"I'm sorry." Noelle left the floor where she had been unpacking on her knees. "I don't know what I was thinking. I guess I got jealous."

"Jealous of what?"

"I can't explain it, just know I'm sorry."

The argument was too simple for Leona's liking. "That's not going to be enough, this friendship is already manufactured and—"

"I think I might have a lead on your mother."

"What?"

"I knew what I had done was fucked up, so I made it my business to do some snooping and my mother was able to track her by credit card. My mom works for a place that looks into credit scores, so she has some pull."

Speechless wasn't what Leona felt, dumbfounded was the proper term. "What?"

Noelle laughed and that twitch was there. The one that made Leona uncomfortable. "I know I…kinda through you a curveball here but it was the least I can do." Noelle picked up the empty box and took herself to behind the counter where she picked up another one and sliced it open with a box cutter.

"Where is she?"

"My mom could only track her with one card and that one has since been terminated, the last purchase made was at a grocery store in Tallahan City."

Tallahan was two-hundred miles from Nome city, still part of Sugenta state but the far west side bordering Pennsylvania. Her mother Liz had always spoken about moving to California. That's where Leona and Remy had learned the term *pipedream*, the irony that she left them both to possibly go sickened Leona. That sickness although devastating was easy to mold into rage.

"This doesn't excuse you for what you did with me and Lauren."

"I wasn't expecting it to. I just did it to be nice, my mother has access to things and it wasn't a hassle, you're allowed to be as mad as you like."

Noelle's lack of confrontation and ease of statement just made Leona want to bicker more. "Why are you being so co-operative? I came here fuming."

"Because I know when I'm wrong and I live it up to it. There's nothing else I can do."

"First you try to break me and—"

"How long are you going to hold that against me? I've apologized for that."

"Now you try and break up my friend and me. There's a pattern there."

"So why are you still standing here, I've apologized, I've listened to Trevor go on about how much he wants you, I even asked my mother, who I don't get along with to help find yours, I'm sorry but I don't know what else you want."

"Wait, what about Trevor?"

Noelle clipped a nail on one of the racks while dropping a box to the floor. "Fuck, yeah don't mention I said that about him. He wants your ass."

Is she being literal or does she just mean in general? My ass isn't even all that nice it's flat. Does Trevor really think it's nice? "How often does he talk about me?"

"Here and there, mostly that he wants to be strong for you but the temptation is there. Sorry, I shouldn't be saying these things."

"It's alright, I don't really know if I should keep hanging out with him if he has feelings like that." *Why am I hinting to her for advice?*

Noelle left her knees once more, stretching out her back and looking over her shoulder at the inventory of boxes behind the counter. "I think you should still hang out with him, you guys will always wind up texting each other so why fight that?"

"Because I have a boyfriend."

"Last time I checked you weren't giving Trevor head, there's no foul in just hanging out."

That made Leona blush, she wasn't used to speaking sex with other females. She had been waiting until Lauren lost her virginity if that day ever came. "I just don't want anything happening."

The twitch in Noelle's mouth entered the shop as she leaned up against the counter, Leona envied the size of her chest reaching for the ceiling. "Does someone not trust themselves?" She smiled. "You know what I learned in all my years of being a *slut?* Urges don't lie, you can either run or pretend they're not part of you, or you can embrace them and sleep well at night." Noelle took one of Leona's curls and playfully threw it over her shoulder. "I mean, how do you sleep now?"

Leona took as best a step back as she could on one foot, denying herself the right to accept a word of Noelle's wisdom. "I should go."

"I guess. We should hang out later." Noelle went back to her shop duties.

"Lauren wouldn't be too fond of that."

"Okay then."

Thinking about it, Lauren was mad at her and Leona wasn't scheduled for work until tomorrow. She could go see Remy.

"You're thinking about it, aren't you? I'm not a bad person you know."

Leona stayed quiet.

It was now five o'clock in the afternoon and Noelle drove. Her car smelt of cinnamon and candy, Leona didn't entirely hate it. What she did hate was the way she drove, cutting off any car that drove just above the speed limit and tempting every yellow light. The cigarettes were another thing.

"So you only smoke when you drive?"

"Yeah," Noelle flicked her stag. "It's the only time I feel stressed and I remember my dad always smoked when he drove."

Leona didn't have a response for that, reflecting on how little traits are often stolen from the ones who bring you into the world. *I guess stubbornness is my cigarette.*

"Where is your dad? This was the first time you've ever spoke of him."

"He left, that's why I related to C....you I guess. Both missing our fathers."

"My father never left." Leona clenched her fist hidden behind her leg.

"I know, different circumstances."

"Sorry. Touchy subject."

"It's alright." Noelle looked over her shoulder and despite the Lexus streaming down the street, she shot her car across the yellow line and entered down a side street. Leona's heart had an asthma attack.

When they arrived at what used to be a place called Tysen's cheesesteaks (according to Noelle), all that remained was a small one story building with panels of fresh wood on the windows. Leona found the brown streaks left by letters that had once been there especially funny.

"Okay I swear that this place had living souls in it the last time I was here."

"Which was when?" Leona held back laughs,

"Last November."

"We can just go to Orangefly."

"I hate Orangefly." Noelle sounded like a toddler.

"Ummm," Leona had already forbidden Ralph's in her head, that wasn't happening. Going through her mental rolodex of diners that were so-so she landed upon one that she had gone too with her mother once. "I know a spot by Narrow's junction."

"Kristy's? That place smells like a petstore."

"That's all I got."

"They do have good cheesesteaks though."

Leona couldn't tell whether Noelle was speaking to her or just out loud to herself. Fifteen minutes later they stopped at the light a block down from Kristy's. Leona's leg had begun to feel that end of day swollen soreness which usually dulled after taking a painkiller. She squeezed at her cast and stuck two fingers down inside, that made her remember Mateo in a dirty way, which pulled her out of reality and back into her mind. It angered her; sitting there next to Noelle of all people. *What the hell has my life become, months ago I hated this bitch and now I've forgiven her twice.*

They found a parking spot around the corner from the quaint little diner. Narrows and Seeder was the block, filled with quiet houses secluded from noisy traffic and seemingly life itself. They were the type of houses that look as though inside were fairytales. For once Leona's imagination didn't bring her below dark clouds.

"One day I want to live in a house like this, I've always had to climb stairs and live behind giant doors with no personality.

These houses look like the three bears live in them." Noelle said, looking around.

"Growing up in a house all my life, the little apartment sounds cozy." Much like Mateo' apartment. She wondered about it. Was all the stuff thrown out? Had Mateo returned to it?"

"I guess the grass is always greener." Noelle stayed quiet after that.

When they turned the corner leaving the shoe store next to Kristy's was Lauren and her mother. Leona's heart needed the asthma pump again. This was bad—very bad; if Lauren were to see Leona and Noelle together, which she did. Even from afar Leona could see Lauren's eyes squint and then widen. Leona wanted to speak, she wanted to yell something that would cancel out what Lauren was looking at. But they were walking side by side, just like friends—the way Leona and Lauren had walked time and time again.

"Isn't that your friend?" Noelle said.

"Yeah. That's her." Leona waved on instinct, it was an innocent wave, like she had been ten years old. It was either innocence or guilt, either way she had waited for Lauren to reciprocate—but nothing.

Lauren turned her attention away from Leona and kept in her stride, trailing behind with bags in hand her mother followed. Leona never broke her gaze, watching Lauren and seeking any ideas which would make things better, but just like Lauren's answer, there was nothing.

"Why didn't she wave back?" Noelle asked as if she were the cute little ten year old now.

"Because I'm with you." Leona fired back just as Lauren's mother shut the car door. "You don't see how messed up this is?"

"I see a friend who's being a bitch over who you decide to keep company with."

"After what you did to her?"

Noelle was now picking at a finger nail, "Have you never made a mistake in your life." Noelle looked up, giving Leona eyes which lead her to understand why men would fall for her. "Maybe instead of making me out to be the grand witch in all this, you should ask yourself how your best friend can throw away a friendship over little ol' me."

Lauren's car drove away, and while the tires made music with the asphalt, Leona's best friend presented her with one minor glance. Despite the window being up her features were as clear as day.

Anger didn't begin to explain.

Nurse, Friend and Listener

As usual Aunt Betty poured Leona a glass of steaming hot coffee while she sat and waited for her to unload whatever news she had up her sleeve. Betty had always been the type to ease into conversations. Even voicemails never explained what she had been calling for, instead they were sixty seconds of a plea to call back so she could then get into the reasoning. Just like voicemails, the tea or beverage had been the warmup act for conversation, whether Betty did that on purpose or not, it was a small routine that Leona grew comfortable with over the years; that one constant that would live to be some memory decades from now.

But despite that comfort and despite the solace away from the frenzy in her head, that frenzy still rattled her nerves. Betty only remained quiet for long periods of time when she was pondering the arrangement of her words.

"So," Betty said, sending a dagger across Leona's throat.

"No one ever starts off good news with *so.*"

"Not true….in this case yes though."

"Okay what?"

Betty sat down in her seat, dipping her tea bag into her hot water, her eyes never left the mug. "The police aren't finding anything on Mateo, that or they just aren't paying it a lot of mind. The private investigator that I hired for your mother has turned up nothing either. They both don't want to be found."

Leona placed the information about Mateo in the back of her head for the time being. "What about my mom's credit card use? The investigator didn't find any purchases in Tallahan?"

"Why Tallahan? He looked into her monetary activity and the only thing he turned up was a withdrawal from the bank on the day before she had vanished."

"How much did she take out?"

"Sweetheart, I don't think details are necessary, they're only painful."

Leona couldn't disagree with her there.

"Why Tallahan? There's only farm land up there, not many places to go shopping and use credit cards." Betty asked.

"My friend said that her mother did some snooping and discovered that my mom used her credit card in Tallahan."

"Lauren? Don't her parents work in law?"

"It's not Lauren, another girl and her mother works with a credit place."

"They don't have the authority to go into someone's records like that Leona."

"Your private investigator did it though."

"My investigator gets paid to go through the proper channels in getting the information legally sweetheart." She sipped her tea. "Are you close with this friend? Because I sincerely find her information to be hard to believe your mother wasn't one to go out to the country."

"I was just in Tallahan actually, I went to a bar."

"And what were you doing at a bar? Cleaning the glasses?"

That reminded Leona of Anne, the bartender with the broken nose and chiseled arms. "I was driving around to clear my head."

"Tallahan is miles away."

"It's not that far if you take the highway." There was a pause. "The police really didn't turn up anything on Mateo?"

Betty borrowed the pause; she was terrible at hiding her sympathy. "No dear, they said they'd let me know if they find anything."

"Which means they don't give a shit."

"Leona," For once Betty's voice was stern. "It's hard to find someone who isn't missing but rather wasn't to disappear."

"I don't understand why he –" *His aunt*, she quickly remembered. "I'm having a hard time staying in that house by myself, like I don't want to go home because it feels giant and empty now." She could feel the emotion in her throat.

"Oh dear, I'm sorry." Betty left her seat and took Leona in a hug. "You're welcome to stay here, you know that."

Before Leona could let tears escape Remy walked into the kitchen, it made the muscles in her mouth almost form a smile until the dark cloud came trailing in behind her.

"Hi." Remy said.

"Hey." Leona exchanged Betty for Remy in her embrace.

"How's Max?"

"He sleeps on your bed at night, he misses you." The instant Leona finished the sentence she felt regret at the sight of the sadness Remy wore.

"Life sucks like that, no one thought about the dog." Emma added with such a cold tone that the emotion from the room had been extinguished.

"Are you ever happy?" Leona asked, avoiding the eyes of her aunt.

"Only when accidents happen and no one gets hurt."

"I don't even know what the means." Leona went to the fridge, pouring herself a glass of orange juice.

"Did you not like the coffee?" Betty asked, reminding Leona of its existence.

"I want something cold." *Besides Emma's soul.*

"Why don't you all go down to the park, it's a beautiful day out, you shouldn't be cooped up inside. We'll talk about all this stuff another time."

"What stuff? Remy asked, stealing the comment that was meant for Leona.

"They were probably talking about your mother." Emma added.

"Are you in this conversation?" Leona asked the one with too much eye shadow.

"I don't mind her talking, at least she's not scared to talk about things with the people who want to talk about them." Remy left the kitchen on that note, leaving Leona to boil.

"Again," Betty said awkwardly, "I think the park would be a good idea.

In an effort to fix things with Remy, Leona took her little sister and the demon on Nome City to the park. Leona and Remy found a bench meeting the walking path in between the bright green fields of grass. People walked their dogs, others rode their bikes, and the breeze took away the sun's heat but left behind its brightness. Emma stalked a pigeon with a twig while silence sat in between Leona and Remy. It almost made Leona laugh at loud at all the black Emma was draped in despite the beautiful weather.

"I don't want you to be mad at me." Leona sliced the awkwardness away with a butter knife of words.

"You talk to Aunt Betty about mom but with me you always change the subject."

"I was speaking more about Mateo than mom."

"I don't believe that." Remy's legs dangled off the bench, swinging back and forth showing her age.

"When we did speak of mom it was just about her private investigator and stuff, I wasn't speaking positively—you always do."

"She's still our mom, just because she's not here doesn't mean that changes."

That angered Leona. "How can you be so forgiving?" Leona watched her legs swing, trying to justify her blind faith with being eleven years old.

"You forgave me when I hid your Sugenta State letter."

"That's a totally different situation, you were trying to keep me here. I can understand that. It's not like you abandoned me."

"You forgave me when I asked dad to see that movie."

For a second Leona had to comprehend just what she meant by that, then she did, and all her will power went into not snapping at Remy. "Don't blame yourself for that, it wasn't your fault."

"Yeah sure—"

"No, I'm serious, that had nothing to do with you. It was out of your control."

"If mom hadn't been stressed she wouldn't have left."

"We don't know her reasoning for leaving—"

"She was mad at me for not cleaning my room the day before she left, it was the one time that I just didn't want to do it and I didn't mean to make her mad."

Leona realized what was happening now, what her sister was doing to herself. The guilt, the blame, the regret—it was all too familiar. And when Leona looked upon her little sister's cheeks, there were the streams of tears even though Remy made not one sound. It was the type of crying that made Leona want to cry too.

"Remy—nothing is your fault, please listen to me."

"The thing about birds is: they only care whether we give them food and don't kill them. It's a false bond, one that I wish I didn't care about." Emma stood before them both, dropping her twig to the ground. "Why are you crying Remy?" When Emma looked upon Leona's face she had the answer to her question. "You're not blaming yourself again are you?"

"How do you know about that?" Leona asked.

"Because I told her." Remy said. "You haven't been around so I talk to her, just like you talk to Aunt Betty."

"Remy—"

Remy left the bench and picked up the twig from the ground. "Let's find the bird Emma." And they both connected their feet with the grass, leaving Leona to once again boil in guilt.

Later that day Leona and Trevor met at Kristy's. Trevor's overly optimistic demeanor was an escape from everyone else dark cloud whether he was putting it on or not. At first, they didn't speak much, the awkwardness from last time had carried over, but then maybe because they have chemistry, they were able to find common ground. At least that's what Leona hoped for.

"I went to Nome College for like a year, but that shit wasn't for me." Trevor said, his V-neck tee asserting Leona's attention to his chest.

"College isn't for everyone."

The look on Trevor's face seemed to like that answer. "Why did you want to go to Kristy's so bad?" He asked.

"I went here with Noelle and they have good chicken wraps."

"Got ya."

They both sat in a booth. Despite the reviews of the place the seats didn't have tears in them like Ralph's and the service wasn't riddled with senior citizens. The waiter brought them there food and Leona spied Trevor's fried shrimp.

"Can I taste one?" She asked.

"Yeah sure."

The little crispy piece of shrimp was better than she had thought, regretting her chicken wrap. Regret reminded her of her actions with Noelle, and Lauren's gaze of discontent through her mother's car window.

"You can't more if you want," Trevor said, pushing his plate to across the ivory colored table.

"I'm okay, but thank you." Pause. "Is Noelle as genuine as she seems? I feel like I've asked you this already."

"I think we spoke about it in the hospital. Why? Are you gettin' bad vibes from the girl?"

"I can't tell. I do know that things just get weirder when we're together and now, my friend hates me because of her."

"The friend from the hospital? The Spanish chick?"

For whatever reason Leona felt a pinch of jealousy that he remembered her. "Yeah, her names Lauren."

"No offence to your friend but she doesn't have a right to be mad over who you hang out with."

From the fiasco with Michael and Mateo all the way down to the phony text messages that Noelle had sent to Leona, she filled Trevor in on everything. By the end, his shrimp had begun to get cold.

"Can I get you guys anything else?" The waitress asked.

"Just the check." Leona replied.

"I'm sorry to hear you've had such a bad experience with her like that. Her and I aren't that close and I ain't that great with reading people. You should just be honest and shit with Lauren."

"I don't think she'll listen to me at this point."

"You want me to talk to her?"

The notion sent her a neutral answer. "Wouldn't that be weird?"

"How else are you gonna get through to her? Ya feel me girl?"

Is he just trying to talk to her? Is he interested? Am I being insecure right now? "I mean, you could try. Shouldn't I like man up or something?"

"You could, but is being stubborn and using brunt force really gonna do shit?"

"You just want to talk to her, she's a virgin you know."

"I was just trying to do you a favor, not everybody thinks with their fun parts all the time."

That eased her mind a bit, although, she couldn't understand where the jealousy was coming from. "Alright, I'll give her your number."

And that she did.

Fast-Paced Meetings

Three days had passed since Leona gave Trevor Lauren's number, and he had texted her. They spoke only briefly and then to his surprise, she wanted to meet in person rather speaking about her friendship through text. That threw him for a loop, a big loop. Maybe it was the fact that he reached out and showed compassion for them both, yet that idea made him feel bad, like he was the good guy. Years of being labeled as just that poured dread over every act of kindness that he just couldn't help himself but execute. So however the meeting would go, he detached himself from it, even if that somehow meant losing his friendship with Leona, so be it. She wasn't interested in him, and he chalked that up to being too nice. He hated himself for that.

Trevor sat on the rickety bus, always seeming to be a second away from imploding on potholes, his hands sweat. Meeting people blind had never been his favorite past-time. His friends had set him up on blind-dates and that had been bad enough, forever training him to hate the unexpected.

Stop after stop he grew more nervous. For whatever reason he wanted the interaction to go well, he wanted to be of help to Leona. Doing things out of the kindness of his heart at least told him that his life wasn't completely meaningless, contradicting the self-hatred he garners for doing so. *The fuck is my problem? Why do I have to think like this?* He asked himself that often, but a solution never presented itself.

But then the old tiny chapel on the corner pulled him from his mad cycle, the very chapel that meant his stop had been next—he pulled the string and the red sign at the front of the bus lit up.

Trevor's feet hit the pavement as the bus breathed exhaust in driving away. In front of him stood a diner called Ralph's; It was an older looking hunk of building that had noticeable little things to make it look new, like the flags hanging along the roof or the signs in the windows. He brought himself in and to his left off in a booth sat Leona's friend, who waved on eye contact. Off in the corner as Trevor walked to the booth, he noticed an old man wiping down the counter.

"Hi," Lauren said.

"Whattup." *Was that too strong or thug? She's going to think I'm ghetto or something. Why do I care? She's sexy.*

But to ease his silent concerns Lauren had smirked at that. "You can sit you know?" She said while he noticed how awkward he must have looked hovering over the table.

"My bad, I'm not a diner person."

"What classifies someone as a diner person?"

"A person who hits up diners on the regular."

Lauren laughed at that, a little too hard and then Trevor could see the redness on her face. "Sorry, it was the way you said it."

"It's cool," *Say someshit else, she gonna think you empty headed.*

"You wanted to talk to me about Leona?"

The waiter had interrupted and they ordered their food, giving Trevor some time to organize what he was going to say, in reality, he had forgotten about the thing. Then it hit him. *If you don't want to be the nice guy, be fuckin honest.*

"Yeah, but once I saw you I forgot about it to be honest."

The redness had returned but it was as if she wanted him to say that. "Why did you forget?"

Be honest, "Because you're sexier than I remember, if you don't mind me—"

"Not at all. I forgive Leona, we don't have to talk about her."

There was that giant loop again, the one that scared him tremendously and excited him at the same time. *Just because good things are happening right now, doesn't mean you can get comfortable,* he reminded himself. "Really? You came all the way here to—"

"Yeah but on the way I thought about how silly the whole thing was, I'm not going to let some girl get in between us. Leona's not the enemy, Noelle is. You're friends with her right?"

Just then a man walked into the diner, his coat was crisp, and his watch said he had money. He had the type of hair that one of the owners of the hospital has: going grey but styled in such a manner than you couldn't picture a hair ever out of place. Lauren had noticed him too.

"I need some information on a kid who lives around here, He had your diner's card in his wallet." The man said to the stunted lady behind the counter, whatever she said back had been too low to understand. Both Trevor and Lauren fell intrigued just by the way the man carried himself. "His name is Mateo Colon and he kidnapped my son."

That's when Trevor caught Lauren with her mouth open. It was cute how shocked she had gotten over it, as if she had some relation to it herself. The eye contact she gave him almost lead him to believe that she might.

"What's the matter?"

"Shhhhhhhhh," Lauren responded to Trevor's concern.

"That sounds like a matter for the police, we here ain't the lost and found diner of Nome City."

"There's a nice chunk of compensation in it for anything you can provide."

"Mateo Colon is Leona's boyfriend, the one that went missing." Lauren whispered to Trevor. Now his interest matched hers and he fell quiet, listening now just as intently as Lauren while not trying to be obvious about it.

"How much money are we talking here?"

"Five-hundred, cash." The man responded, placing what had to be five-five hundred dollar Hanks on the counter.

"This is seven." The woman said.

"I'm a kind man, that's two-hundred for cooperation."

The stunted lady in the stained apron slid the money off of the counter and squeezed it into her jean pocket. "The kid works at O-Dera about a mile from of the city, you know, the fast-food joint."

"Why would he work so far from his home?"

"I've only spoken the kid once or twice, Mateo Colon ain't the type of name you forget, it's catchy. I remembered that little fact cause it's odd as you pointed out. That's all I know."

"Thank you ma'am." And just like that, the man's crisp white shirt was out the door, as the waiter stopped at the table with Trevor's and Lauren's food.

"Mateo kidnapped that man's son…should I go stop him? Tell him that Leona is his girlfriend?" Lauren asked, staring blankly at her flatbread Pricewich.

"Shits the right thing to do, but that guy didn't look alright. He looked like a villain out of a movie."

"Yeah, something is preventing me from moving." Her eyes left the flatbread and met Trevor's, the whites around her pupils revealed her instinct.

"What?" Trevor asked.

"Watch my flatbread." Before Trevor could comprehend, she was out of her seat and running down through the diner. The old man with the wiping down the counter in the corner lifted his head but never turned to look.

Dangerous, she could be hurt, that guy is shady, Trevor's mind said to itself. He shot up from his seat and told the lady at the counter to hold their food, apologizing too many times in the process. And then he copied Lauren, darting from the diner and scanning the parking lot. She was nowhere to found. The pounding in his chest tightened his airways. The seconds ticked. He wanted to call her name now. *Where the fuck is she?*

Suddenly to his left she walked, clutching a piece of paper and a smile. Her jet-black pony-tail made his lips pucker,

"You could have gotten fuckin hurt or someshit, don't do that. You saw the mothafucka, he was shady as fuck." Once the words stopped Trevor was just as shocked as Lauren. But that smile of hers only changed in attitude.

"Nothing happened, I'm alright…why are you so upset over me? I thought you liked Leona?"

His skin was caramel but that didn't mean that it was incapable of blushing. Before he could respond, even though he had not one word ready on his tongue, she was showing him a piece of paper with an address.

"This is where Mateo was last seen." Lauren said proudly.

"You're a good friend to Leona, she's going to cry." They both walked back into the diner, the food had remained untouched.

"I'm going to google it," Lauren sunk her face into her phone and Trevor watched her lips mouth out the letters as she read them from the paper. She had the little crumbled scrap laid out on the table, her finger traced over as she read. He imagined what she kissed like, what it would be like to have her sprawled out on a bed with no clothes concealing her body, which lead to other thoughts that forced him to look at the old man in the corner to ease his trouser trouble.

"Did anything pop up?"

"It's the address for a pawn shop." Lauren said confused.

"Is that what the guy said it would be?"

"He didn't say anything, when I explained the situation all he did was ask about Leona and then gave me this address."

Trevor didn't like that. "What did you say about Leona?"

"He wanted to ask her a few questions so I gave him her number in exchange for the address."

"If he has her number then he could have just given her that over the phone."

"I know that now, I was just trying to do something nice for her."

"No but why would he give you that address if he knew that, shits sketchy."

Lauren shot him the eyes of a puppy dog. "That's my word."

"What? Sketchy?"

"Yeah, that's so weird."

"I guess, I think that guy is weird and you need to warn Leona rather than directing her."

"You're right. Why are you getting yourself mixed in with this stuff?"

"I don't know, it's not something that I put too much thought into. It all just kinda happened."

"Are you attracted to me?"

Another loop, this time with no seconds to spare, no time to prepare an answer and no way to avoid her eyes.

"You're very straightforward huh?"

"I'm not like most girls, I don't play games, and if I want something I get it."

He noticed a slight shake in her hand, he suddenly realized that she was nervous and forcing herself to be confident.

"I am attracted to you, I wasn't in the hospital but when I saw you today...I don't know."

"Were you not attracted to me in the hospital because Leona was there?"

Trevor wasn't sure on how to answer that. "She had made me feel less alone in the hospital—sometimes you can feel like you're the only one living in there while everyone else is hacking up a lung or dropping like flies."

"When you think of her now what do you feel?"

"Why are you so hung up on her?"

Lauren retreated her lips with no rebuttal, he couldn't tell whether she was angry with him or herself.

"I'm just curious, this is dumb. I shouldn't have gone to this place so quickly with you. You weren't even coming her for me."

"Well I'm here for you now, just because the plan changed doesn't mean you need to question it."

"I'm being weird."

"Who's to say I don't like it?"

"Why?"

"Because for once I'm not the weird one." He laughed and then she joined him with dark red cheeks. "Weird things happen, but I'm sure you didn't meet Leona when you were looking for her."

"You're not going to be able to put up with me though." She picked at her food, making that the first time it had been touched. She didn't eat it, she pulled little pieces away and moved them about on her plate. The bashfulness on her was growing on him.

"Why would you say that?"

"Because I'm a virgin."

Although his response had taken half a second, he was instantly flooded with a flurry of warming sentiments: *I'm not alone. She is too. We could lose it together. Is she the right girl? Would she want to? Does that mean we have to be platonic?*

"I'm a virgin too." He said.

It had been the first time that he told anyone that and the unreadable mask that Lauren wore now made him want to dash out of the diner. *What if she was joking?* His heart sunk.

"Are you just saying that, or are you being serious with me?"

"Being serious. I came close a few times but it never happened, I always chickened out."

"Then this was officially a date, and we're going to see a movie after this. You have no choice in the matter." Lauren smiled.

"I see no need to argue that."

Then they finally ate their food, Trevor loosened his face to not let the smile show.

In the Forest

Mateo stepped over branches, kicked through fallen bark and tangled his way through tall grass, but no matter how deep he took himself into the dark green brush Bradley was nowhere to found. Two days it had been since Bradley vanished, leaving nothing but a trail of toys he must have tried to carry with him. The action figure with little chips in its paint was the only clue, left at the foot of the family of trees that held only darkness. Mateo had never known Nome to have such land, sheltered his entire life between stone buildings and ambulance sirens. He had dreamed of running away just like Bradley, except instead of biding his time to make a clean getaway he would have left a note. As he tripped over a foot long-branch not two centimeters thick, he realized that he had run away, and now he was chasing after someone who had as well.

"Bradley!" Mateo yelled. His voice was now hoarse. It didn't occur to him that when Anne broke the news that Bradley had fled his search would have been more than five minutes, this thought two days in. It was smart of the kid though, vanishing not after breaking Anne's nose, but doing so when everyone least expected it.

"Bradley!" That's when Mateo came to a sudden stop, a small red little fox or what Mateo had believed to be a fox stopped in front of his path. They gave each other a sharp look and both remained still, almost like out of a Bugs Bunny cartoon.

Do foxes hunt people? I could probably take him down with a kick of my boot. What if Bradley came across one of them? His fear would have gotten him killed, if not the fox some other animal. Shit.

The fox turned to face Mateo, which is when his heart played the drums. For the first time in a long time Mateo felt fear. The eyes of the little beast were little dots centered in a greenish marble. The animal didn't blink, instead it took tiny slow steps towards, its head close to the grass. Mateo bent his knees a bit. He didn't make any movements in case the little red ball of fur would mistake them for hostility.

"Get away, go!" Mateo said, but the animal continued, smelling the ground now with every paw sauntering against the grass. Mateo imagined what it would be like to fight the thing, if he could maybe take his belt off or grab a branch for defense. Were there others? He wondered. Was this going to be some sort of ambush?

The streak of red flew before his eyes and Mateo fell to the ground, closing his eyes in immense fear, the harder he closed them hopefully he wouldn't feel any pain.

When he opened them, the fox was pouncing a lizard.

The breath returned to Mateo, his heart slowed to a point that wasn't normal. The grass tickled his elbow and the mud coated it like icing on a cake. His jeans were covered in the stuff, his black shirt even as black as it was advertised that he was in a forest. He rose to his feet and gave the fox one last look. The animal wasn't paying him any mind, but on his own rested the worry of what other living things were in the forest and had they gotten Bradley.

As Mateo went on his way, the only sounds being his footsteps and insects, something else danced on his eardrums. It was like drops of water against leaves, except the sounds were too much in rhythm and too close to Mateo' heels. He turned around with caution, as if he expected to get slapped across the face. The fox was sitting behind him, both front feet as straight as arrows giving the ball of a fur the posture of a cute solider.

"Are you following me?" Obviously there wasn't an answer, just those marble eyes which now seemed a little less terrifying. To get the answer that Mateo desired he took a few steps forward, turned around and there stood the fox once more. 25% of him worried that maybe the little carnivore was just toying with him, needing more a chase before sinking his teeth into Mateo' sweat and tattoos. But the fox sat idle, too relaxed to be a predator at the moment. So Mateo went on his way, accepting that he now had company.

The sun had now given the sky a pink backdrop, and that was the only part that Mateo could see through the tall intimidating oaks and maples. In all their beauty they were still in a way scary. He had to be at least two miles into the forest by now, and with every drip of sweat Mateo was reminded of his own mortality; not as bad a thought when you have at least another living organism by your side for the venture.

"Bradley!" *The kid couldn't have gone...* Mateo' thoughts were interrupted by the fox's howling: the short little screech sounded as if the fox had stubbed his toe. Mateo thought it was cute, his voice was deeper than the little vixen's. Every time Mateo called Bradley's name, the fox howled along like a little sidekick, somehow that made the sweat evaporate from Mateo' forehead, or maybe that happened because the night's air was approaching.

Mateo stopped, pinching his eyes then looking around himself. He had spent the day alongside trees and noisy bugs, and yesterday investigating the area all around the farm. Wherever Bradley was, he didn't want to be found. Mateo looked at the fox in frustration, eyeing him as he sniffed around the grass, moving little pieces of fallen tree with his nose. Suddenly, Mateo had an idea. He removed Bradley's action figure from his pocket, running his thumb over the chips in the paint, and then he bent down to meet the fox. It was the first time feeling the softness of his fur, the tininess of his head and the dampness on his nose—the nose that would be his new found hope.

Mateo put the action figure in front of the fox, and for a minute, there was nothing, and then, the fox took off running. That angered Mateo, his energy was below the soil. But he took off after the fox anyway. If it wasn't for it stopping every now and then to gather its route, Mateo wouldn't have been able to keep up. He chased the fox for yards, tripping and skimming his flesh on different plants that Mateo thought he'd never have to come in contact with. *Please don't be poison ivy,* he thought after every brush with unknown greens.

After a steep chase down hills, and through branches tangled like television wires, the fox stopped and sniffed at the ground. Then, he rested, rolling around on the grass and soil like he was in a McDonald's ball-pit. Mateo watched him in confusion and then his eyes shut for the briefest of seconds. As soon as they opened the fox brushed up against Mateo' leg—he was fainting.

It took him every ounce of his strength to stay awake; the dryness of his tongue, the dreariness behind his eyes and the weakness in his legs all did their best to tear him down.

"Where is he? I followed you? Where is he?" *I'm talking to a damn fox, I'm losing my shit.* That's when he put two and two together. As heavy as his eyes felt, he lifted them to the above, where the pink sky spun around him. Luckily, he found what he was looking for, the run had paid off. Up in the tree sat Bradley, looking down with a heartfelt yet defeated face. Mateo felt his eyes close in the moment.

Leona danced in a tight red dress, the room had faces that he had never seen before. They were almost faceless. But their claps were crisp, routine and all synchronized. They were watching Leona dance the salsa, rooting her on. Mateo looked down at himself to see that he was wearing a full white suit, the gold bracelets on his wrist sounded like the claps except louder. When he looked up the crowd was waving him on, and Leona stood their smiling, waiting for him to join the dance floor.

Behind himself he heard he name being called by a faint but familiar voice. It was feminine as well, and when he tried to move forward to Leona he was stuck. The tips of his shoes couldn't penetrate whatever it was that blocked his path. When he looked up at Leona she stood their crying with bags at her sides. The crowd sat motionless as a soft chilled hand grabbed his, pulling him into the dark abyss behind him. The warm lips and peppermint smell took him. When the delicate flesh removed itself, Noelle's face smiled, giving him one last peck before, Mateo woke up to the green of the leaves and the darkness of the sky. The grass below his head was wet, which forced his head from the soil. Next to him sat Bradley staring at him with the cadaver eyes. The fox's weren't any more welcoming.

"I think I'm going to name you 'Finder'." Mateo said to the fox.

The walk back hadn't been as bad as Mateo was telling himself over and over when looking for Bradley in the first place. Somehow the kid had found water, maybe it had been his own supply stolen from Anne's fridge, but there was no way of telling since no sound left the kid's mouth. The house, in they went. Anne was more surprised to see Finder in Mateo' arms rather Bradley alongside next to him.

"Are you out of your mind bringing that rodent into my house?" Anne said as the fox jumped out of Mateo arms and into the living room where it perched itself on the couch.

"That *rodent* found Bradley." Mateo said.

Anne did nothing but give the child a cold look and then took it back, Bradley wasn't as kind and made his way up the steps where Finder followed him.

"Swanson thinks you kidnapped Bradley."

Mateo wasn't as surprised as he knew he should have been. "Did you tell him otherwise?"

"Yes, but he ain't that high on takin my words for things."

"So what's that mean now?"

"Walk with me." Anne went through the screen door of the house and down the steps, Mateo followed. The night air had felt ten times cooler from how it was two seconds ago.

"Once he sees you, he's gonna lay hands on you. His type needs some sort of retribution to make themselves feel better." Anne said.

"So? I can handle myself."

"And if you? What will that accomplish? I need you to leave the farm."

That stung Mateo in all his vitals. "I'm not leaving Bradley."

"I told you from day one to worry about yourself and not get involved but you had too. And now you've angered the one person who funds this whole operation."

Mateo stopped walking. "What does that even mean? You never explained to me about Bradleys' mother, why you put up with his father and now you're banishing me from—"

"You need to go back, people need you."

"Anne, how the fuck are you going to tell me that now? Huh? When this whole time you've bullshitted me into believing that I need to be by myself and get things straight."

"I still don't know your personal reasons for agreeing to stay here, but what you did for Bradley tonight showed your selflessness. If you can go home and apply that to whatever is waiting for you, then you'll be just fine."

"What about my car?"

"I'm sorry."

"What about me seeing Bradley...he's like a little brother to me."

"I'm sorry, but he made the choice."

Confusion filled him, sweat coated his hands and his heart hit the base once more. "What?"

"I asked him, do you want Mateo to stay longer or do you think he's ready to go home? The whole running away, well, how you acted proved to us that you're as good as—"

"You set this whole thing up?"

"I didn't think Swanson would—"

"I almost died out there. Why did you go through all—"

"Your aunt Rosa is dead Mateo."

"What?"

"Go home, I have a bike you can have."

The sky whirled again, and the heaviness behind his eyes returned, except this time they were lined with tears.

My Broken Prince

Leona sat, tracing her finger over the crack in the marble looking table. Comprehending was one thing, believing it was another. Lauren had no reason to lie, nothing to gain, and was far too enthusiastic to believe otherwise. The side-realization to it all was that even after all of Leona's mistakes, Lauren was still there. In the corner Hanky chewed on a piece of bread, wiping down the counter and living in his own bubble, perhaps the size of the one that Leona felt like she was in right now.

"Mateo wouldn't have any reason to kidnap anyone. This doesn't make any sense. Maybe he's acting out because his aunt died."

"I don't know Leona, the whole thing is sketch, but! We do have a clue, pawnshop or not." Lauren held up the wrinkled piece of paper. "I just don't understand why that guy hasn't contacted you yet."

"None of it makes sense so don't be surprised. Again my only guess is that Mateo is acting out."

"That's the logical assumption."

Leona eyed Lauren's plate of cheese-fries, an appetizer of an excuse to meetup. "I'm sorry about Noelle."

"I don't want to talk about her, if you're going to be friends I just don't want to know. I'm sticking by my gut instinct that she's nothing but trouble."

"I won't talk to her any longer. I already have Trevor's number and I don't need her for anything else."

Lauren remained quiet, picking off of her cheese-fries and moving the bits of crust around the plate.

"Something is on your mind, is it something about Noelle?" Leona asked.

"No."

"Okay then what? You're acting weird."

"Trevor and I kissed. When we met we turned it into a date and he kissed me at the end."

That unknown, rogue and guilt laced jealousy filled Leona, blocking her airways in manufacturing words. *Why do I care? I should be happy for her.* "You sure you're not rebounding a little bit too quick there?" Leona was surprised that of all the combination of words—those were the ones that came out.

"Okay, I don't mean this in any way to cause a fight....but don't you think that's jealousy talking?"

"Why would I be jealous when I have Mateo?"

"Because you liked the nurse and now he's with me? If anything, I'm doing you a favor by crossing him off your list, you don't have to think about him anymore."

"Wait, wait," Leona laughed, not the type where it was because of something funny. "Do you think that he chose you over me or something? Because seriously, I was the one that said no. I made it clear that I only wanted a friendship, if I actually wanted him—which I don't then I could have him."

On Lauren rested a reservoir of expressions, they moved like an ocean's current. For once, Leona was the beach.

"I'll reiterate myself—I wasn't looking for an argument. But he chose me—me." The waves were now angry. "Get over it Leona, like you said, you have Mateo. I watched you stay over at his house night after night, I'm allowed to have a boyfriend."

Where is this coming from? She had it all for years. "Can you calm down—"

"No, first you hang out with that—girl—Noelle and now you're getting jealous over a kid who you shouldn't have been ogling in the first place. I want him, he's mine."

Does she fear I'll take him away? Mateo only ever got angry when he was insecure; anger is fear. "Okay, relax. Please. I don't need you mad at me for something else now.

And just like that the tides went back out to see leaving an indent of regret across Lauren's face. *At least she knew that she was acting crazy,* Leona thought.

"Are we still going to check out the pawn shop?"

"You're the one with the car today Cole."

Inside Lauren Torres' car the tension had buckled into the back seat. Leona sat shotgun with her index finger digging into her thumb. Naturally she blamed herself; to get Lauren angry took more than a lot, it took numerous wrecking balls, and even then the girl refused to utter a curse word.

"Thank you for driving me." Leona said while holding hands with feeling stupid.

"You're my best friend Leona, just shut up."

"I don't like when you're mad at me."

"I'm not." But the way Lauren handed the words to reality said otherwise, like someone spurting out gallons of blood and saying that it's just a minor cut.

"I've been friends with you for about five years now Cole, I know when you're mad."

"That shows how much you learned in high school, by now you should know it takes me a while to cool off."

"Fine."

THUD. Leona could feel the back of her head hit the cushion of the seat, the velocity made the cushion feel like a stone. The screeching of the tires and the deer's limp head bouncing off the steel of the hood plucked Leona from the passenger seat and dropped her right back to the day her own car had collided with another.

"Oh my god." Lauren brought both her hands to her mouth. "I'm a murderer."

"I'm okay though." Leona grabbed her neck. "No whiplash here, let's worry about the dumbass deer who thought he had the speed of an Ethiopian."

"He had a family somewhere." Lauren cried, how the tears drenched her blouse so quickly reminded Leona just how much she loved Lauren.

Down the block from the pawn shop the engine shut off and Leona watched her friend stare out in the distance as if her eyes had been borrowed from a blind person. The last time Lauren had been shaken like a cocktail, her pet cat Lucky had died in freshman year.

"I mean, if I had jumped in front of a car with my neck you wouldn't have felt bad you would have considered me a fool." Leona laughed at her own joke because Lauren kept a face of ice, one that had two streaks on both sides to make it look like it were melting slowly. "Do you want me to leave you here while I go in?"

"No," Lauren whispered, "I'll be fine."

"Ay, the cops thought it was funny."

Again, Leona's humor was met with deafening silence.

"Okay then, remind me to get you frozen yogurt on the way back."

"He'll never even get to take a lick of frozen yogurt, no cheese-fries, no lick of yogurt, not even a lick."

"You're staying here."

"I'm fine." Lauren started to cry.

"Yeah, and I'm Bambi."

The sheer horror on Lauren stole the comedic effort from Leona's heart.

'Sorry, too soon." Leona hopped on one foot out of the car and struggled to yank her crutches from the back, although she knew that she had made it look effortless in an attempt to not disturb Lauren's mourning. Halfway up the block was where Leona felt the pinch of anxiousness flicker in her chest. There was no game plan, just a narrow search of needles in a haystack for a vanishing boyfriend. Whoever she was to speak with might as well be on their day off. The whole trip may just be sour grapes. Maybe Mateo is working there and this is his hideout—a new life started over in secret all to avoid Leona. The plethora of outcomes presented themselves with ever click of crutch to concrete, emitting the sound to the likeness of a tap dancer who lost the will to dance.

At Thew Pawn, the sign said above the cold steal of the door handle which kissed Leona's palm, clearing her palate of concern for the time being. Sprawled out before was the expected pawn shop layout but more extravagant. There were novelties littered all over the shop and on the walls like: a pink flamingo sporting a mustache, a candy machine that also blew up balloons, a typewriter with gloves attached. The oddities escorted Leona from why she had come in there in the first place.

"May I help you Kaye?" An old man wearing suspenders and a striped shirt asked her while oiling what looked to be a miniature bike. The man's hair was grey and like cotton candy.

"Just looking around." She lied, too coy to present her reasoning. The absurdity of the shop had seemed to make her the gazelle stumbling into the lion's den.

"I can't argue that until your presence teases my pockets. Let's hope you're not the sole soul to remind me that no one cares for with Velcro on the end."

Leona scratched her head, trying to find where the shoelaces were. "No offence but why would anyone want them?"

"To make the ends hold hand. How many times has someone bumped into you in the city while holding hands?"

"Never."

"Cause pairs are better than strays. Who wants those little pieces of plastic on the ends? Tapping away at the sides of one's shoe like an applauding Neanderthal. I'd much prefer to look down and see my laces in unity."

Leona observed the man to be wearing loafers, the laces were absent, but there looked to be at least eighteen holes. She considered questioning that but the near riddles were migraine inducing.

"Why does that typewriter have gloves attached to it?"

The man put down his little bike and the thing drove itself away. Leona put a hand to her face to conceal her childlike smile. The man went to the typewriter, if Leona had just walked in, she would have mistaken the man for some sort of clubfooted, contemporary Ebenezer Scrooge. When he reached the strange piece of writing machinery, the man's hand riddled with spontaneous gray hairs waved her closer.

"Feel the material Kaye." He said.

"It feels like rubber."

"Ever heard of pencil ink?"

Leona racked her brain. "Can't say that I have."

"Course you haven't, liquefied lead was barred from public use right before the great depression." The man held up a jar wearing a faded label matching the color of his hair. "Put the gloves on."

Leona followed the man's order, stretching on the gloves which were as tight as cleaning gloves but as warm and heavy as snow gloves.

"Type something."

I love Mateo, she typed instinctively.

"Oh sorrow, I wish you had written something a tad bit less sentimental," The man held back his guffaw. "For my example will add a damper, type *not*."

And so she did.

"Now use any part of the glove like an eraser, it doesn't have to be rough, just a little breeze of the finger."

And so she did, wiping away the word *not* and replacing it with the cloud color of the paper.

"That's amazing, regular erasers leave dirt behind."

"Well it's a special kind of lead, poisonous to skin Kaye," He guffawed at that. "Only I hold onto such dangerously convenient specimens." The man placed the jar onto a shelf and helped Leona remove her gloves.

"Why do you keep calling me Kaye?"

"I like to give my customers nicknames, helps me to get a little closer, I remember people better that way."

"Why Kaye though?"

"An older name, and the shortening for the word *okay*. You look like a stubborn old fashion minded human, therefore Kaye." The man turned his back, dragging his foot back over to where a pile of odd looking pieces of electronic equipment made the shop ugly; wires and colorful scraps of metal wrestling each other on the smooth surface of the counter.

"I came for something." Leona said.

"So you fed me a fib?" The man said un-looking.

"To be honest I was caught off guard by your inventory."

"To be caught one must already be running, therefore you came in here with your guard up?"

"Yes, the man who sent me didn't give much background, and I've never been in a pawn shop before let alone one that resembles *Pee-Wee's Playhouse.*"

"State your purpose then." The man sunk his hands into the miniature pile of rubble and began to intricately move things around.

"My boyfriend went missing, and there's a man looking for him, he gave my friend this address when she asked him whether or not he had any information on him."

"Mateo Colon, Rosa's nephew. So the little tike got himself a girlfriend. Why is it that when one other people gain in age we become aware of our own?"

"How do you know him?"

"Rosa Alvarez and her husband never rolled in money Kaye, given that circumstance and the oddities that reside in my shop, most of Mateo' toys were adopted from here."

It always was a funny thing to picture Mateo as a child let alone playing with toy cars and action figures. What she would do to own just one of them now. "I'm honored to meet the man that gave his childhood a little bit of light, but that still doesn't answer why–"

"Swanson sent you here?"

"Yeah."

A look of empathy waved over the man's face like a tide coming to shore."

"When you know someone as a child it often hurts more when you lose them. Mr. Swanson is a man who enjoys sending messages in the forms of lessons."

"He wants to hurt Mateo." The anger boiled. "How do you know this man?"

"Mateo' aunt isn't then only one who's fond of my product for their young one's. As bad as the man is, he cares about his son. Kidnapping him isn't something that would give Swanson a reason to invite you to dinner."

"Mateo didn't kidnap anyone!"

"That's not for my ears to be convinced Kaye."

"Fine." Leona shot herself to the door frame as if the thing had been the barrel of a gun and she were the bullet. "I never got your name." She said with the door handle in hand.

"Mathew."

Inside the car, Leona shimmied her way in as if the outside had been something she was climbing out of. No matter how many times she stuffed herself into a car it never got easier.

"What happened in there?" Lauren asked, finally breaking the chains of her shock.

"Long story, I'll tell you while you drive. You can take me home, I need time to think."

"Okay."

Time at the house felt as though it had been drenched in anxiety and Leona changed seats in the living room too many times to count. The television remained off. It probably wasn't good she knew: to sit around concerned about someone who decided to vanish. Justifying it was impossible but still, stubborn reasons were in abundance and Mateo persisted; the pain only existed as a flicker, the worry was the flame.

There was something so reminiscent of the reality which hugged Leona. Little clips in her psyche brought her back with the speed of a fighter jet to the cold isolated night where depression kidnapped her and Mateo was the only one who came to her frail calls. Dark skys holding the moon above nothing but the screech of Mateo' Mercedes were the nights that Leona felt she held as debt to him. And no amount of hurt could take it away, or the happiness which he fed her without barely lifting a finger.

Rosa Alvarez: the woman's death made justifying Mateo' vanishing somewhat possible. The unexpected tragedy–it had to cripple Mateo. And that was the reason Leona needed, as small and unconfirmed as it may be, there was a keyhole of light that gave her hope that maybe his reasoning really did have nothing to do with their love.

The knock on the door was loud, or maybe it just sounded that way because her nerves had already been dancing. In that second, Leona pondered whether it was a hallucination, but as the seconds stacked one after the other, the miniature drum played its song once more, confirming that it wasn't Leona's imagination. *I can't speak to anyone with my heart racing.* It dawned on her that the house only had one occupant, one very scared occupant now. *What if they force their way in? Pretend that I'm not home–the lights are on, fuck.* There was the rapping at the door again, but this time....

"Leona it's me."

His voice was like an antidote, it sung through the door and replaced the drumming in her chest with a different rhythm. Leona took a moment to comprehend the vocal chords on the other side, to accept that her prince–had come home.

And as if her leg had never been broken and mummified into the stiff white plaster that weighed it down now, she galloped to the door, with tears skiing down her flushed cheeks. Whimpers filled the room with every step. At one point the soles of her feet knew what it must be to walk amongst the clouds. She opened the door, and there he was–Mateo Colon.

Explain Later

It was a blast of passion, a cannon of lust orchestrated by uncontrollable fingers; they danced across each other's flesh without law. Fingernails dug like shovels, teeth broke skin like feasting wolves. The sweat came and went as quickly as people going in and out of a city building. One moment Leona pinched her eyes shut as the salty moisture would overflow into them. The next moment she had been freed of sweat, sprinkled with Goosebumps and instead, she vacuumed up the perspiration off Mateo with her fingertips, and sometimes her tongue.

"I'm sorry," Mateo said with a mouth slipping away from Leona's lips.

"Shut up–not now." She stood on both feet, her back joined the wall across from the now empty dining room table. Leona barely noticed the cumbersome weight hugging her one leg. Mateo kept surveying the cast, she sensed it– every time he pulled away from their embrace to find another spot to let his kisses roam. "It was a car accident." Leona forced out. "The day after you–" She kissed him, it was all she wanted and the only thing that mattered. The past could be dealt with in the future.

"I'm sorry," As Mateo kissed, the guilt melted onto her tongue from his. He grabbed her face, the curiosity filled her for the briefest of seconds and then overflowed out. The upside to his remorse was the aggression in his hands, flinging her onto the couch yet being careful enough with her leg. Once her back met the fabric, his hands yanked at the elastic around her waist. The cool air tickled between her legs and the thong slipped down like an elevator.

By the end, the room carried a humidity. Stray hairs stuck to Leona's face while it mirrored the ceiling. Her breaths mimicked a marathon runner's; Mateo sat his bare behind on the end of the couch were her cast occupied, he lifted the thing and placed it over his crotch, guzzling a glass of water so clear it took away the dense airs in the room. She had wished her cast wasn't there, barring her leg from his manhood.

"Can you tell me about it now?" Mateo asked, never giving her eye contact.

"I think that you have more explaining to do than I, my car accident was just me being angry. You weren't the only one that vanished."

"You're mother?"

"After the day you left me at the mall."

"Did she give you a reason?" He manned up to looking at her this time.

"Just like you, no."

"I needed space, I'm sorry. I freaked out."

Mateo was lying, she could tell. He only looked at the floor when he was concealing the contents of his psyche. As much as he despised her analytical nature, she had picked it all up by now: the cues to right before he gets mad, the denial of his feelings all the way down to when he's about to say something. He looked to his side, which meant he was about to, most likely an addition to his lie.

"I just needed to get away. I knew you would make me talk about how I felt, and I couldn't. There was no way of turning my emotions into words."

"So where did you go?" She ignored her gut, the current question was boiling too much.

"I originally went to this pub outta town. That's where this lady Anne took me in."

The wheels started turning in her mind, the coincidence was almost comical. Too many questions ran to the front of the fence bashing their faces against it like zombies with equal amount of curiosity.

"I went there...Anne's pub.... where did she take you?" Leona sat up, ripping the sticky flesh from the fabric of the couch.

"To her farm," That's when Mateo told her everything, from torching his Mercedes all the way down to finding Bradley in the forest. In return Leona exchanged what had happened at the pawn shop, what she found out and how Swanson put Mateo on his radar. There was two things she failed to mention, but with her rectitude towards honesty they had to be dropped into his reality, secrets were her enemies and unlike the expression Leona didn't want them close.

"When I was in the hospital," she started, "I met this nurse and we became friends."

Mateo extended Leona his discomfort, a mask that advertised the anger holding it on.

"He developed a little bit of feelings for me." she watched Mateo put the finger on the trigger of the 'let's start a fight' gun. "But nothing happened, I shot it down. He's dating Lauren now."

"Are you staying friends with this kid?"

Why even ask me if when I give you the answer you don't like, you're going to throw a fit? "Yes, but he's dating Lauren so I don't seen the big deal."

"He's fuckin attracted to you, that's the big deal. I don't want him near you."

"He was there…" If she finished the sentence there would only be more fighting, yet Mateo vanished, maybe he deserved to hear it. "When you weren't."

Silence.

"I'm sorry Mateo, but like, nothing's going to happen. I'm also friends with Noelle, I know that may be a surprise after our history but we found common ground and I forgave her."

Mateo turned his head almost in slow motion. It was here, arriving just as expected and there wouldn't be any way to stop it—his rage.

"Why the fuck would you be fri……" Mateo paused, giving his attention to the beige tiled floor. Leona waited, and waited, nothing left his lips.

"What?" *Why aren't you continuing to jump down my throat…deep throat…sex again?* Her thoughts betrayed her sense. "Say whatever you want, at this point I really don't care." Pushing her sex covered body off the couch took way too much trouble than predicted, but she did. Making her way past the stoic Mateo and reaching the bottom of stairs where a pair of warm arms wrapped around her bare waist.

"I'm sorry." Mateo inserted into her ear with a deep and heavy melody.

Leona spun around on her bad leg, meeting Mateo eye to eye. She kissed him, for a long while, and throughout that long while his rock like body melted into her grasp. They somehow wound up back on the couch, coiled, entangled in a pile of what could only be love. Everything and nothing occupied the head which rested on Mateo' fuzzy chest.

"I love you." Leona gave him in a whisper.

"I love you more." In the room sat the peace Leona had been looking for. Although somehow she knew it was the eye of the storm. She pondered why; Mateo was back, which meant there would be no more lonely nights in the empty house and no more time spent mingling with her sorrows. Mateo was there physically, so why did it feel like all a dream?

Leona ran and ran, through headstones that sat covered in moving vines, dented by Mother Nature, and worn by her wrath, the cemetery was never ending. The soles of her size seven converses beat against the soil which kept moving under her feet the way a treadmill does. The fog grew thicker and then it subsided, growing thick again and subsiding, the pattern was maddening, better yet scary.

"Dad!" Leona screamed. "Mom's gone! Mom's gone! I can't find her! Please help!" Her voice gave sound but felt as though it didn't. She could not feel a thing except fear. It was a great fear, one that sent cold sweat down her arms and legs. All she wanted was a response from her father, something to let her know that everything will be okay.

The hushed melodic whisper stole her from the left, a faint figure standing stiff in the fog, the beings arms hung like a cadaver. Instantly Leona regretted calling out for her father, for what she may have to see would be unforgettable. His lifeless decomposing body, a shell of what he used to be was what she was afraid to open her eyes to.

"Open your eyes." The voice was Remy's.

When Leona did, there was no decomposing corpse, just her little sister, gawking with dismay, as still as a light post.

"What is it Remy? Why do you look like that? Are you upset with me?"

"You're the reason she left." As if Remy was standing on lightning fast moving walkway, now her bemused body stood before Leona.

"I'm sorry Remy, I never meant to let you down."

"If you had gone with me and dad to the movies, you could have stopped the accident, but you had to be selfish." Remy took two steps forward causing Leona to take two steps back, behind her was the edge of the cemetery, below it was an abyss of rock hundreds of feet down blanketed with fog.

"Please Remy, I can't have you hate me. You're all I have; you've always been all I had." The tears graced the tips of her eyelids.

"There you go again, it's sad—you always make it about you."

"No, no, no, that's not my intent, I do everything—"

"I, I, I, that's all my ears hear. If it must be all about you, then you should enjoy this lonely fall to the bottom." Remy's delicate hands contradicted themselves, pushing Leona over the edge and into the dense unforgiving fog below.

"What!? What's the matter!? Mateo jumped out of what must have been a sleep session. His arm removed itself from Leona's clammy body.

"I'm sorry, I had a nightmare."

"What about?"

"I can't remember." Leona lied.

"I'm sorry."

"For what? It's not your fault babe."

"For leaving– for everything. I don't deserve you."

Leona rose, taking herself from the couch and around the bend of the living room, at the staircase she stopped. "I don't ever want to hear you say that again, it's the farthest thing from the truth. Now carry me upstairs."

And that Mateo did, taking her up two flights of stairs and landing her in her fluffy bed covered in her purple blanket which, held the chill of the room.

"Lay with me, my mom won't disturb us." Leona laughed.

"This feels weird, I always imagined in your bed, and now I feel like we're breaking rules or something."

"The bad boy is scared of being bad for once?" Leona pulled him closer, wrapping her arms and legs around Mateo' warmth. She desired getting under the blanket, but laziness nailed the idea to the bed.

"I'm not a bad boy, I never was."

"You are, and you were. The fact that you don't like that label makes it okay. It's one of your best redeeming qualities. And hey, the bad attracts the good." She pointed to herself and Mateo laughed.

"Before I left…I don't know."

"What?"

"I had reasons for leaving, and…"

"Okay, I mean I kinda figured that. What else then?"

Mateo fidgeted, his hand loosened, the warmth seemed to evaporate from his body. "Nothing, just what you said." His words were abrupt, with little room for a response.

"You can tell me anything you know that."

"I know."

"Do you miss it?"

Mateo shifted to the wall, extending to her bewilderment. "Do I miss what?"

"Relax, what're getting all defensive for? Your little friend Bradley. Do you miss him?"

"He never really spoke."

"Remy barely speaks but I miss that girl when I'm away from her for two minutes."

"No, he was like a mute or whatever you call it." Mateo draped his arm back over Leona, the cuteness in that nearly crashed her train of thought.

"That still doesn't answer my question."

"Yeah I do, he felt like a little brother."

"You said Swanson treats him bad?"

"Worse than my mother treated me."

"Where's his mother?" For some reason the question made her uncomfortable.

"Buried under a tree a few yards from the Anne's house."

"Did you ask her what happened?"

"It's a big mystery."

"To Anne?"

"To me."

"I think I know where we can find out."

"You don't have to get involved with this, the guy Swanson—"

"Is looking for my boyfriend. It's my business."

"You have to worry about your mother, I'm not worth—"

"If you say you're not worth my time one more time I'm going to neuter you, why do you keep saying that? After everything we've been through, after what I," Leona thought back to her dream. "After everything, you should know that you're my life. If anything, I don't deserve you." Why there was a hint of anger residing on Mateo' face, she couldn't fathom an answer for. Before she could drum up more to say Mateo was by the window, peering out through her tangled blinds.

"I don't want to hurt you anymore than I have." Mateo said to the window.

"You have never hurt me, and you never will. Your problems are my problems now."

"Leona when will you see that I'm more trouble than I'm worth?"

"When will you see that you might be equal trouble as your worth and I'm okay with that value." Leona sat on the end of the bed, scoping Mateo' chiseled back. "Look around us babe, search the house, you're the only one I have left. Whether or not you think you're some disease I'm blind too, I see someone that loves me, problems or not. So stop."

"Fine. What is this idea of yours?"

The next day Leona intertwined an arm around Mateo' bicep to keep balance, grasping onto one crutch standing before the business that held a sign which read *Thew Pawn This.*

"I don't understand how a pawn shop will give us answers, you have school to worry about, a job, and you're taking me on a field trip to a pawn shop with a tiny Ferris wheel in the window."

"I've showed you my stuffed animals, complete with their names and make-believe occupations. If I trust you, why can't you trust me?"

Mateo had not a word for a comeback, instead Leona lead the way into the cozy shop which had already sucked her in with its miniature universe—a small gateway into Mateo' past, did more than intrigue her.

Inside lacked Mathew or a sales clerk. One customer browsed: an awkward looking girl with glasses the size of coasters. But everything else remained from the pile of entangled machinery to the rare toys and other odd equipment waiting for a home.

"We have to find Mathew, he's the owner." Leona whispered.

"When are you going to fill me in on…" Mateo took his arm back for himself at the sight of what looked to be a toy red car, no larger than a banana."

"I'm good, don't worry about me breaking my neck or anything." Leona said as Mateo picked up the car, surveying it like an alien finding a new world.

"This is my car, look– it says *C.C.*" Mateo showcased the carving on the side.

Leona almost got jealous at how tight he held the thing. In that moment, for whatever reason she thought about her mother and danced with how Mateo suggested that she should be worrying about her as well. As much as the crevice inside her gut agreed with that, anger punted it away.

"I want to buy this, what are the odds that this thing would be here?" Mateo gushed.

Pulling Mateo to the side and away from his new pride possession she pulled him down five inches to where she could whisper a bit, whoever the girl was, she didn't need to know their business.

"The owner knows who you are." She explained. "He also knows your aunt."

Keeping up with his assembly line of bewildered gazes, he gifted her yet another one. "What are you talking about Leona?"

"If I had told you sooner you wouldn't have come."

"Mathew isn't here right now, nor will he ever be again. You both should go. Purchase the car if you will, but then you must go." The girl with the oversized glasses directed her plea to the shelf of rainbow televisions that sat before her. Upon more focused examination the outside of each TV was encased in a form fitting lava lamp.

"Are you talking to us?" Leona asked the girl.

"Well you two are the only ones in the shop I presume, unless you're privy to the supernatural. If you are I'd much like to meet a ghost."

"Miss, we don't mean to bother you." Mateo said.

"A shame then, you've failed."

Leona spawned a dislike for the way she the girl was speaking. "Excuse me but, Mathew was here the other day, we spoke, who are you exactly?"

"Marsh, I work for Mathew. I'm going to rewind to what I said before, Mathew is not here. Nor will he be again, I need you to take yourself and Mateo out of this shop."

"We never told you his name." Leona said, feeling a surge of confidence shoot down her bad leg.

"Lucky guess," Marsh finally extended them both a glance, but nothing more, speedily walking to where the broom was. She began to sweep, the girl's awkwardness brought did not mix well with Leona's protectiveness.

"You're a really bad liar, no offence."

"None taken."

"Leona, maybe we should just leave."

"No, we came here and I'm not going to be denied by someone who thinks she can be snooty for no reason. Mathew was really kind to me."

"Mathew isn't here!" The girl screamed, slamming the old broom against the ugly brown floor. Both Mateo and Leona stood motionless in the room's tension.

"Leona, I'm going to the car." Mateo snaked the keys from the top of Leona's handbag, holding the door open with the heel of his foot. "Are you coming?"

"In a minute."

"The girl wants you to leave her—"

"Mateo, in a minute." With that the dainty bell above the door jingled and Leona was left in the room with Marsh.

"Why are you so godawful stubborn? I tried to be nice. I even tried to be patient and if you look at that clock it should show how patience is one of the hardest things." Marsh watched the zebra stripped ticking machine do its job.

"Where's Mathew?"

"Tick tick tick, with every tick our lifespan goes down a second. Patience," Marsh laughed. "Patience is nothing but a waste of time."

"Forgive her Kaye, like me time has poured fire on the girls' verbal filter." Mathew emerged from a backroom wearing a luchadores' mask. This was the point in time where Leona realized she was dealing with insanity.

"Okay, this has gotten too crazy for me."

"You don't like my mask? An old friend gave it to me from a trip he took to Mexico." Mathew removed the red and green flamboyant headgear. "Here, give it to your boyfriend, it's better than the mask he's wearing right now."

Leona had no choice but to accept it, the man's hands seemed as though they wouldn't accept a refusal. "I came here to find out what you know about Swanson, that's all. I want the bounty taken off of Mateo' head."

"Not an easy task, Swanson is much like you a stubborn man. And that's all I know of him. As personable as I am and as human as I like to make my customers, I don't know much of their personal lives. Now, I need you to go. And please, do not return."

"Fine," Leona said, clutching the mask. "But I'm not stupid, I know you're Mateo' father." Without looking behind herself and without waiting for a response, Leona made for the door.

"Take the car too," Mathew Colon said. "It's his, please."

Leona turned around, first gazing at the man's contrite. Then she took the car from the man's shaking hand with the same care of removing a Jenga piece.

"Becareful," Mathew said.

Not knowing what he fully meant, Leona left it at that.

Richter Town, Anne's Farm

The little car left Bradley's grasp at the sound of the tires hitting gravel outside the window. His skinny legs drew him over, just to verify whether or not it was indeed who he thought it to be. His father had not been to the farm since before he had run off. Anne denied Mateo kidnapping him at first, or at least that's what she claimed to have done. Now it was a different tale, one in which Bradley wasn't all against.

As directed beforehand Bradley removed the paneling to the back-wall in his closet. Two feet across and five feet top to bottom, Bradley stuffed himself into the crevice and adjusted the panel back to the way it had been, the homemade handle on the back made that easy, patiently waiting was the hard part.

Maybe it was a few minutes or maybe long seconds but eventually the clatter had arrived downstairs. One sided yelling it was. His father's voice boomed. Harold could not make out the words, but the deep almost ruptured stereo sounding tone of his father explained enough.

What had to be pans and pots hit the floor downstairs, glasses shattered like they were angry, and doors slammed. For moment, one door slammed repeatedly and with every slam shut hit father bellowed a word simultaneously.

Why does he get mad if he doesn't care? Bradley thought, wishing that he could at least adjust his elbow position. And then there was severe quiet, Bradly could not liken the feeling to anything else he's ever experienced. There was one movie though, where he remembered seeing the atomic bomb going off. It was quiet after that. The giant swimming mushroom cloud was the most peaceful and frightening thing he's ever seen; he could imagine the cloud hitting his room at any moment.

The door shot open, and the hand which did the job had to be made of steel. Bradley hushed his breathing, his legs shook with flames of fear.

"I left you with him for a damn reason you bitch, it's been days now. I swear to fuckin god if you have him in this house I'll do worse to that ugly face of yours."

"I've been dang on waiting for him to return myself, you should be out looking for this Mateo kid not tearing apart my house."

"I'm tearing apart your damn house because his toys are in your fuckin living room! You're telling me that was you playing with fuckin action figures you lying redneck?"

"It's called house cleaning, you want your son to live in a clean house now am I right? If he returns."

The pause had been brief but long enough to let Bradley know that Anne had said the wrong thing.

"You want to run that by me again? Let's take a look at who the fuck let that kid stay in this house to begin with."

The rubber soles of the boots smacking the floor set the scene for Bradley. There was little doubt that Swanson was walking towards Anne. The urge to release the wood panel and put an end to the charade was tempting. But Anne's plans had always been solid, so Bradley continued to hold the handle while the shaking from his legs migrated to his hands.

The soft yet precise eruption of flesh on flesh forced Bradley's eyes shut, as if they could do the same for his ears. The room was now rid of noise. Bradley waited, and waited until Anne finally spoke again.

"You can hit me all you'd like, it ain't gonna bring your boy back."

"Fuck you. I gave you my son and put food on this time so that the little shit could stuff his face, clothe his body and put water on that pale skin every day and you up and lose him. I should have put you six feet into the ground instead of Karen."

There was an earthquake in Bradley's hands, the wood panel shifted because of it. Wood against wood poked its head into the room for the briefest of seconds and replacing the rage in Bradley was now the hope that his father did not hear it.

"You have possums or raccoons up in this house?" Swanson said with a voice so deep it sounded satanic.

"A critter can easily get into these walls, why?"

"Don't pretend like you didn't hear that."

"Hear what?"

"Something is in here, and I have the best instinct in me that it's my boy."

Bradley swallowed, doing his best to contain the trembling shooting up and down his arms, wishing that he had closed the closet door just a little more to not bring attention to the area.

That's when Swanson began to tear the room apart, Bradley was sure of it, and a little worried that his toys would be destroyed.

"Where is he?!" Swanson yelled. "When I find him I'm running a knife across your throat. You think I can't find someone to babysit his ass? You think you're irreplaceable?"

"I don't know what you're talking about." Anne stayed calm which in turn made Bradley settle down somewhat. But as things hit the wall and got tossed about, the fear continued to travel. Then the worst happened, it all suddenly stopped.

"The closet, he's in the closet."

"Swanson, you think I'd let you do all this if the boy was feet away from you?"

"Let me? It's the perfect scheme of yours, hide the boy in plain sight."

Bradley swallowed three more times, listening to the rustling at the bottom of the wall panel.

"You should be worried about Mateo, not distrusting the woman who's been raising your son for years, watching you hit him every day."

Most of Anne's plans were hard to decipher, but Bradley could see what she was doing this time—she was stalling. Which meant that she was scared as well.

Bradley could hear the creak of the closet open. That didn't make sense because he heard rustling at the bottom already, if Swanson hadn't been searching then what was the noise?

"Holy shit!?" Swanson bellowed.

"I told you!"

"Why the fuck do you have a fox in this house?"

"Get it out of here!" Anne screamed at the top of her lungs. Bradley could breathe again—for now.

Later that night Anne sat next to Bradley at the dinner table. Sitting idly was a big bowl of cloudy white mashed potatoes and veal covered in a creamy light brown gravy that glistened under the light.

"It should hold him off for a while, until he gets to Mateo."

Bradley said nothing.

"I trust Mateo and I'm doing this for us. I can't keep watching him hurt you Brad, enough is enough already. You'll hide, and we'll just hope this goes our way. I believed that there was a light in Mateo, but now I'm hoping that the darkness puts it's out. Sometimes when you know enough about someone you can predict what they'll do, and when you can do that all they need is some steering. If this doesn't work I promise, we'll run."

Whatever Anne meant by that, Bradley hoped she was right.

The Secret Holder

Leona sat, landing her head in every direction that was physically possible. Mateo' weights, his shiny black television, the scrape revealing tan paint on the very right corner of his bedroom doorframe; being back at his apartment allowed her to breath normally again.

"How did you keep this place while you were gone?" Leona asked, still with the head of a squirrel.

"I sent money orders to my landlord. I need the number to the hospital you were in."

Leona assumed why but asked anyway. "To see what happened to your aunt?"

"Yeah."

"Um, not that it's more important but what about that the lock had been replaced?"

"It can wait." Mateo put his new cellphone against his ear, walking into his bedroom to make the call and leaving Leona with a tinge of offence.

Leona did wonder about the lock pad, originally it had been a dulled grey with streaks of wear and tear running down it like tears. Now, upon return the thing was a new gold color which stood out like a sore thumb. She wondered if Swanson had broken in and maybe the landlord had replaced it after. But Mateo had yet to speak to the man.

On her good leg she hobbled to the counter where junk mail, fitness magazines and papers that Mateo probably didn't need were scattered about. If one had just stumbled upon it without knowing they would have assumed Mateo had been looking for something. With impact it hit her, he was never that much of a slob, and someone had been looking for something.

Mateo came through his bedroom door, there wasn't a bad look on his face, more a confusion; that made both of them.

"So what happened?" Leona asked.

"They couldn't disclose any information to me over the phone, I have to go there in person. I'm going to go today while you're at work."

Trevor, Trevor, Trevor works there. They don't know each other though. Why do I have a bad feeling? "We could go before I have work, I want to go with you."

Mateo gave his eyes to her leg and she instantly knew what his response was going to be. "I could probably do it quicker if you didn't go."

"But I want to, I'll walk quickly. These papers…" She decided to change the subject. "They're usually organized. Mateo, I have a really bad feeling that someone was in here. You need to call the landlord."

"My landlord wouldn't have let someone in here while I was gone. That's illegal and against my lease.'

"You think Swanson cares about that?"

Leona had never laid eyes upon Mateo' landlord Henry, and after doing just that she had wished she never did. The man had a forest of bushy black hair, only on the sides of his shiny dome. What bothered her most was the way he shaved his chine and left all the coarse black hair around his over-sized lips.

"When I saw the door open I had f-figured you had c-come b-b-back. The hallway c-cameras caught nothing out of the o-o-dinary. My guess is somebody fell or dropped something a-a-and the d-d-door broke open. The lock was flippin old."

After Mateo and Leona walked away from the man, Mateo knew the question before she asked it.

"Yes, he always had that stutter."

"I hate you for knowing what I'm going to say next." Leona lied. "To me, it sounded like he was covering something up. Who falls and breaks a door open."

"I don't know, but investigating it ain't going to un-do anything." Mateo held the passenger side door open for Leona. The walk he took around the car to the driver's seat tortured her patience, holding onto refutes was never Leona's strong suite. As soon as the door opened so did her mouth.

"Are you just waiting for something to happen? Like you're being too prideful. You don't know what this guy is capable of. Instead of acting like a sitting duck maybe you should put the fire out before it comes to you."

"You're instigating things now Leona, you ever think that maybe the man wants me to go after him? Or maybe he let it go, Bradley is back at home now."

"You let this Anne lady just tell him that you kidnapped Bradley? Why didn't you stick around to tell him the truth?" It was as if her fury had started the car. Or it was Mateo choosing to put his energy into driving so that he wouldn't lose his patience."

"She wanted me off the farm, I'm not one to start trouble."

Suddenly Leona realized just how weird it was for Mateo to drive her car, she missed the Mercedes, in turn handing her some resentment towards Anne. "You know, as much as you went to that farm to start over and rid yourself of all these *problems* you had, it really feels like you just took on a whole shitload more of them."

"Everything happens for a reason."

"Since when did you become a positive thinker?" She didn't like it for some reason.

"Since I have you."

But that changed her mind.

After an argument, Mateo summoned enough reason for Leona to remain in the car while he pushed himself through the craziness of the hospital waiting room. At the front desk, a young brunette with a slim face and pouty lips types away at a computer. The thin gold chain sparkled and rested just above a little bit of cleavage. Mateo yanked his eyes to hers, which immediately were drenched in flirtation.

"Hi, how can I help you?" She asked.

"My aunt was…passed away here and I was wondering if I could get any information on what happened to her."

"Oh, I'm so sorry to hear that." That's when the phone rang and she was stolen from their conversation. It lasted at least minutes by the time Mateo took notice about how long it was. Now she was wrapping a hair around her finger. *Guess she flirts with everyone,* he thought, now letting his attention span wander amongst the hospital noise.

Then, with the horror and speed of a lightning bolt, it was before his eyes. The air in his chest escaped like it had been trapped for centuries, Dizziness almost took him at the knees. He now knew what it was like to experience pure dread.

Noelle walked down the hall beside a nurse. It was when Mateo went to look away that she noticed him as well. All of the energy that she had been previously using with the nurse fell into a shaky smile, one that was laced with pain, lust, love and everything else that Mateo had wished to never encounter ever again.

"Mateo…." Noelle said it from afar but it arrived as a poison whisper.

"Sup," was the coldest thing he could think to say. The nurse rounded the corner holding a vanilla folder, and then he stopped in his tracks, turning around to give Mateo eyes as if he knew him.

"I didn't know you were back, you should have called me."

"Why would I have called you? How does that make any sense? You and I never happened, you understand that? You're the reason I left."

The nurse was now before them both, with more approach towards Mateo than Noelle.

"Do I know you bro?" Mateo asked, now with a spine of fire.

There was a reluctance on the nurse's face, until Noelle saved him from his own sinking ship.

"He's Leona's boyfriend, you remember Leona? The girl you changed while she was unconscious, the one with the broken leg. You were there when he wasn't." Her stare had not one blink, with eyes as dry as the hottest dessert beaming into Mateo.

"That's one way to put it, not how I would have worded it Noelle."

"What do you mean that he was there for her?"

"Ooooh, I'm sorry. Leona hasn't told you about her friendship with Trevor?"

And then Mateo remembered, relieved at the notion that it actually hadn't been a secret. Which meant Leona had nothing to hide. Rationality could bury Noelle's farce. "She did actually." Mateo said proudly. "Thank you for taking care of her while I was away."

"It's no problem, I was just doing my job. I hope she also told you that I'm dating her best friend."

"Yes she did. Did she tell you that Noelle?"

"No, but I'm sure when we hang out she'll fill me in on all the deets."

The stare-down between Mateo and Noelle was enough to sever the hospital in half. Instead, Trevor did that for their stare-down. So yo Mateo, what exactly you here for? If you don't mind me asking."

Slowly and reluctantly, Mateo pulled himself away from Noelle's gaze. There was still part of him that wanted to toss her against the wall and taste the softness of her lips. "My aunt passed away here, while I was gone. I need information on where…"

"I got ya. It's okay. What was her name?"

"Rosa Alverez."

That same look that Trevor wore when first lending his sights to Mateo returned. "I know where I can get you that info, you can come with me if you want. I've heard the desk clerk don't really consider anyone else's pace."

"Yeah, that's fine."

The two of them squeezed by sauntering doctors, sickly filled beds on wheels, beeps and seemingly miniature sirens that wreaked havoc on Mateo' psyche. Knowing that his aunt had spent her last moment's aside cold machines with equally cold doctors and no family was enough to again bring him to his knees. It hurt. The pit was heavy in his stomach leaving in its wake a nausea and uneasiness that made him want to sleep, better yet—die. And then on top of that Leona had spent her days in the very same place following her mother and boyfriend vanishing selfishly. It all felt like one big overly sad novel.

"This was her room."

"How do you know?"

"I remember rooms. Sometimes the patient's family comes back to see it, even when it's occupied…since it is the place they remember seeing them alive last."

Mateo stood as quiet as the empty room itself, jumping between tearful looks at the unoccupied bed and Trevor as he brought himself to a lonesome computer sitting in the corner. The nurse typed, and while the clicking filled the room, Mateo brushed his hand along the surface of the empty white mattress. He cried, silently, with his face turned to the wall.

"It looks like somebody financed her burial–a family member." Trevor said, causing Mateo to suck in the moisture on his face.

"What do mean? She lost contact with everyone, no one would have done that."

"I'm just reading the disclosure records, that's what it says. I don't have enough access to verify who but didn't you just want to know where she was anyway?"

He did, but now that was beyond the point. "Where is she?"

Mateo walked back through the busy hallways himself, leaving Trevor to go attend to hospital business. From what he overheard a patient had gone into cardiac arrest while in the bathroom. Trevor wasn't what Mateo had expected, he wasn't sure what he was expecting, maybe the equivalent of himself: some sort of replacement. But Trevor seemed less of a threat and maybe that's what still had him worried. From what he learned in his twenty-two years on the planet—the quiet ones hold the power.

With her arms leaning on the front desk, holding up her two heavy breasts, Mateo spied Noelle nose deep in her phone. The only business she had left in the hospital had to be with Mateo, she was waiting he assumed. And that sparked outrage. Even as his forehead began to throb he realized that the emotions he was feeling were most likely engendered by his aunt. Whatever they transformed into and directed themselves at wasn't his concern though. Like telepathy, Noelle's mascaraed eyes met Mateo midway down the hallway, which is when he waved her over. An empty staircase was what he remembered passing before and an empty staircase was where he would take her.

Mateo walked and she followed behind, her fruity yet cinnamon smelling perfume wafted around him. That boiled to the service things that he wished did not exist anymore. But apparently they still did.

Inside the staircase Mateo quickly browsed for cameras without ever craning his head and then spun around to grab Noelle by the shoulders, shoving her slender, soft body against the wall. The way her lips fell open on contact made Mateo look away.

"I need you to stop talking to Leona." Mateo grunted.

"Not happening big boy."

"What do you want?"

"I'm looking right at him." She extended her head as if to kiss him, but Mateo jerked his head back. "You're lying to yourself, I do like the paws on my shoulders though, grrrrrrrr."

"I told you, it was a mistake. I was weak. You have to let this go Noelle."

"Why did you leave? Was it really because of me? You couldn't face her could you?"

"I'm not talking about this–not with you." Mateo released his grip, turning his back to her and realizing that this wasn't going to be as simple as empty threats and mutterings through the teeth.

"Then with who Mateo? Cause I know you have even mentioned it to Leona, she doesn't know."

"Don't call me Mateo, and I don't need to talk about to anyone because it never happened." Mateo turned around, confidence at his foot soles. Noelle's gaze wasn't as intimidating, because after all, she couldn't prove a thing.

"Is that the card you're playing?" The long, pink and maroon nails clicked against the concrete wall, propelling the body topped off with jet black hair towards Mateo. "You think that I can't spin this thread my way? You don't think that Leona trusts me enough? Ask her friend Lauren." One done up nail poked at his stiff chest. "You're the one who left, I was there on day one when that cast was put on her leg, begging for her friendship....for her trust. The funny thing is, I look like the villain." Noelle smiled a cold, narcissistic smile, with broken eyes that wanted to spurt tears. "But I'm the one holding onto the truth to save you from her scorn, to protect someone that used me." The nail dug deep into his chest, for a second Mateo wondered if it would break the tight black fabric of his t-shirt. "Before her, I was this close," She measured about an inch with her thumb and index finger. "to actually being with you and—"

"Enough! What do you want me to say? What do you want me to do? I don't feel the same way as you." Mateo tried his best to extend her the sincerest mask at his disposal.

"Stop lying to yourself, you know that's not true."

"Stop lying to yourself and accept that I don't. I love Leona!"

The stairwell fell silent, leaving in its wake the corpse of whatever confidence Noelle had left. Mateo turned his back, leading himself in a half pace.

But then that shrill, scheming noise which was Noelle Santiago's voice took the stage once more, resurrecting the limp pride that Mateo thought he had extinguished seconds ago. "Your insecurity binds you to her, you know that right?"

"Shut up."

"That weak, innocent little boy who clambers for his mommy only stays with Leona because it makes you feel safe. She takes care of you right? Like a little baby."

Mateo bolted around, nearly taking her by the shoulders again. Something inside his head stopped him, maybe Anne's voice, maybe Leona's, he couldn't tell. "Watch it."

"But with me, I'm the girl that truly satisfies you." The nail, along with three others pranced along his chest. "I'm the one you really desire after stripping away all that sadness, that fear, and low self-esteem. It's why you keep crawling back."

The hands met her shoulders with a tight squeeze, shoving her back up against the wall. The anger sped through his veins like a speed boat, but she was loving every second of it.

"You're going to stop talking to her, I mean it."

"Hit me, go ahead. Do whatever it is that you want to do, at least I stand here and see you for what you really are. At least I don't lie to myself and pretend that you're this savior prince who needs fixing. I know that you're fucked up. I know that you're a piece of shit, and I like it. Because frankly, so am I. The difference between Mateo Colon and Noelle Santiago—I accept it." Noelle pushed Mateo from her space with both hands, the cracking of one nail was felt right below his collarbone. "I don't need someone to baby me, I don't need to feel safe. I need someone who likes me for me. Which you do."

"It's pathetic that you can't let go, I hope you know that." Mateo pivoted to the door and Noelle blocked his path. All five feet of her summoned all the courage she had left.

"I'm not crazy and I'm not pathetic. I'm certainly not wrong. I know more about you than Leona does, I know that without even needing to ask, you know why?"

"Stop."

"Because, those nights where you cried after sex, the nights where you held me and said to never fuckin leave." Noelle finally cried with a quivering lip. All the muscles in her face acted like a crowd trying to hold up a giant wall. "After saying all that, the fuck would you leave?"

"Sometimes you have to leave before you get left." Mateo said through a grunt. "I'm not talking about this, it's over. Nothing is going to change, so please—let it go." The sincerity which had been called upon earlier made hopefully its final appearance.

"No. I want what I want. I don't care how many lies you tell yourself—or Leona."

"Nat—"

"I don't care what everyone calls me, I don't care how mad you get, how stupid you think I am, or how long I have to wait until you're shit gets fucked up. But I know it will. Because people like you and me, don't get people like Leona. What she stops being a narcissistic, shallow little twat and wakes up and realizes that—"

Mateo' hand clenched into a fist and the second the fingers coiled into his palm, Noelle had her hand over it.

"You see this? Because I do." She said. "You want to hit me. You'll never change. Your anger will always be there. But some people won't." Noelle Santiago gave Mateo Colon her back, hopefully she was wrong—and he'd never have to see Leona's.

A Cast of Mystery

Leona found Emma's face unavoidable. Her gloomy mug tore down the emotion in the room. *Does this girl ever smile?* Emma sat in between a fidgety Remy and Aunt Betty who sat with her back as straight as a ruler with her hands folded as if she were in grade school. Leona's little family made her laugh on the inside. *They're a motley crew in their own right,* she thought. Even with the black eye shadowed Emma filling the room with teen rebellion, the occasion was a rung below joyous: the cast of Leona's leg was going to be cut off by a doctor any second. It would have been fully joyous if Liz Price had been there and if the cast hadn't existed in the first place.

"It's going to be a dark frightening forest under that cast." Emma said.

"Thanks."

"Well it's good that the thing is finally coming off and you won't need to hobble around like a wounded animal anymore." Aunt Betty added.

"Thanks again, you guys are making this feel like New Year's and Christmas all wrapped in one." Leona shot a glance at Remy who was unnervingly quiet.

"It's funny how we're getting excited for a leg that's only going back to the way it was before if you think about it.

Humans are strange." Emma said, seemingly out loud to herself.

No you're strange, Leona thought.

Just then the tall blond haired doctor marched in holding what had to be the cast saw. It reminded Leona of the thing that her mother used to use on the heels of her feet; an item that had to be at least eight inches long with a tiny little plate at its helm.

"You ready to get this off, I could leave it on if you like?"

If it had been another doctor, a little less attractive, the joke would have angered her, but his smile tickled her shallow side. "No, you can have it. Maybe nail it to your wall to remember me by."

"I don't think I'll go that far."

"My old cat had to wear a cast before it died. Couldn't use its hind legs. Death was a present." Emma said while creating a room full of saddened faces.

"Emma, you're my family and I love you, but somethings can be worded less like a eulogy." Leona said.

Then, the cast saw vibrated its spinning plate of metal down onto the off-white hunk of turmoil that Leona had almost grown accustomed to. Once the wrapping underneath was peeled away by the gentle doctor amongst the eyes of her interested family, the skin hit the room with a raisin like wrinkle and grapefruit pink hue. It almost made Leona vomit.

"That looks like something out of a My Chemical Romance video." Emma said.

"Thanks."

The four of them walked from the hospital. With each step on her wrinkly leg Leona wobbled a bit, as if the thing had been put onto her thigh for the first time. *Is the blood not getting down there or something?* She wondered.

At the car Emma took the back while Remy hopped into the passenger seat. As Leona played claw machine with the inside of her bag for her keys, Betty grabbed her by the wrist.

"I need you to speak with Remy." Betty said.

"What's the matter?"

"I don't know." Betty said it as if she had just walked up ten flights of steps. "Nothing seems to make her happy, she barely speaks—"

"Like usual."

"No, less."

The parking lot around them was swarming with vehicles, horns that held no restraint and ambulances that frankly, brought down Leona's mood. But off in the distance, there stood a boy. His face was of need, lost but longing for something. And then his mother picked him up under the arms and carried him to their minivan; his face an ocean of comfort. Leona looked at Remy.

"I haven't been there for her."

"Don't blame yourself." Betty gave her response to the pavement. "Why don't you take her with you, and I'll take Emma."

"I have work at four, I'll have to drop her off."

"That's fine Leona, just spend some time with her."

"Okay, I'm sorry that I haven't been around much."

Disdain, it was something Leona hadn't expected on Betty. If anything, the assumption was that Betty would have denied Leona absence, but apparently there was a different storm on the horizon.

"I don't Mateo. I know that he left you at a very bad time." Betty began.

"Okay…"

"I know, that you're mother wasn't fond of the boy. And I also know that you two have had your issues. I've never taken a strong stance against your relationship. I've never seen the problem–until recently."

The storm had hit and Leona hadn't stocked up for it, let alone knew it was coming. "Where is this—"

"We're midway through the summer, Remy has spent little time with you, and you haven't shown the slightest interest in school. All your energy either goes to missing Mateo or being with Mateo. And sweetheart, I mean this in the best way for you possible–he's trash."

If it had been a second longer that Leona's mouth hung open, a fly would have flown in and made it his home. "Okay." Leona said. For the briefest of seconds, she and her aunt held a stare, and it was broken by Leona. She ripped open the door and said "C'mon," to Remy, who without question followed Leona to her car.

Inside the car, Remy surprisingly broke Leona's tension filled silence. "She's right you know, you can get mad all you like, but one day you're going to have to listen to or lose us."

The words tangled at Leona's lips, and after a second of trying to untangle them, she remained quiet.

"How many things are you going to let get ruined because of him?"

Leona halted the car right before a green light, screeching the tires and biting her lower lip. She debated on kicking Remy right out of the car which in turn, made her consider Remy's words. She pulled the car to the side of the road.

"I'm sorry that I haven't been around."

"For someone who hates mom, you act like her."

The storm was still hitting.

"You were a hypocrite with Hank, and now you basically vanished just like her. For some guy who treats you badly. I'm not stupid, I know when people are bad."

"You don't know how he treats me Remy. We've been over that so please calm down."

"No," Remy un-did her seat belt and removed herself from the car. She walked aimlessly up the side of the road one foot on the hardened black roadway, the other in the grassy dirt. It took Leona less than three seconds to catch up to her by foot.

"Are you crazy!?" Leona yelled over the engines of passing traffic. "Get back into the car!"

"It used to be about us. You used to care."

"I still do care. I said I was sorry that I haven't been around, Remy, please get back into the car."

"You'd rather spend time with someone who probably doesn't even know your birthday."

"Remy," That's when Leona heard the leaves in the brush rustling, a heavy rustle that instantly revved up the motor in her chest. "Remy!" Her little sister jolted her head to her right and suddenly the animal emerged from the green wall of crowded leaves. While it was in midair, all four feet soaring over the ground and a ducking Remy, Leona noticed it was a deer. Missing Remy by half a foot, she hit the ground on her rump and Leona bolted to her, yanking her from the soil and shuffling her tiny body back to the car where she belonged.

Inside was a mix between laughing and crying from both parties. Remy was the first to hush herself, then followed Leona. The interior of the car filled with an awkward pause.

Leona eventually turned the engine on an let the air condition fill the car with not only a cool refrigerator like air, but also a bit of much needed noise.

"I'm not wrong for my feelings." Remy muttered.

"I never said you were."

"Yes you did."

Leona pulled the car away from the side of the road and drove, wishing that Remy's rightness was in the rear-view mirror.

Leona didn't make the slightest effort at hiding her glances towards Remy, munching away on cheese-fries at a noisy mid-afternoon Orangefly. Kids hit their highest pitch while waiters and waitresses looked like human pin-balls carrying platters.

"How can you tell that he's bad for me?" Leona asked.

"I know you. You've been one way my whole life, then suddenly you're picking fights with mom and leaving home."

"That's it?"

Remy's eye's never left the plate, "No, there's more that I can't put it into words. It's like these cheese-fries, no one had to tell me they're bad for my body but I somehow know they are."

"I'm sorry that I haven't been around more."

"That's not what bothers me. I have Emma to as company, she isn't as dark as her lipstick."

I find that hard to believe. "Then what is it that's bothering you?"

"Every time I see you, mom is always something you avoid."

Leona stirred her thoughts with avoidance as the main ingredient with anger as the spice. "Because she left. I'm trying not to pass off your forgiveness as your age but, I don't know Remy."

"You think because I'm young I'm stupid."

"No, just two different perspectives." Leona couldn't grab hold of a solid explanation.

"Just like you can't see how bad a boy is for you, other people can't see their own faults either."

"She left. Without any explanation. Agree to disagree."

"People leave." The cheese oozed off the end of the limp fry in Remy's tiny fair–skinned hand and plopped down on the white oversized plate below. "You were going to leave for Sugenta State. You left to live with Mateo. Blood is thicker than water."

Something about that reminded Leona of her father, Patrick Price. Remy could have been wearing his demeanor and speaking his voice it had been so nostalgic. Leona came to realize that her father would have taken the same stance. His vast stubbornness fell into every facet of life, especially when it came to blood and loved ones.

"I would have at least kept in touch if I had gone to Sugenta state, and when I lived with Mateo I still called."

"Agree to disagree."

That irked Leona. "I meant to ask Aunt Betty, did she happen to find anything on mom?"

"She didn't tell you?" Remy finally dragged her focus away from her plate.

"No..."

"She called off her private investigator. The guy turned up nothing. Dead end."

Why is she cold and withdrawn about that but when it comes to being mad at the bitch she's Mother Teresa? "Oh, so what that means we just stopped looking?"

"I don't think she wants to be found."

"Yeah, and how does that not piss you off? How are you not fuming like me? You just forgive her like she forgot to cook dinner."

"Hey."

"Like she's our mom, you should be mad, you should miss her like I do. I need her." The tears were welling in her eyes to the point where it stung.

"Leona."

"What?"

"I lied, she sent a letter to Aunt Betty. I didn't lie about the investigator though."

"Why... would you lie about that?" She somewhat knew the answer.

"Because I know you, and what it takes to get you to be honest with yourself." Remy ate the last fry and smiled.

The letter slept encased in an envelope, neatly torn open by Aunt Betty, who even when ripping open mail left no trace of sloppiness. Off-white was never so unsettling, a small insignificant piece of paper altered into a message of pain in the form of ink, Leona shook with it in her grasp.

"You don't have to read this now honey." Aunt Betty said.

And Leona heard but did not listen, removing the folded piece of paper from the envelope and lifting it's flap to reveal way more text than she had anticipated. Sprinkled in with the mystery of what it could possibly say an ounce of hope. Of what? Leona didn't know. Escaping from the kitchen of her aunt's house and slowly sinking away from the awkward eyes of Remy and Emma, Leona began to read.

Lucille,

I'm sorry for doing this to you. I'm sure by now you've taken in my daughters. There's a lot you don't know. About me, about my life, my husband's life, and I need my daughters to be away from me. I'm not a good mother. I'm not worthy of their beautiful smiles, positive outlooks, and rock solid shoulders that have carried my personality throughout the years. In time, maybe you'll understand. Just let Remy and let Leona know how much I love them. I'm writing this not so much as an explanation or to take the blame off myself in anyway. I write this purely to say I'm sorry.

Upon reading the last word, Leona balled up both the envelope and paper until the tips of her fingers dug into her palm, and hurled the small ball across the kitchen and into the sink.

"Leona," Aunt Betty said once more.

But again instead of listening Leona made a bee-line for the sink as if she had forgotten to read a word. She picked up the ball of sorrowful text and turned on the stove, crisping one end against the blue flames as if it were a Marshmallow. After that she put the fireball out and brought herself to Remy.

"Don't ever ask me to speak of her again."

Falling Skies

Immediately Trevor realized the newest light in his life had evolved into darkness. Thanks to the plague stretching from early childhood all the way down to an ailing grandmother in his adulthood, nothing which was bad could catch him by surprise anymore. Nothing cataclysmic or of sorrowful coincidence could bring the same heart flutters he once had as a young boy. But, the searing yet numb pain was there, filling his vitals, attacking his psyche and sucking the moisture from his mouth.

She's not into me anymore. Trevor declared through the hurricane in his mind. "It's okay."

"I just broke up with my boyfriend, the relationship had been a long time and we were very close. I don't want to start something with you as I'm standing on ground zero." Lauren said. Her eyes reminded him of autumn; brown with a beautiful hint of hazel. "I understand. I really don't know what else to say."

"What are you feeling?"

What do you think I'm feeling? "I don't know."

"I'm sorry,"

"You don't have to be, shit happens."

"I really do like you."

"Are you not attracted?" He felt dumb asking, knowing full well that wasn't the issue.

"No no, it's not that. I just–"

"I know, sorry for asking, that was stupid."

Lauren put both her hands to her face, covering it as if she were playing peek-a-boo. "I'm such an idiot, I'm stupid oh my god."

"Relax, it's not that serious." Yet it somehow hurt like it was. To calm her down he imagined grabbing her by the face and kissing her soft innocent lips, even now in a time where she loathed herself, she couldn't muster of the nerve to let out a swear-word.

"It is serious, I didn't set out to hurt you, I had good intentions."

"I know that, at least it didn't go further than it did."

"I wouldn't have minded to be honest."

Did she mean what he thought she meant? "What do you mean?"

"I wouldn't have minded losing my virginity to you. But I don't know, it would be awful now."

Then why say anything? Why fuckin bring it up? Trevor yelled on the inside but let nothing seep to the surface, fumbling with any semblance of a response, to his shame, that may lead to peeling the clothes from her virgin body. "Why would it be awful, I know Imma probably sound like a horn-dog but I wouldn't mind losing it to you either."

"We can't." Lauren's face went stern.

"Okay."

"That wouldn't make any sense, it's just that sometimes I wish I could experience it. And I don't know, I'm stupid." She once again grabbed her face, and the diner they sat in finally tore at his patience. With one obnoxiously loud party of four sitting behind them two rows back in a booth, yelling at a baseball game on television, Trevor had wished they had agreed to meet in a library instead. It was a small family owned place called Vesti's, which had more white people in it than Trevor wanted to acknowledge.

"Then no offense but why did you bring it up?"

"I don't know, it sounded good in my head, like I was paying you a compliment of some sort."

Her innocence only made him want her more. "No, it just made me want to have sex."

"You haven't even had it though, so how do you want something that you've never had hmmm?" She was trying to be cute and Trevor felt the guilt in not being able to feign amusement better. "I'm sorry."

"Stop apologizing, it's done. Let's just move on."

"Can we still be friends?"

It was like being shot inches from the chest with a nine millimeter and then having a switchblade jabbed into your kidneys. But being the soft hearted nurse that he will most likely never morph out of, he said, "Yeah, of course."

Trevor sat idle on the bus, staring at nothing in specific while listening to *I don't want to know*. It was a song by rapper Sean Combs and although the lyrics were about cheating, something about the sad melody which hinted at closure brought him comfort. There wasn't much that he wanted to do otherwise let alone think about. Usually on bus rides to and from wherever, Trevor would either write poetry, play video games or maybe look for better jobs online. But today he wanted to be one with his bed.

A ride home was offered by Lauren, in numerous pleas. She even went as far as pulling up to the bus stop on the vacant corner in front of the dilapidated former eye glass shop and pleaded for Trevor to hop in. Three polite declines later and she was on her way.

Clunk clatter clunk, the bus slipped its noises right under Trevor's blue Beats headphones and rattled his nerves. Anger was on the cusp of filling him from head to toe. *I'm too nice, that has to be it. I have the nice guy syndrome.* He beat down on himself inside his head, as if he were the victim of a terribly violent mugging that wouldn't let up.

"You gonna read that?" Trevor could hear faintly. He half cocked his head to the right where a balding man sporting a loosened tie and balding scalp pointed to a folded up newspaper on the seat in between them.

"No."

The man took the newspaper with hands that held knuckles covered in coarse black hair. "Maybe you don't give a shit about your hearing but the rest of the bus don't need to hear that bullshit, turn it down."

Is he talking to me or himself? Trevor wondered. But the man's unmoving dark eyes answered his question with a disdainful antagonism. So Trevor removed his headphones. "Excuse me?"

"You're blasting the music, no one wants to hear that shit." The man unfolded the newspaper and gave his attention to it, leaving Trevor with the decision of whether he would feed into the man's bullying or sulk back into his depression. After stomping out a fiery anger he chose the latter, and turned off the music completely.

"Thank you." The man muttered.

Trevor paid no mind, leaving his empty caMichaelrous eyes to the equally empty seat before him. *I want to die. I don't want to do this anymore. What's the point if I have a shitty job, no prospects for a relationship, barely any family. I'm a worthless person. I wouldn't want to be around me.* The self punishment continued. As bad as the cycle tormented, it felt good to wallow–to hate unforgivingly. There was an almost euphoric relief to it, way better than pretending to like himself.

"I apologize for being rude."

Once again Trevor had to ask himself if the man had been speaking to himself. He shot the man a glance and the one he received in return answered that.

"It's okay." *I probably deserve it.*

"I was just laid off today."

The man's casual delivery seemed insane. "I'm sorry to hear that."

"Nothing lasts kid," The man said to the newspaper. "I worked at my job for twenty some odd years, gone like that."

"How are you so damn calm right now then?"

The man laughed. "I just yelled at you for listening to music, you call that calm?"

"Calmer than I'd be."

"It's out of my control, the hell is getting angry going to do about it. Sometimes you gotta embrace the bad. It's all we're really guaranteed."

No response came to mind for Trevor. He searched for a deeper meaning out of the conversation, maybe something to apply to his own life to raise his head above water–but nothing.

For the remainder of the bus ride Trevor chose to look out the window. The streets were dimly lit by a lowering sun, spreading it's reddish glow across check cashing places, small grocery stores, old woman pushing wagons; at times he loved his neighborhood of Raisetree–a small community located at the heart of Nome City, other times the urban setting just made him feel like a stereotype. *I'm not better than any of these people, but I don't want to be here forever.* Why he felt bad for that notion he had no clue, it was just another low pulling him along under his black cloud. Which is when he left the window and yanked on the stop cord

Trevor stepped off the now overly crowded bus filled with yelling and strollers. He took his time heading home, from placing the little gold key in the first banged up bulletproof door of his building to inserting it in the next similar door of the vestibule a few feet away.

Once upstairs, on the third floor, he let himself into his apartment and called for his little sister. From down the hallway he could see her purple book bag lying on the floor, despite all the times he reminded her not to leave it there. He hollered for her to go get it, but he received no answer from her. The television made no noise, and the dimness to lazy eyes could be mistaken for heavy smoke. Trevor shut the door behind himself, pushing it closed with the tip of his index finger. His feet were already moving.

Down the dark hallway, past the small table decorated with candles and little figurines Trevor rounded the corner and at the kitchen there was still no sign of life, until he spotted the yellowish beam coming from his grandmother's room like a ship finding a lighthouse in a hurricane.

Feet from the doorway and centimeters from grandma Julie's bed sat Robin. Her head craned at Trevor for the longest of seconds revealing a face which had surely been hysterically crying, he was now sure of it because she did just that as a motionless Julie laid on the bed, clearly not breathing. Trevor could relate, the breath escaped him. He held back the tears and fought a mouth that needed to quiver. His efforts failed, the tears fell, the lips moved liked sad worms as screams bellowed from his belly. Robin held Trevor on the floor as Trevor held Robin, they were years about but in that moment could have been mistaken for little children.

The heavy footsteps beat down from the hallways as the EMTs burst through the door. Their flurry ceased once they spies the Bailey kids.

At the hospital, Robin was huddled away by their Aunt Delores, a two-hundred pound woman who advertised all the food she ate with giant forearms, a round huge belly and calves that must loathe their job.

"If you would have been home to remind her to take her meds she wouldn't have died. But you don't care about that do you boy?" Aunt Delores bellowed. "Leaving your sister to watch her grandmother die. Go home, Robin comes with me tonight."

Trevor remained wordless, gazing at the heavy look on his little sister's face. Part of him wondered whether his aunt was right. But then again, solid thoughts had become hello, which is how Trevor could over-look Robin's lack of vocal disagreement.

"Will you call me about the funeral arrangements?" He asked.

"Yes." Delores shuffled Robin away, through the double electronic doors of the hospital and out of sight. It was at that moment where his heart felt as though it was lifting weights. He missed Robin already but expected his Aunt's wrath. After waiting a bit to make sure Robin was squared away in Delores' car, Trevor left the hospital and walked the long stretch of the dull and musty parking lot.

Aunt Delores always did favor Robin over himself, maybe it was a feminine thing or maybe it was because she felt he was the sole reason for his mother's absence; the mistake of a child who drove his mother to her very breaking point, distancing herself from family, running away to start over. It was easy to feel like the pointless mistake, one that hurt everyone and only grew like a tumor over the years.

The over hanging parking lot lights illuminated the fog of the night, seemingly interchangeable with the dark pit of death which used to be his home but now will remain as the place Grandma Julie to her last breath. He walked, taking his time and listening to the engines of the cars go in and out of the lot. It reminded him that it wasn't just him in the world going through tragedy, that also had to be another plus to being a nurse; from broken limbs to patients in cardiac arrest, in comparison he was okay. Just like the cars in the parking lot, people come and go though. Maybe he could change that.

After three knocks and holding his breath, she opened the door. The fear had already taken him, but once he grazed the smile on her face, it had vanquished.

"Trevor?"

"My grandmother died."

"I'm so sorry." The smile melted away.

"Lauren and I broke up."

"Come inside."

Black and White Night

Mateo washed the glass until there was not a fiber of a stain remaining, holding it up to the light until it looked clear, solid and with a sparkle in his hands. Cleaning as of late made his anxiety evaporate. Order and routine was refreshing. Although, the strain behind every scrub or ever swing of the broom was sponsored by a stifled rage, Mateo was grateful for his new found appreciation for discipline in the form of being a neat freak. He wasn't grateful for the looming haze of uncertainty that was Noelle Santiago.

From the moment he awoke in the morning to the instant he laid his head on the pillow at night, she stabbed at his stability. Mateo' relationship with Leona–already a fragile mess of unpredictability did have at least one underlying constant: it was in their control. Now she held the destruct button. And that was terrifying.

Not more than the rap at his door though, a heavy beat that sounded like police. *Who the fuck is this?* Mateo brought himself to the peep-hole, only extending it a brief glance revealing two men in sunglasses and dark coats on the other side. *They're not police, could they be of Swanson's?* Another jarring rock-solid knock broke his thinking. He took steps back out of reflex and next came the twisting of the doorknob–then silence.

On Jefferson Street, where the only sounds were cars pulling into their driveways and homeowners speaking with their dogs. The Price house now occupied a distraught and bewildered Trevor. Leona could tell immediately that he wasn't himself. The flush and reddening eyes, the words that tumbled from his lips rather than the usual melody of words of his which could make any situation the terminally-ill smile. Even his earrings appeared like Broadway with all its marquees shut off.

"Lay on the couch. Would you prefer coffee or tea?" Leona asked, shuffling Trevor in.

"You don't have to get me anything, I'm alright."

"Coffee will only keep you awake and give you jitters, so I'll make you tea." Leona lifted his head from the couch and stuffed a fluffy silk pillow underneath. She left a stare next to his silence and then made for the kitchen. Something poured out from her soul and into reality seeing him in the house again. There was a tiny crevice in her heart for Trevor and suddenly it's lights turned on. She could see the irony in the situation: he was there in her time of need, now she was playing the nurse.

Mateo tip-toed back further, shutting off the kitchen lights, muting the television and putting on his shoes as if he were against a gameshow time-limit. There was no activity at the door, which only stirred his heart more. He shut his eyes in an attempt to calm himself, listen better and gather a plan of action just in case the worst, whatever that may be were to happen. Then, the prologue to it did.

"I-I-I- saw him t-t-the other day, I don't know." It was his landlord Henry's voice. The annoying stutter, the nervousness, two and two clicked in Mateo' head and whatever was happening his gut was yelling to take action. *Two guys, possibly weapons, nowhere to run,* he said to himself and then—was interrupted by thuds. The hinges on the door teased at popping off, the door itself looked to be about ready to retire.

"You're g-g-going to break it!" Henry screamed. Then there was a pause, and the thud didn't hit the door, it sounded to be flesh on flesh.

That's when Mateo eyed the window.

Leona sat down on the adjacent couch after gently handing Trevor a bowl decorated in a blue lacey design with stick figures riding on horses. It had been her mother's favorite bowl.

"Soup?" Trevor asked.

"Yeah, chicken noodle. Comfort food does a better trick than tea."

"Thanks." He sat up and placed the bowl on his lap, waving his hand over the soft grey heat which wafted the aroma over and under Leona's nose. It made her want some too, but instead she watched him sip from the spoon.

"You're welcome. Do you want to talk about anything?"

"No, not really. I just felt alone."

"Why did Lauren break up with you if you don't mind me asking? I mean, I'm not completely surprised." The look on his face translated that she had not used her words wisely. "As in she just got out of a relationship and barely knew you."

"You answered your own question there."

"I'm sorry."

"Don't be, shit happens."

"Did you like her?"

"I liked the idea of her I guess. I don't know what I want. I do know that anything that takes me out of reality for a little bit is addicting. And maybe that's my problem."

The way that *addicting* melted from his tongue connected with her so well that the goosebumps on her arms did the wave. "Aside from tonight, what's so bad about your life?"

"There's too much in my head to put that shit into words. So I smile instead."

It was back—the lust. Something about him penetrated her gut, it was still there and so was the guilt. "The smiling is for everyone else, but what do you do to help you?"

"What do you mean?"

"You said whatever helps you escape, so what does? And if it's bad how do you deal with the people who tell you to stop doing it?"

"Are you asking me that or yourself? Maybe the question is what do you know is bad for you yet you keep holding onto it?"

Mateo shut the window from the outside, leaving but an inch of space to not let the thing lock him out onto the fire escape. Three stories below were parked cars who were as good as firefighters looking the other way in case he jumped. Luckily there were two other fire escapes below his own. The traffic on the streetlight filled pavement mocked a race track, but the buildings in the distant horizon—the Nome City sky-line—was a library of comfort. For a moment, Mateo had snuck away from his worries on the other side of the glass and come face to face with a world that didn't look so inventoried with sorrow. Only a moment, and that moment had come to pass.

The cracking of furniture stole him, glass broke, yells happened. He couldn't decipher what furniture, or what the glass that now sprinkled the floor used to be, but Mateo Colon didn't need to be a linguist to understand the screams came from Henry.

Holding his breath, Mateo counted to three in his head. Then with only the sliver of the whites in his right eye grazed the window to see what was happening. The two men, hugged by black over-coats that were two warm for the seventy-five degree weather outside were making a joke of Henry. One man searched the apartment, the other back-handed Henry while he lay on his side. There was blood, in little spurts it looked like miniature fireworks with every smack. Part of Mateo stood behind the notion that he could take them both, the other parts were so stupid.

"Everyone says Mateo is bad for me, I've dealt with this from the beginning of our relationship and I don't know." Leona said.

"You're starting to believe the voices?"

She couldn't imagine agreeing. "Maybe, but it's more that I'm also starting to not care and accept it."

"Does that make you feel bad?"

"How did we get on the subject of me? It's not supposed to be about me tonight." She spied a smile on his face and that sent her over some accomplishment.

"I don't want it to be about me, I said that I like to escape remember?"

The smile jumped from him to her. "I love him, and it often feels like that costs me everything."

Trevor sipped the soup, she could have seen six presidents take office for how long it took for him to respond. "And you're okay with that?"

"I know he's bad, and I know that loving him makes me bad, but I don't care." A surge of energy pillaged her goosebumps, the crevice where Trevor had occupied her heart collapsed, and the anger towards her sister—from all the things that she said of Mateo boiled to the tip of her fingers.

"What happens when he hurts you?" Trevor injected.

"What?"

"You know he's bad for you, and it's fine if you accept that shit—but what happens when his bad really hurts you, I mean directly?"

"That won't happen."

"What's bad doesn't discriminate with who it what it hurts. I know that for a fact."

I let him into my house, I make him soup, listen to his problems and then he has the nerve to tell me that Mateo is bad for me? I thought he was different. "Maybe you should leave." Leona said with words covered in ice.

Trevor rested the spoon in the bowl and placed it on the table in front of him. "If that's what you want." He rose.

"It is."

Once Trevor rounded the couch she blocked his path. "What?"

"You really think he's bad for me or is that just you being jealous?"

"You want me to leave so I'm leaving." Trevor's lips shut tight.

"Answer me."

"What does it matter?"

"So you didn't mean it."

His lips opened, and the jaw went forward. "I did, and I'm also jealous yeah." Taking a step around her, his attempt at walking was once again blocked by five feet of Leona.

"Take it back."

"Where is he?!" One of the men yelled at a cowering Henry.

"Please." Henry cried. "Please, I-I-don't know."

What followed next was flesh being snapped and teeth being broken. *I have to do something,* Mateo thought.

"He has the kid, he's been here. You're going to get in touch with your tenant."

Henry didn't respond. With perfect timing the traffic down below came to a halt, revealing the low whimpers coming from the bloody lips of Henry.

Mateo' adrenaline borrowed the power from a water geyser. The choice was clear now, and the situation was no longer about him—it was about the innocent man fighting for his life on a floor that wasn't his. Mateo stuck out his right leg, counted to three...

"The window!"

And kicked back.

The glass shattered into the apartment and through the sparkling sharp flakes and specs Mateo flew through the sanctuary that was his apartment and landed on his two feet—in a boxer's stance.

Trevor held one wrist with one hand and the other wrist with his other. Leona's back kissed the wall and they were face to face.

"I need you to calm down, it's not that serious." Trevor said in a fabricated calm tone.

"Get off me."

"You're just going to hit me again."

"Don't talk badly about my relationship—you don't know anything about love."

Trevor's brow scrunched up into thick wrinkled lines, and everything under was one shade away from being tomato red. "You don't know my life or what I've been through!" He released his grip, spinning around, throwing his hands to his face.

Leona woke up from a state a mind that left her in a state of stupid. If she had a time machine she would have gone back and never opened her troublesome lips.

"Hey," She took his forearm. "Hey, I'm sorry. I'm an idiot." The hand that finished the arm Leona had in her grasp was wet. "Look at me." She said. And then he did, through poorly concealed sniffles and strawberries for eyes. "I'm sorry."

"It's ight."

"No it's not. You've been through hell."

"So have you."

"Don't make this about me."

"From the minute you came into my hospital it was about you." The strawberries melted into two deep forests of bold brown. Those big lips, which she had denied thinking about, were beasts she couldn't fathom playing with, they made their war cry.

"Trevor, no."

"No what?"

"No to...."

Trevor's long finger's gently met her chin, raising it into a forbidden light. "Finish your sentence."

Mateo handled the first burglar like the man had never fought a fight in his life. The second one was trained in something—what? Mateo didn't have the time to figure out. The man's kicks were thunderous, connecting to Mateo' thigh, then his shin, and finally beating against his ribcage. The second man was coming to his feet. Suddenly the apartment was no-longer Mateo' home, it morphed into a room filled with weapons, possible allies to save his life.

"Just give us the kid...and we won't kill you." The man who had with the kicks said.

Mateo spun around as quickly as he could and connected the tip of his sneaker with the man who struggled to get to his feet. That one was now out cold. Without hesitation Mateo lunged at the first man, swing for swing, three missed and one connected. The assailant stumbled backwards. What the man lost in footing Mateo gained in confidence.

"No to this…you know we can't." Leona said.

Trevor took one of her hands and interlocked their fingers, using his other to caress her cheek.

Mateo and the man exchanged shots, and the second man started to come to. One jab from Mateo, two from the man, three from Mateo, three from the man. Mateo was only getting angrier by the second.

Leona knew he was going to do it, she could sense it coming like a storm. She had to stiffen her legs to prevent them from trembling. She squeezed Trevor's hands from preventing her own from shaking. The choice was asking to be made— push him away or let him kiss her.

The first man stepped back to catch his breath, wiping the blood from his lips and forehead. The mask he wore was that of defeat but perseverance was there. Mateo understood that to defeat these men, he'd have to put them down as close to death as possible—If he wanted to survive himself. But like a whisper in his ear, there was the wild card, fabric against his next problem: the second man pulled a nightstick from his belt, once he did that the first man smiled through his crimson portrait of a face.

Trevor's lips were big, warm and skilled. The kiss started at her own, but it traveled quickly to between her legs. On instinct her formerly anxious hands took Trevor by his face, urging him closer and somehow communicating that his tongue was more than welcome to play with hers. And so did, and so it felt so good that she wanted more and more.

Mateo now had the first man in a choke hold, as if to signal to the second, if he came any closer he'd snap the man's neck. Perhaps that would sully the weapon in the man's hands. But he wore a crooked smile. It was game to them both. Maybe not a game but more a bloody sport.

The second man took steps forward, casually as if to say *snap his neck, see what I care.* And it did put the man in a tighter grip, Mateo wasn't even aware of his own pressure until the man's nails were digging into his forearm. That's when Mateo thought, *I'm going to have to kill him and then kill the second man. It will be self-defense. He's not stopping.*

Suddenly, through the hole in the wall with teeth of glass that used to be a window shot a little red blur. Through the room it went, latching onto the arm topped off with a nightstick. The blood spurted from the arm, matching of the color of who Mateo called Finder. Never had he been happier to see the little beast.

Mateo put the first man to sleep and then tackled the second, putting him in the same chokehold and sending him off to his own nightmares. It was a way better alternative than murder.

Mateo sat on the floor, sprinkled with red as Finder jumped on the couch and perched himself there like the little soldier he earned himself to be.

"I-I-I think in t-t-the lease I s-said no pets. Y-y-you can keep him." Henry struggled to say.

Leona pushed Trevor off by the face. The legs began to tremble and the hands went back to shaking.

"We can't I'm sorry. I'm sorry. That shouldn't have happened."

"Then why did it?"

"I don't know, moment of weakness. You're not the only one who's in a shitty state of mind." Leona paced, replicating the moment where Trevor had his hands over his face. *I'm an idiot, I can't believe what I've just done. You didn't fuck him. That's all that matters. Mateo will never know. This never happened. If Trevor says anything he'll just look like he's trying to start shit.*

"You can label it anyway you'd like but—"

"Stop!" Leona screamed. "It was a mistake, please. I'm an idiot okay? I'm weak. I act on emotion, it's why I met you in the first place. You think I broke this leg for shits and giggles? No, it was my fault, my own motha fuckin emotions controlling me like they always do, making me the shitty person that I am—"

Trevor grabbed her by the face and went in for another kiss. This time her hands did not grab, they stiffened instead. And one smacked him clean across the face, as hard as she could with all the emotion that she had just spoken about.

The house sat quiet, for only mere seconds. But those seconds sure felt like hours. Trevor's heartbroken brown eyes previously a strong and attractive forest, now, were nothing more than pathetic and pitiful.

"You should go."

Trevor pulled his puppy dogs by the leash and made for the door.

"Don't contact me for a while."

"Okay."

"This never happened." Leona said it with confidence but wasn't so sure that he understood.

"To me it did."

"No, it didn't. And for the record, it should never have been about me."

Leona locked the door after him.

The Beautiful Witch

"Well, she's right about the whole not making it about her. No girl in their right mind wants to be treated like Cinderella unless they're chock full of daddy issues or running on E with self-esteem." Noelle said without a doubt of certainty.

Trevor walked beside her down a cobblestone path centered in *Middle Park*: Nome City's biggest park located smack in the middle of the city. Never was there more noise than Frisbees being hurled, chatter amongst people enjoying the grass, or the barks coming from the canines who frequent with their owners. All that alongside the happy sun, Trevor's mood wasn't as bad as he expected it to be lying in bed last night.

"Then why did she kiss me?"

Noelle shot him a long look, one where Trevor felt as though he was in the wrong. It was scarce in his mind how many times she had made eye contact during their friendship. "She kissed you?"

"Yeah, why is that so shocking?"

"No reason." It took maybe five steps before her façade fell to the cobblestone. "That never happened understood?" She stopped, in return leading him to stop.

"That's what she said, why are you backing her on this?"

"As her friend, you don't mention that to anyone."

"You've been my friend longer—"

"Are you listening to me or hearing what you want to hear?" Her skin competed with the fire of the sun in the sky. "Never mind, you're right this is none of my business."

"It isn't, I just wanted your opinion on the shit."

"I believe she was acting on emotion, you were in the right place at the right time. Don't get into your feelings because she has none for you. She loves Mateo, you don't stand a chance." Her demeanor had changed, like a lion who had spotted its prey.

Trevor couldn't understand why it worked her up so. *Is she jealous or something? Does she have feelings for me? Why's this so personal?* Why are you taking this personally? I thought you liked Mateo, them breaking up would only benefit you."

"In a field that you know nothing about, just move on from Leona and forget about her. If what you're saying about her telling you not to contact her is—"

"Why would I make that shit up? What do you mean I'm in a field that I know nothing about? You don't know me like that."

"You're a virgin right?"

He had never told a soul aside from Lauren. Noelle didn't even give him the slightest glance when asking, she was pure ice. To pinpoint that so easily, so assertively, made his manhood shrivel up. Trevor was left speechless.

"What's the matter? Am I right? Yeah I'm right. So I'd listen to what I'm talking about." She stopped walking, stepped in front of him and pierced him with eyes so heavily done up with mascara that she looked like a sexy raccoon. "I've had more sex in my life than good conversations with my family. I know how to read men. I can predict them and figure them out with one look up and down. All but one. So when it comes to relationships, I may not be cut out for one but I'm a fucking supreme court justice of the law of attraction so don't argue with me about this, understood?"

"You're crazy." He said, but couldn't find it in him to give her eye contact.

"You don't know the half of it, I mean you will but, yeah you don't know."

They sauntered without a word, down the path, passed happy couples, happy couples with kids, elderly people taking their time to nowhere, squirrels that looked as though they owned the park and joggers who made Trevor feel like he was missing out on life somehow. He would fuck Noelle, in less than a heartbeat. So much sexual experience, so little empathy for other people: something was attractive about her iciness. Maybe he envied it. His niceness had always been the chink in his armor, and there walking next to him nearly bouncing out of her blouse stood a girl so hardened by the world yet still so strong that he craved her in a way. The shame over-shadowed that, he was a virgin, a virgin who fell for any girl who crossed his path apparently. "

"Why can't I get a girlfriend?" He asked.

"Because you want one. It's a shame, you're a good looking guy, and your duck is probably bigger than average right?" No-elle asked as if she were inquiring what the weather would be tomorrow.

"That's a little personal."

She laughed, nearly mockingly. "That's humble of you, but still–another reason why you can't get laid."

"Why because I don't want to openly speak about my private parts?"

"Precisely. You have shame in your body, shame in sex. Let me tell ya, that just oozes confidence. But I mean, maybe some crazy bitch with low self-esteem will find that attractive."

Her responses left Trevor empty but angry, and in dire need of any semblance of a rebuttal. Unfortunately but not unsurprisingly nothing presented itself.

"Again, you know I'm right. Let's take the subway, you have time right?" She asked.

"Yes."

On the train to somewhere Trevor had no clue of, they sat next to each other. Noelle didn't shy away from letting herself be smashed up against him on the crowded subway car. Despite the heavy racket of gears and metal wheels screeching against metal tracks, Noelle's nails clicking away at on the screen of her phone still filled his ears first. She was playing candy crush; a puzzle game filled with bright colors wrapped in cheery punchlines and taglines. Trevor couldn't help but analyze her. *She knows how to escape, or maybe she's just happy the way she is. Something makes her attractive, and I want it.*

The train doors opened, releasing them both from the graffiti stained interior and sour smell. Noelle stepped off first, and Trevor's eyes fell directly to her rear-end; a round and massive jiggling hunk that filled her zebra stripped leggings, teasing Trevor's manhood along with many more. Something about the way she walked lead him to believe she knew just where he was drooling over. *I'm pathetic.* He thought.

"Where are you taking me?"

She kept steady in the lead. "Scared of a little adventure? When was the last time you did actually venture away from just home and work?" Noelle shot a glance back, there was a demeanor he's never seen before.

"Leona's house."

"No need to mention her."

And so he kept his trap shut. Following her down crowded blocks that held fruit stands, and stores packed next to each other like it were some designed movie set to mimic Manhattan. It was new to Trevor, never venturing farther than where he was obligated to be. It was a welcome escape, even with the end being a mystery.

Then the streets transformed into tranquil concrete paths of scenic houses covered in vines and stoops that welcomed people to relax, but only few souls took upon their offers. Immediately, without a hesitation Trevor wanted to live there. And then, without any warning, he remembered his dead grandmother. *For a second I thought I didn't have any problems.* He remembered his true home, what death it carried and that no matter ow pleasant the moment may be, it was back there at the end of the day; with a sister who had most likely lost her joy for life. Tranquility was a treat, so he sopped up the scenery, bathed in the quiet and let his eyes follow that voluptuous rear-end.

The block then turned down next was on a dead-end street filled with but six houses and two trees, in a u-shaped layout. It had for whatever reason reminded Trevor of sesame street. The fourth house in from the right Noelle carried her thick thighs up then stoop and Trevor held himself at the bottom.

"I'm not going into some random apartment building, you want to tell me what we're doing?" He said.

"It's my step dad's building, relax." She smiled. "I guess trust is the sister to your shame. Come in." She unlocked the door and her rear-end disappeared inside. Trevor followed.

The interior was beyond beautiful. The chandelier stole Trevor's attention first, then the idle fireplace. Smacking his sense was wealth he realized. He took back the wish he secretly planted in the universe traveling over, instead of wanting to live on that other block he wanted to live in a place like this.

"Make yourself at home, I'm going to use the bathroom." Noelle proclaimed.

Trevor took himself to the fridge. *She's actually being nice, if she's trying to take my mind off my shit maybe she does have a heart.* Trevor marveled at the two ice dispenser's on the outside of the fridge. One said *Normal* and the other said *Temp Changer.* After pouring himself a glass of sparkling soda, he placed the shiny square glass under the temp changer and out fell two cubes of ice, popping into the soda and evaporating two seconds later. Following that, the soda had been ice cold with little flakes coating the surface. Like a little child he smiled at how it was.

Leaving the kitchen Trevor walked into the living room where standing in the doorway he was met by a semi naked Noelle. Her hair hung loose in black curls. She wore nothing but a red laced see-through bra and a matching thong. He couldn't make out the sweet between her legs, but her nipples were so flowery pink and round that they screamed through the delicate lace of the brazier.

"What.... are you doing?" He struggled to ask.

"Taking your virginity." Noelle pushed herself from the wall, her nipples could cut glass, and he couldn't deny feeling if they could for himself. With every step closer with her sparkling toes he could make out the one thing that's he's never seen in person, that vertical slit which now revealed just a little bit of hair right above it.

"Noelle,"

"Shhhhh." She kissed him, wrapping her warm slender hand around the nape of his neck and pulling him so close that her hair conditioner rented space in his nostrils and her nipples confirmed just how hard they were.

Trevor didn't fight it, and they made out standing up until she brought him to a massive bedroom with an equally massive bed. The walls matched the color of her only articles of clothing. It was all he had time to notice as his eyes fell closed with every stroke of her tongue against his. Once his back hit the sheets she got on top of him and put his had underneath her thong where the warm and wet said hello to his fingertips. *I didn't know it got that wet. This is really about to happen.*

That thought was blown away by her smooth dancing fingers unbuckling his jeans. In his chest, his heart took off. *She's going to see. Someone's actually going to see my dick.* Once the zipper stopped moving Trevor opened his eyes. The ceiling held yet another chandelier, it was off, and also now were his jeans, leaving him in his boxers. He looked down to see Noelle gazing at the only fabric concealing his manhood. Then her long fingers, tipped off with those devilish nails slipped under the elastic on both sides of his waist and slowly pulled down. Out stood tall his manhood, and the excited smirk that Trevor had hoped to see advertised on Noelle's face was present, turning into her biting her lip. Before he could wallow in his ego, her lips where stealing him away from reality; sucking up and down, making his virginity disappear in her tight throat.

After a while, a longer time than he had expected her to go for, he finally took control, tasting, feeling and entering that one area which he had a strong doubt of ever actually coming close to. It was better than he expected.

Then they laid there, on top of messed up sheets stained in things that Trevor was proud to have put there. The room's hazy made his skin sticky, or maybe it was other things. Either way he didn't care, relaxation wasn't familiar but he had it now.

"Can I ask you something? I need you to be brutally honest and speak from a place of truth." Noelle asked, cutting through the steaminess of the room. All Trevor could comprehend was her massive chest budding up to the ceiling, nipples still so hard.

"What?"

"Now that you've had it, how bad do you want it with Leona?"

"Pretty bad, but I'm not thinking about that right now."

"What about her friend?"

"Not really actually."

"Do you really want her and Mateo to break up?"

Trevor felt like she knew the answers to her own questions but maybe talking would lead to more sex. "Yeah,"

"Be honest, does she have feelings for you?"

Why does she care? "No, she made that clear, I told you that."

Noelle rolled over, letting her breasts fall to the side, squishing against each. Trevor grabbed himself, to make it harder, and then her lips met his, kissing him like he had just returned from war. Then they retreated, and a smile arrived below her devious eyes. She left the bed, and Trevor watched her rear-end jiggle while she walked to the dresser. He wondered in that moment, who's bed had they slept in. Before he could ask, she yanked a camera from behind a small television set, seemingly turning it off.

"What's that?" Trevor sat up.

"A video camera." Her smile grew wider. "Everything that just happened is on here. Don't worry, I still thoroughly enjoyed this. You're really good for a first timer."

His ego chuckled but his confusion screamed. "You fuckin video tapped me?"

"Relaxxxx, no one will ever see it unless you decide to open your mouth about your kiss with Leona, this is to just disprove that."

Both his fists clenched along with his ass cheeks. His penis shriveled back to before he had hit puberty. "What are you talking about?"

"What you just said about them breaking up, her having no feelings for you. The second you tell Mateo that you both kissed, I'll show him this and it'll look like you're just sabotaging they're relationship. The boy who just fucked basically their enemy—me." Her smile was sickening.

"You video tapped me having sex with you."

"I know, and if you don't want it on Pelpage, then you'll also keep your mouth shut. I have a good history with making sure dirty laundry hits the internet." She brought herself to the bed, crawling on it like a cat until she was before him. Her long nails pushed him down against the pillow and she tugged on his now tiny penis. "What's the matter? Am I making you shy?" Despite his dismay he was getting hard just with her touching. "There you go, see....this was a better alternative that what I had planned. I was so scared, that I debated on pushing you in front of the train, drugging you, putting you into a coma somehow." She squeezed his penis just enough where it felt good. "But this way, you got something out of it, and I got piece of mind."

"You're crazy."

"But I get what I want. Nice guys finish last. And hopefully after today, you won't be a nice guy. Hopefully after today you'll see just what needs to be done to get your way in this world."

"You took my virginity and put it on camera."

Noelle released her grip and straightened her back as if her round pink nipples the size of Snapple lids weren't staring him in the face. "If you told Mateo that Leona kissed you, he'd have power. They'd make up and all would be well. But if she were to leave him, then he'd be heart broken, realizing just how low of a person he is and who he should really be with; who really suites him best."

"You're seriously out of your mind. Things don't work like that."

Those thin eyebrows of hers jolted down. "If he didn't love me, he wouldn't have fucked me, over and over and over. You don't keep coming back to someone you only want to fuck. He's the only guy that ever has come back. Even when he thinks he's in love with someone else."

Are those real tears lining her eyes or is someone cutting an onion? "You sound like you're delusional."

She began to laugh, which then turned into a cackle. Then she grabbed a pillow and gave it an up and down. The way her grin made love to it scared Trevor tremendously. Without warning she placed the pillow over his face and held it down with all her strength. His hands grabbed at her while the breath in his lungs screamed for more. The moment when she wouldn't let go, and he desperately needed more air was when he knew that he might die.

Then she released her murder, and threw the pillow against the window. Before he could utter a single sound she had smacked him twice across the face.

"Don't you ever call me delusional again. Maybe if you want Leona you should have faith in my plan, because if they break up because of me, then you may actually get the bitch. And hey, now you know how to please her." Noelle left the bed and left the room.

Trevor laid on the bed not knowing what to make of any of this. Noelle had black mailed him, and the one thing that gave him hope that maybe he could be with Leona was now something that truly never happened. His grandmother was dead, his sister emotionally dead, and now his virginity was gone to a girl who didn't have a lick of feelings for him. He might as well be dead too.

Noelle came back in the room fully dressed, putting on her earring and checking herself in the full length mirror. "Are you sure you've never eaten pussy before today?" She asked.

Relief Effort

Mateo knew beforehand that she would have wanted to go. It wasn't going to be convincing Leona something had to be done, it was convincing her to stay and let him handle it.

"And what if something happens to you? As it already almost did." Leona stood like she had been from some sort of military academy.

"I handled it didn't I?"

"A destroyed apartment, roughed up landlord and a black and blue face isn't what I call handling it."

"Listen to me," he said with nearly an echo in Leona's empty house. "If I don't handle this, they're find you and you won't be able to fend these people off, the police can't get—"

"No, no Mateo, I'm not debating that we need to handle this—"

"There is no we right now. This isn't your problem. I don't want you getting hurt."

Leona stole the face of a defeated puppy, in cute fashion searching for any semblance of a rebuttal to keep the argument a float. But after some time, she accepted defeat, lending him an anxious look decorated with sensitive beautiful lips. "I just don't want anything happening to you." She rested her head against his chest, wrapping her arms around his waist and bringing them in tight.

"I know, but the same goes for you and that's why I need to go clear my name before it escalates. Henry's pain is on my hands, I refuse to let yours be on it too." The words nearly tripped on his tongue as Noelle puckered taunted in the back of his mind.

"I need you to call me, constantly."

"I will, and you need to do the same. If you suspect anything suspicious."

"I'm going to head over to my aunt's for the night."

"Alright." He kissed her forehead.

Anne knew that he was coming. Mateo made the call early in the morning. The call was brief,

"I'm coming to the farm to clear things up."

"I had a feeling you would, I'll see you tonight?"

"Yes."

Mateo rode the motorcycle above the speed limit down the empty streets, and tinkered with it on the more crowded of streets. He had to tug himself into focusing on the roads, his thoughts had been chained to what was ahead. *How am I going to clear this mess up? How can I clear a name that's already cleared but fabricated into shit that I agreed to take on? When I confess that I don't have him, everything unravels.*

It all weighed on him, the only thing Mateo could bring himself to do was keep a clear mind, focusing on the black tar with the yellow line going down the middle; the wind beat up against the eye protector of his helmet, pounding away with every yard that the wheels accelerated down.

When he arrived at the farm, it began to rain. Even though he had only been away for little time the land was almost foreign. But then again, one sight of that tree with the lone swing now being drenched by the downpour brought him back to the night where he first heard Bradley's sorrow.

Mateo' Timberland boots hit each step up to the door matching the thuds in his chest. Trying his best to engineer his fear into confidence, he knocked on the door. There was no answer. *This is an ambush,* he thought. Then he knocked again, a few seconds later Anne opened the door. She appeared to have aged 10 years, then Mateo realized it was just the grey in her hair; she had apparently stopped dying it.

Anne said nothing, leading Mateo to the dining room where the table sat completely empty with only Bradley at its end. The smallest smirk twitched at the boy's mouth. *He's happy to see me,* Mateo realized. After he pulled up a chair and sat next to Bradley, Anne positioned herself in a chair across the table. Her mouth hung open and shut closed in an effort to find a place to begin.

"My plan was to protect Bradley. Against the wishes of his father, I thought that I could take the dang boy and rid him to a place free of this life. Of the things that I kept from you."

"What are—"

Anne raised her hand to signal not to speak.

"When I took you in, I knew that you were cut out for this life. I knew you were truly lost." She laughed. "Hell, at first sight of those vacant holes in your face I thought I was looking at two cemeteries." She paused. "But then, you showed me that you wanted to change, you actually bought into all my persistence and discipline will reap you a better soul. I couldn't drag you in any deeper. But now, the choice is yours. I was wrong to shield Bradley from his father. Sometimes shielding shit just makes you a bigger target." Anne rose and exited into the darkness of the other room. Mateo sat, patiently, but curious. And then, Richard Swanson appeared from the darkness.

"Anne's Cousin Hector, who then turned into the stranger boy named Mateo." Swanson took the seat Anne had previously filled. And dread filled Mateo.

"Hello." Mateo said.

"I'm not here to kill you, if that's what your gut is calling 911 over right now. No, far from."

"Those guys in my apartment, they make that kinda hard to believe."

"I can understand that." Swanson combed his hair with his hand, his polo tee once again appeared like it had wandered onto the wrong body. "But those weren't my men."

"Listen sir," Mateo felt the salutation was necessary to stay alive. "The fact that there were men trying to kill me in the first place means you're caught up in the wrong stuff or have way too much power to begin with."

"They weren't trying to kill you either, they wanted Bradley."

"And I don't like the way you treat him either, he's a good kid."

Was it compassion on Swanson's face or did he have to take a shit, Mateo wondered.

"Why do you care about this boy, you have no relation to him what so ever?"

"I know a good person when I see one. I know them because I'm not one."

Swanson took one of the biggest inhales Mateo had ever seen. "Those weren't my men, and they wanted my son. Are you familiar with the NCF?"

Nome City Family, "The mafia?"

"Nome City Family, I prefer to call my organization."

"You're the fictional Terry Golia?"

"I'm glad common folk like you still think I'm fictional, I wish my enemies saw it that way as well. This farm here, it's a recruitment station. Every now and then, Anne over there pulls in some lost sap with as much deadly intent as he has emptiness in his heart. Obviously, Anne didn't think you were as lost as you think you are."

"And you think I am?"

"Just the opposite. The State is one of my leading opponent gangs. They want to see me dead but more importantly my hire."

Mateo looked at Bradley seemed to loathe every minute of the conversation. "Were they the ones responsible for my attack?"

"Ding ding ding." Swanson laughed. "Do you know who The State recruit as their members?"

"I know nothing about this stuff sir." Although, it somewhat intrigued him. Anne brought herself back into the room with a blank face. As if no one had been in the dining room she put on a pot of coffee with in the coffee machine that rested on a small bookcase.

"They recruit ex-marines, ex-FBI agents, ex-navy seals, men who were once established, tasted glory and then there was no more glory to be had, no families to come home to—nothing to live for. And you, took down two of them by yourself, one with a deadly weapon."

"Gotta do what I gotta do."

"I want you to come work for me. To protect my hire, to be an underground king."

Mateo' mouth nearly hit the floor. One minute ago, the mafia was nothing but legend. Now he was being asked to join by its kingpin, a man who had been rumored to run it for twenty years. "I can't do that."

"My enemies know, that you don't have my son. They will no longer come after you. But under the NCF you'd have even greater protection, greater wealth; a better life."

"A life of crime."

Swanson smiled and rested his glance at Anne who poured herself a cup of coffee and sat herself down in the reclining chair off in the corner. When his thin lips met the mug Swanson turned his attention back on Mateo. "They say crime doesn't pay, but look around you. There's food on the table, coffee in her mug and clothes on our backs. Bradley is set for life when I'm gone. Anne too. Crime always pays, but you have to pay it back."

"I have people who care about me."

Swanson leaned in, the overhead light beat down on his crisp hair. "We all do, but now imagine one day you're gone. What're you gonna leave behind? You're gonna go to school now and rack up a few hundred grand over a lifetime? Please, I can triple that for you in a month. What's a better way to be self-less to the ones you care about than giving your life to them. The way I see it, if I get taken in by the boys in blue today, at least the ones I love are taken care of forever. When you need to pay your debts to people, when you need to give your life or makeup for all your fuck-ups, a better life by giving yours—you can't go wrong."

That struck a chord in Mateo' chest; a way to make up for what he did with Noelle, a way to give Leona the life she deserved. "I can't. I'm sorry."

"You'll change your mind." Swanson responded without a hint of doubt. This type of encounter," he gestured to himself and Mateo. "Doesn't just happen by chance. Something was meant to come out of it. I don't know if you're a religious person or not and that shit may sound funny coming from a man who's wrapped his hands around more necks than a bear catching fish in a stream, but I am. And I believe that this part of the story wasn't just for nothing. We'll see each other again and unfortunately for you, you've most likely already been sucked in. I see it in your eyes."

"I hope you're wrong sir." Mateo stood from the seat. "The men that came after me…"

"There won't be any more, if there are any problems call Anne and I'll have it handled."

"Can I speak to Bradley alone?" Mateo asked.

Swanson and Anne followed. In the doorway Swanson lingered. "I'm an asshole to him because he needs to be tough to take my place. Please understand that." Swanson left the room and Mateo got on his knee alongside Bradley.

"Did he kill your mother?"

Bradley nodded yes.

"If you ever need anything, Anne has my number. Don't hesitate to call me okay?"

Bradley nodded yes again. When Mateo stood Bradley took him by the wrist and then pulled him in for a hug. The tears filled Mateo' eyes.

On his way out Swanson stood outside and waved him over. "Take a walk with me." And so Mateo did. "I got you something for taking care of my boy." They walked to the barn where Swanson yanked open the door giant doors to reveal a silver Mercedes. "Leave the motorcycle here, and remember what my offer, it'll stand as long as I'm alive."

Girl's Night

Leona gave her best shot at lightening the mood, but Remy's stoicism in the passenger seat danced with Emma's black cloud in the back seat. Dancing to Madonna in the front, Leona made up her own lyrics to Barbie Girl and nudged at Remy to sing along. But the girl was in her own world, leading Leona to turn the radio off.

"Okay, let's all just be grumpy pants."

The car stayed silent.

"What's wrong with you guys?" Leona asked. "We're having a girl's night; we deserve to have a little fun. When was the last we all hanged out like really?"

"The last time I saw this girl Noelle I had my fingers nudged into her spinal cord." Remy said in a deadpan worse than Emma's.

"And I don't like new people." Emma added.

"You don't like people in general." Leona said. "We were all new to each other at one point. Lauren is a sweetheart and Noelle is fun. Just try to keep an open mind."

The car hit a giant pothole and the girls bounced from their seats.

"Damn." Emma said.

"Sorry, they need to repave the streets."

"No it's not that. I was hoping we'd die."

Later that night at the Price house, Remy and Emma sat on the couch next to each other while Noelle sat on the one across from them. Leona spoke with Lauren in the kitchen.

"Those girls are miserable and Remy and I aren't seeing eye to eye about mom. That note she left really hit the nail in the coffin for me."

"I don't think that's how the expression is used. You guys don't have to agree on everything you know, you're going to disagree sometimes. If you agree on everything it would be sketchy." Lauren wrapped a curl around her finger, leaning on the kitchen counter while scrolling her phone.

"I get that, but it'd be a lot easier if she just understood where I was coming from."

"She's eleven, that's not easy. Why did you invite Noelle by the way? You know I can't stand her."

"Well that doesn't make this night any more awkward." Noelle said, bending over into the fridge. She yanked out a can of coke and opened it where she stood.

You could have told me she was standing there, Lauren mouthed. "Sorry, but there is a slight rift between us. It's not every day my friend *curses* me out through text." Lauren spun around to meet Noelle.

"Guys, I didn't orchestrate this night so we could all mope and jump down each other's throats. This is the moment where you two make up and move on. We all do stupid shit. You're both my friends so let's move on?"

"I'm over it, I have no hostility." Noelle proclaimed in between sips.

"I'll try my best." Lauren muttered. But Leona knew that wasn't going to happen because Lauren removed herself from the room.

"She's a stubborn one isn't she?" Noelle asked.

"I wouldn't say stubborn so much as she sticks to her beliefs."

"How's Mateo doing?"

She knows that's a sore subject between us. Is she stupid? "He's fine, taking care of some personal stuff. No offence but you know that's the one person that causes problems with us, why bring him up?"

Noelle finished off her can of soda, guzzling it like it were alcohol. "The only way for him to not be an uncomfortable topic is to confront him as if it's normal. I choose to move on, can you?"

"I can. As long as you can. All I ask is that you're genuine."

"I've made some mistakes but I've learned that being transparent is the best way to go. If it makes you feel better I just had sex with someone. Mateo is the last person that's on my mind."

Her honesty or what she labeled as transparency caught Leona off guard. Her actual words didn't sink in until Leona's face sprung its way back from being in shock. "Oh, okay then." She tried her best to fabricate a laugh. "If you say so." As Leona walked from the sink to the doorway Noelle said the last thing she had wanted to hear.

"Trevor told me what happened."

The world collapsed, the walls spun like tires, the air could have been a hazy smoke at that point, but she never turned around to face the girl. "What are you talking about?"

"The kiss–he told me. Said not to bring it up to you but like I said, transparency is best."

"He's lying." Was the first thing that Leona could grab from her faculty.

Just then Remy brought herself into the kitchen, wearing a pair of innocent eyes and filled with a bubbly energy. "Lauren and I got Emma to play a game of Candyland, you can have in on the next game if you want?"

"Sure, yeah, you got it, just wait for me in there." Leona was now on autopilot.

"We don't have any apple juice? Just because I'm not around doesn't mean you can slack on grocery shopping." Remy explained with her face nearly kissing the refrigerator shelves.

"Okay apple juice, got it."

"What's wrong? Why do you seem tense?" Remy asked.

"We were just speaking about Leona's ex Michael. The boy was saying some stupid stuff."

Leona's shoulders relaxed themselves but her psyche snickered at how easily Noelle could come up with lies.

"What was he saying?"

"It doesn't matter, boys are dumb. Just wait for me in the living room and I'll be in there in a minute."

"No I wanna know what he said about my sister."

Leona and Noelle exchanged a stare and Noelle's eyes held amusement.

"Are you lying?" Remy asked.

"What? No." Leona said. "I just don't care to go into detail over what an idiot has to say about me."

"You're lying, what is it?" After not getting an answer from Leona, Remy slowly drifted her head to meet Noelle, but the enigma held her tongue.

"Remy, I'll tell you later okay?" Leona pleaded.

"I'm not going to forget."

"I don't expect you to."

And on that, Remy walked back to the living room with stiff legs that wanted to stay in the room.

Like a reflex, Leona went back to Noelle, this time extending her most defensive gazes.

"What did he tell you exactly?"

"That you guys made out and that it almost went further."

"The second part is a lie."

"Not to be the one to state the obvious here, but if you guys made out then there was the slightest possibility of it progressing, no?"

"Okay so fine, yeah whatever, you know. So what? You're going to tell Mateo and ruin my life?" Her defenses came crashing down much like a demolished building.

"No," Noelle's face scrunched up. "Why would I do that when I've been trying to drill it in that noggin of yours that I'm on your side here? I'm over Mateo, completely."

An unexplainable laugh wanted to slip from Leona's lips. "So then why bring this up? Why is it that most of the time I get this dark feeling about you?"

"I can't explain what's in your gut." Noelle pulled a chair from the table and plopped her massive behind in the seat. "I'm a dark person, but I mean what I say. I'm not trying to sabotage your relationship."

"Then you're watching it slowly collapse to make your move?"

Noelle left her eyes to her hands, which picked at a nail. "That's a bold assumption, especially after I just said I don't want Mateo," Her eyes met Leona and she rose. "I told you before I just fucked someone. I've been hanging out with you this entire time. If I wanted to sabotage this relationship you and I have and more importantly the one you have with Mateo, wouldn't it just be easier to tell you that he cheated on you or something?"

"I guess." *She makes sense, but why is it so hard to digest with her?*

"I could have done so many things to break you two up. If I wanted Mateo why would I sit here and watch your relationship crumble, to me, it's far from ruins. But to you—seems like another story."

Leona watched as Noelle took a spot again against the counter, waiting to see what Leona would have to combat her brutally honest observation. "I don't know why I kissed Trevor—"

"Is Trevor that black nurse Remy told me about?" Emma surprised the room with her satanic excuse for a voice.

"How long have you been standing there?" Leona asked.

"She just walked in." Noelle answered.

"But I've been in the doorway since Remy came back. I'm not fond of board games."

"This doesn't concern you Emma."

"You're my cousin. As weary of my lifestyle beliefs you are, we're still blood. And this one here wreaks of none in her veins." Emma brought herself further into the room, standing before Noelle as if they were to have an old west duel.

"Jesus Matteo I'm starting to think that the one who had her fingers in my back months ago is the only one that loves me." Noelle handed her words to Emma covered in that devious smile of hers.

"Your smile is authentic only because you enjoy confrontation. Under it you're scared and over thinking what your next move will be." Emma paused. "Now you're wondering what else I know since I got that right."

"Emma please, don't make this night anymore harrowing."

What's going on?" Remy asked, bringing even more dread to the bags under Leona's eyes.

"Are they going to fight?" Lauren asked. "I have my money on Alice Cooper."

"Who's that?" Remy asked.

"I'm not the enemy here." Noelle said unblinking.

"You have an obsession with Leona's boyfriend. It's why you speak like a condescending villain. Leona's just too stupid to realize it."

"Hey, I just told her I'm skeptical."

"But what's your motives?" Emma turned around seemingly to read the floor. "Could it be that you're hiding things in plain sight? Maybe you are trying to watch her relationship blow up. Maybe he did cheat on Leona."

"What's your fucking beef with me?" Noelle exploded, grabbing Emma by the shoulder and spinning her around.

"Don't touch her!" Remy yelled and Leona could see Lauren holding her back.

"Because I don't like fake. I wear dark makeup and look like shit but at least my shit's real. You? You're trying to hurt my cousin. And I'll figure it out."

Leona couldn't tell whether she wanted to cry or yell at Emma Melissa Price. "Everyone needs to take a chill pill and not make this a witch hunt. The point of tonight was—"

"So that she could continue her façade of loyalty to you." Emma pointed at Noelle with an index finger decorated in black nail polish.

"She has a point." Lauren said.

"She always does, even if it's as dark as the sky." Remy said.

"What is it that I have to do…to prove that I want to be your friend? Leona's friend, without being accused of anything? Hmm? I barely know you." Noelle said to Emma. "And you're in my face like I've already hurt your family."

"Someone who wants a friendship doesn't chase it. People chase things for personal reasons." Emma spoke as if she were a lawyer speaking to a jury, still with little emotion. Why constantly badger Leona if you didn't want something for your own gain?"

Noelle ran her slim fingers through her hair. The butterfly motions of her eyelashes answered Emma's question instead of anything verbal. "I'm leaving."

"Noelle." Leona said, with every fiber of herself feeling bad and embarrassed. As the girl with jet black hair toured through the living room, scooping up her purse, Leona latched onto her arm and was met with a whisper of the word *Stop.* She was gone out the door before Leona could drum up anything else to say.

"What is it with you and her? Why are you so clingy?" Lauren asked as both Remy and Emma stood one side of her.

"I'm not."

"Yeah you are....oh my god....I see what's happening here." Lauren brought both hands to her face. It looked as though Remy had shared the same thoughts.

"Whatever you're about to say better be well filtered because I'm not in the mood for anymore outlandish conspiracy theories."

The pause that filled the Price house showcased how well Lauren is at being anal with her thoughts. "Don't take this the wrong way. I'm saying this as your friend who cares about you and only serves you honesty."

"Lauren, just say what you have to say."

"You're substituting Noelle for your absent mother."

"Oh my fuckinggg goddd Lauren really? Are you being serious right now?"

Remy and Emma exited the room like squirrels.

"No, listen." Lauren took Leona and wrapped her hands around her hands. "She's emotionally unavailable, condescending, withdrawn—"

"A bitch." Remy said from the living room.

"Watch your mouth Remy." Leona said.

"She's very close to your mom in personality, and with what you're going through it's only natural you surround yourself with a challenge—the feminine emotional challenge that your mom once gave you."

"We only chase for our own needs." Emma said, bringing herself to wear Lauren had just released her soft grip of Leona's clammy hands.

Are they right? Am I really this fucked up? Leona asked herself. It was a terrible notion to wrap her head around, but it made sense. That was when her pride followed Noelle out the door and the one's standing before her became the support group. "Fine. Maybe that's right, but that doesn't change the fact that I hate the woman."

"You don't." Remy brushed passed Emma. "Being mad doesn't mean you hate."

"I don't want to have this conversation again."

"Listen to your sister." Lauren added.

"Just cause mom left doesn't change the fact that she's still mom. If you didn't miss her why would you want to replace her?"

"We can find her." Lauren stood next to Remy. "The four of us with our heads together can do this."

"But you have to promise us something." Emma deepened the room with her vocal chords. "Girl's nights will no longer include that greasy Barbie doll you think is your friend. You won't see her anymore."

"Emma's right." Remy agreed, "From day one we knew that she was no good. You can't have two people ruining your life, that's not how stories go."

Remy's comment was a dagger in her side. "Is that comment aimed towards my boyfriend?"

"Yeah, but you know how I feel towards him."

Lauren's fluttering mouth advertised that she had to stop the conversation from swerving. "One thing at a time, look, what's happening here is that you're going to agree to not see Noelle any longer and we're going to find your mother before the summer is over, correct?"

They think it's all so easy. Finding someone that doesn't want to be found with a daughter that doesn't want to go looking, yeah easy. "I can barely find my socks in the morning let alone an adult woman. And what's Remy going to do? Use her doll-house to—"

"Hey, I'm not stupid."

"I know you're not Remy, I'm just saying there's not much we can do to go find someone."

"Not true. Lauren and I wouldn't be much help, but you and Remy know your mother. And both of you have the gumption to find her." Emma said, taking a seat at the dining room table. "The problem here is working together. If you two would get along for the common cause, the wilted field may sprout flowers."

"Why does everything sound like an Edgar Allen Poe story with you?" Leona asked.

"She's right." Lauren added. "It can't be that hard to find someone you know so well who, to be honest most likely needs to be found."

With the three innocent faces, one heavily darkened with black eyeliner and black lipstick, Leona couldn't say no. Despite her own reluctance and the heavy weight of sadness that tagged along with just thinking about her mother, Leona could only say one thing. "Okay, we'll look for her."

"It's the effort that matters." Lauren responded.

So then my mother shouldn't matter.

The Eyes That See Through

Driving a Mercedes was like breathing to Mateo Colon; he was breathing again. Awoken from a hazy black mental coma which only seemed to tug on his flesh with every opportunity. That had to be hell. If hell existed, then what he was looking back on was just that. Pain, sorrow, uncertainty, hopelessness: all ingredients which made him today. And all ingredients which he hoped to forget. The engine was a controlled explosion, much like himself. In his rear-view mirror: dead mother, a dead father, a dead uncle, a dead aunt, a girl who holds his mistakes like nuclear weapons and now—an offer.

Why am I still on this? How can I even contemplate such a proposal? He did ask himself these questions, over and over again, but that engine roared. *This is what Leona must see in me, the same thing I see in this car.* The engine holds a beauty; nothing but controlled chaos making something shiny go fast, for nothing but fun. The danger the car's capable of, the darkness its windows promote and conceal all spurred by fire. *I wish that I could drive my life at the speed limit for her, but I know it won't last.*

The empty highway held trees flashing by and houses which forced his attention away. Even growing up he'd look away from them. Houses were nothing more than status symbols, unobtainable mounds of sheet rock which would never be in his life. *Why even look?* And that train of thought remained today. *Leona may be the light at the end of the tunnel, but sometimes that light gets corrupted by the thing chasing it.* That he said out loud, annoyed by the insanity behind it, the negative outlook which she would surely smack from his head if she knew it was swimming inside.

His foot stomped the gas, the Mercedes roared, his madness swam. Mateo was coming back from an out heading towards his one in. *If I want to keep her around, if I don't want to hurt her—it has to stay behind me.* 'She needs me,' was on the tip of his inner tongue, prevented by insecurity. *She doesn't need me. She only thinks she needs me. Just like I need this car, it's all just an insecurity. I'm bad for her.* If oil was self-loathing and self-esteem was water, they were finally mixing. Much like all the times he drove his Mercedes in the past, no matter how much he tried, the engine could not steal him away from where he had grown from; just like he could never steal Leona away from whatever she was running from. But in any case the engine sounds and its effect still felt good.

Finally back in the confines of his neighborhood *Stray Park,* an area of concrete and tar decorated with small department stores and apartment buildings, Mateo drove with no intention on stopping home first. Where he was going deserved his presence, deserved his vulnerability and more importantly deserved his mercy. All of it was owed; from the day that Mateo asked for Leona's number, to the instances where he spied on her, all the way down to this minute. *At least this means I have a conscience; I'm not completely dead inside.* Mateo stopped at the red, and a black cat scurried across the street. That brought Mateo back to the days where his classmates would create legends that because the town was overrun with Stray Cats, that's how the town came to getting its name. Mateo liked to believe that because the town had its name, all the cats came flocking to it. As he pressed the gas he wondered if the same had rung true for him and Leona; she's the closest thing to Heaven Mateo could find.

Ten minutes out of Stray Park, Mateo's Mercedes met the road that turned like a snake, yet held as many cars as a jammed bridge. Sitting there his legs shook. He bit at the side of his finger, right where the skin was rough and flaky. People on the sidewalk seemed like beings in a world not in the same universe. Isolation was riding his passenger seat. Even though he was doing this to get closer to Leona, the journey just minutes from his neighborhood, felt like one to Antarctica.

Around the bend on Colonvian, onto a small side street down Bancroft, two minutes lead him to the giant black gate which looked like it had been stolen from a haunted castle. In he went, parking in the front and using his memory to bring himself to the spot—Patrick Price's grave.

Below the headstone which read *Patrick Price, Father, Husband, American Hero* sat a small card creased and folded down the middle. On the front sat a blood red rose with a coiled green vine underneath. Mateo' first thought was Christmas because of the colors. Then his mind went back to where he was, a cemetery that is Leona's heartbreaking sanctuary. A place where a man who once served his country, then his town all while serving his family rested yet still guided his daughter when needed. *How can someone who's dead still lead someone whose living? That's a true leader.* Mateo thought, *not like me.* And then it was down to business. He looked around, the only entities around him were tall trees and a white house on a hill to stand witness to his words, which he wouldn't keep inside his head. The birds spoke, but seemingly in a whisper.

"I know that I don't deserve your daughter." Mateo paused, not exactly knowing what to say, but having too much to say at the same time. "She's a perfect person, and all I want is to make her happy and keep her safe. That's really all I ever wanted. Yeah, I'm selfish in wanting her for myself, and I'm sorry for that. But I do know, that I don't deserve her. I'm well aware that I've made her into something that she wasn't. I'm well aware that she puts aside the things in life that she should most dedicate herself to for a better future but instead she spends her time on me, and I'm beyond grateful for that, I am. I'm sorry for what I've done. I'm sorry for all the times I've upset her, and I'm really sorry for how much she cares about me. I've fucked up, but I really really never meant to hurt her." Tears filled his eyes. "I love her with all my heart, and every time I've messed up was my own weakness, my own insecurity. I take the blame for everything. And every day I see her eyes, the ones that look into mine with this passion for me…." He cried, tripping his words in his throat. "For me, a kid whose father left him, whose mother hated him, I'm grateful for her. And I mean that. I just want to take care of her, so please, don't hate me. Please, don't see me as some bad boy whose being selfish because I really do love her with everything I have. I'm just scared. I'm really scared sir."

Mateo envisioned Leona in his place, standing over her father saying whatever it is that she says. The pain was odd, and finding a cure for relieving it wasn't coming from Patrick Price's grave, nor was it apparent anywhere in Mateo' landmine field of a psyche. Why Leona comes here when answers are as scarce as sound he couldn't comprehend. *Another area where we differ,* he thought. She doesn't always need to know right from wrong. *Maybe she's the bad one,* he laughed. *She is after all with me.*

With what had to be at least five minutes with his dark jean covered knees in the dirt, Mateo rose before the cold grey headstone and still, waited for any type of sign or message; anything that would let him know he has her father's graces.

But nothing.

There was a bitterness which swarmed him like a swat team, and fending it off proved to not even be an option.

Why does everything have to be so hard and ambiguous? What do you want me to do? Leave her? I'll always go back. I can't just forget her and move. But I don't feel good enough. Not even close.

That's when the piercing scream broke through the thick silence throughout the graveyard. It took Mateo half a heartbeat to locate it's origins, which had to be the white house up on the hill. North it was, now holding a charcoal colored smoke as if the house had been puffing away on a pipe.

Another scream graced the graveyard, this time sending its duress into Mateo' boots. *How the fuck do I get up....just climb...fingernails in the dirt.* He told himself. And that he did, hopping the small fence which seemingly was built incase small goats wanted to enter, and he dug his hands into the side of the hill. The summer leave colored grass sided with gravity as Mateo could feel his own weight in his waist, fighting him with every new pull-up. The hill wasn't a total vertical wall, but it wasn't favoring the horizontal side either. The screams began to ease into a pattern, mixing in helps and pleads to god; with each one Mateo forgot about the task at his fingertips and pushed the muscles in his arms to a point where the veins wanted to meet the world.

And then,

Mateo met the top of the hill, standing up straight against a house that emanated heat; walls that sounded like pizza cooking left his ears as he bolted around their corners to the orange and black sparking front door. Without hesitation Mateo busted through. Smoke hovered over a staircase like a storm cloud and instinct sent him up. *Right or left,* the hallway asked. He chose right. The room he entered was pitch black and there was no oxygen for taking. *Grade school, firefighters visit,* Mateo hit the floor where the air wasn't pleasant but at least existed. Before his stinging eyes was a bedroom in flames but no sign of life.

Mateo crawled to the other end of the hallway; this proved to be more difficult that climbing the hill, with the fuzzy hot rug scraping against his forearms, his elbows and the fabric of his jeans. But he reached the other room, passing and only an empty bathroom along the way. The screams were the same from down at the headstone, except louder and sprinkled with wet, death-welcoming coughs. *Grown woman and toddler,* Mateo eyed them both from the floor, huddled in a rocking chair that wasn't rocking. The ladies golden hair was the only color in the room.

The two were both over his shoulders now and Mateo ran down the steps into the black pit.

"You're never going to amount to anything, you know that right? Bad people are hereditary." His mother said as Mateo drew on the ground with a hunk of green chalk. "Do you know what hereditary means? It means you get everything your father and I have; the drug problems, the insecurity, your father's knack for quitting when the going gets tough."

Mateo listened but did not accept. The giraffe before him, as wrong as his color was kept his tiny soul from telling her to shut up.

"My mother used to tell me that you know." His mother flicked a cigarette butt to the warm concrete beside him, a few inches closer and it would have been his cheek. "Bad people are hereditary." She laughed. "I should have done it. I shouldn't have brought you into the world knowing that." Her guffaw was embarrassing, drawing the attention of the others in the playground. Mateo didn't have to look up to know that. "I littered this world with someone that not only has my vile heart but also your father's piss filled sternum. High hopes for you alright, you little shit." Mateo looked up into her rotted balls of excuses for eyes and felt the breath being taken from him. He could not breath for a good three seconds and then, the air exploded in his lungs.

His eyes opened to a light blue sky holding one cloud, masculine voices and a head that simulated a dozen hangovers.

"We're taking you to the hospital for smoke inhalation, don't move." One voice bellowed.

But Mateo sat up on the grass, coming into view of two dozen firefighters, a fire truck and an ambulance. Sitting in-between its back doors was the lady with the golden hair and her baby.

"You need to lay down sir,"

"Are they okay?" It pained Mateo to speak.

"Yeah thanks to you. You saved both of them. You got some good karma coming your way kid."

In the ambulance Mateo sat, explaining numerous times that he didn't need a trip to Nome University Hospital. After breathing tests, flashlights shone into his mouth and blood pressure monitoring, it seemed as though the paramedics might listen. The one filling out the paper work now somewhat reminded him of Leona. Maybe it was the brunette curls or thirst for perfection. Whatever it was it eased his pounding head for the moment.

"You saved people today I hope you see what difference you've made. Those two are forever indebted to you." She said, scratching away on the clipboard with her fancy pen.

"They don't owe me a single thing. I did what was right."

"How did I know you'd say that? It's like cropped hair and tattoos make for men who love denial. You were here for someone today? The cemetery?"

"Yes."

"I guess I can excuse your denial for some sort of self loathing, I just owe thanks when someone changes my task from seeing burnt bones to putting bandages on flesh wounds."

"You'd rather treat the living than know there's nothing left to do."

"Exactly."

"When you've done as much shit as—"

"Oh stop, we all make mistakes. I promise you those two will remember you a lot more than anything you've ever done to people you've *hurt*. That doesn't just apply to this situation."

If the pounding in his head hadn't been putting on a concert, her words might have resonated.

Leona opened the door and immediately ignored the person occupying the doorway. "Is that your Mercedes?"

"A gift from Anne."

Leona's arms coiled around Mateo' neck, they were cold, and he welcomed that.

"Why do you smell like my cooking?"

There was the truth and the less complicated answer. "Anne had me clean her chimney, I came straight from there."

She released her embrace and brought herself to the shiny new piece of eye candy. Mateo' legs didn't want to do anymore moving.

"Why do I find it hard to believe that she just gifted this to you?" Leona ran her hand over the roof of the car.

"Did you sell drugs to get it?"

Mateo spun around at minimum speed to see a teenage girl with hair as black as her eye shadow.

"I'm Emma, Leona's cousin. You must be Mateo."

"Nice to meet you."

"I see you've finally met the black plague." Leona said while smirking at Emma.

"I am nowhere near the greatness of the black plague, that's too much flattery for one day." Emma said, never entirely leaving Mateo with those raccoon eyes.

Leona shut the door once everyone was inside, Mateo slowly brought himself into the living room where Remy sat painting her toenails.

"Hi Mateo," Remy said.

"Hello Remy."

"Why are you walking like you fell out a three story window?" Leona asked as Mateo sat.

"Just a lot of driving today, body is stiff."

"He's lying." Emma said.

"I'm not, but thanks for the accusation."

"Emma can you not start another witch hunt, I've had enough fir at least six years." Leona sat nearly on top of Mateo on the couch across from Remy and Emma. Mateo pulled her closer while restraining any sounds of agony.

"Witch hunt?"

"Emma and others, lead me to ditch Noelle among other things."

Mateo was listening, but couldn't pull himself away from Emma's drifting gazes. Her eyes were more decorated than Bradley's yet they seemed to hold more death and more life simultaneously.

"Come to think of it, help me fold my laundry downstairs." Leona shot to her feet, pulling Mateo up by the hand despite his reluctant body. Once downstairs she stood on her toes and kissed him, again coiling her arms around his neck. This time the pain amongst his body subsided. She closed the door behind them both and locked it, pushing him down on the couch and getting on top of him and the pile of clothes beneath him.

Now the pain was gone entirely and there wasn't enough passion that he could fit into his kisses. Grabbing her by the face, sitting her at the end of the couch. A switch was flipped somewhere inside Mateo Colon that translated into bite-Hectors and hair pulling.

"I love you," he said, resting his head on her chest.

Leona rubbed his head. "Where did that come from?"

"Me. I love you and I'm sorry for not being better."

"Mateo, no, you don't need to be better." She lifted his chin with two fingers. "You're everything I need you to be."

"No matter what I do, I don't feel like I am." Mateo sat up, resting his head in his hands. "I feel like I'm bad for you sometimes. Nearly everything that's happened to you has happened because of me."

"Like what?" Her voice held not a lick of wiggle room.

And Mateo could not think of a single thing other than what she did not know. "I don't know."

"Exactly, you're just getting down on yourself." She hurled a sock from the pile of laundry at his head. "I mean, I appreciate your ambition to be better, but there's no need."

"I don't get what you see in me."

"Nobody does, but I'd to think that if I did you'd be replaceable."

"What?" Sometimes there are trigger words which set Mateo' heart into panic mode, that being one of them.

"If I liked you for your tattoos or your car, in my eyes you'd be a dime a dozen. But when you can't put your finger on why you love someone, that's love." Leona kissed him, softly. "Okay?"

"Yeah."

Silence filled the room like a flash mob. "I don't know what I'm going to do about my mom. Remy wants me to go looking for her. I have no idea where to even begin but I promised I would."

Answers were few and far between roaming in Mateo's brain. "Tell her no?" He laid back down, maneuvering Leona to lay on top on him.

"I tried to, but her along with everyone else believes I'm a detective."

"Does part of you want to find her?"

"No. To be honest, I couldn't care less. I mean…a little. I don't know. One minute I do, one minute I don't." Leona shifted her bed, then kissed him roughly on the lips.

Kissing was better than the conversation so Mateo let her vent in the way she needed. It happened and escalated faster. Her kisses went from a handful to a dozen, changing from little taps of her lips to nibbles, to straight bites wherever it seemed fit. This in turn raised Mateo below, to the point where he thought it may rip his jeans.

Grabbing Leona by the shoulders, Mateo put her beneath him, leaving her no say. If the cushions had been made of stone she would have surely broken her back. Once comfortable, with their eyes beautifully aligned, Mateo let his own frustrations free. With his manhood intertwining them both, serving their passion with thrusts, Mateo finished quickly. All over her stomach rested his feelings. And then there was a rap at the door.

"One second," Leona said, absent mindedly touching the stickiness on her person.

"It's important." Remy's voice rang through the door and Leona instinctively pulled up her leggings.

"Get dressed," Leona mouthed as Mateo threw on the wrong shirt. But Remy knocked again, this time as if she would take the door off next.

Leona opened the door to a crack and poked her nose to the other side. Remy's voice was no longer what it had been, instead it melted into a light whisper. For what seemed like eons, Leona held the door, and then shut it as softly as Lead spoke. When she turned to Mateo her face was white.

"Trevor killed himself."

Good Mourning

Even dressed in all black formal wear, Noelle still looked like a slut. Her massive chest blossomed up from what attempted to be a V-neck. As shallow as it was, mentally demonizing Noelle shifted Leona's attention from the demons of the day; one of them being the coffin holding Trevor.

His family resembled people who were waiting at the department of motor vehicles. There were no tears, no sudden outcries of sorrow; not even so much of an out of place act of body language. They seemed bored—all but his sister. If one didn't know better, they would think she was the only one aware it was a funeral. The girl had reminded Leona of Remy, with a slender frame and innocent look upon her face. Except this girl was coated in tears. Robin was her name. Leona had overheard one of the older Bailey women say it. Unlike picking apart Noelle's self-esteem, scoping out Robin was only making things worse.

No one spoke aside from the priest: an Irish man whose wrinkles and bed head said that this wasn't his fulltime gig and that he was called on a whim; as after the ceremony he removed his collar like a work-tie and hauled himself away in his dilapidated Honda Civic. Off waiting on the only paved road in the cemetery, Robin stood by herself as family members paid their final respects to what now was a mound of dirt. The ugly sky concealed that it was dusk with grey clouds and wet winds.

"Your brother was a really good person." Leona said standing aside the quiet little Robin.

"It was my fault. I left him alone."

Shock attacked Leona's heart. "No," she said in a gasp. "You can't—"

"I left him when he needed me most, you think people are indestructible." Robin followed a woman whose mug could have been stolen from a pit-bull. Into the woman's car she went, whisked away by quiet wheels and tinted windows.

"It's a shame, but then again it's not for you I guess—now your secret will be buried in a cheap cemetery across from a corner store that's a front for drug dealers." Noelle's voice was too loud for Leona's comfort, too honest for reality.

"I have nothing to say to you." Leona said, eyeing Mateo who leaned against his car yards away in solemn boredom.

"The cold shoulder again? This hot and cold act sometimes makes me feel like we're dating."

"This isn't a time to be fucking joking, Trevor was a good person."

"Anyone who fucks me isn't a good person, no matter how hard they build up their lies."

Why her words twisted in Leona's kidney with a poison blade she didn't exactly know, maybe it was unexpectedness. "You two had sex?" *They've been friends for years, I guess that's not too surprising…depending on when.* "When did it happen?"

"Recently. I took his virginity. It's weird knowing that you're the only person someone had sex with their entire life."

I've never wanted to smack someone so hard. Everyone's right, she's not my friend nor is she a good person. She just has my mother's tone. "You and I are done Noelle. I don't think we should speak anymore."

"Remember that when the time comes." Noelle said laced with ice. As she cat walked her way out of their banter, Leona couldn't help her tongue.

"What's that supposed to mean?"

"It means I was the one that tried, who messed up but still tried to be a friend. You'll want to remember that. It'll hurt less."

And then the girl was gone, nothing but brake lights, memories and questions in Leona's eyes.

Over to Mateo she went as he still stood leaning against his shiny new black Mercedes, another piece of the universe that held more questions than anything useful.

"You never explained to me what else happened on Anne's farm; how you got Swanson to get off your back."

"This is the time that you choose to ask about this?" Mateo' face had that *how can I argue with him* look about it. Despite its nature, it only made Leona want to argue more.

"Yeah, I don't want to think about certain things." She said walking around to the passenger side.

"You can't bottle up what just happened."

Look at him being a hypocrite. "I just don't see the need," she sopped in Mateo' cologne as he plopped down in the driver's seat. Like an ocean mixed with aftershave, it always soothed her traffic jam of nerves. "I'm not, for some reason I don't feel anything. I mean, I'm sad but I'm more numb."

"Okay." He started the car and after a moment of silence they were on the streets.

"So tell me."

"Tell you what?"

Annoying. "What happened at Anne's."

"She explained things to Swanson and he called off his bounty."

"Just like that? And then you get a new car for nothing? Am I supposed to just swallow that?"

"Yeah, along with other things."

"Like what?" The smirk that wanted to evolve into a smile on Mateo' face answered her. "Oh, this isn't a time to be dirty Mateo."

"When is? You said you didn't want to think about things."

"Can you just answer me? I don't need to feel like I'm dating someone in the mafia."

A car horn blasted to the side of the Mercedes. Mateo had nearly sideswiped a purple Volkswagen. The driver's curly hair made her appear like a lioness who learnt how to give the finger.

"Are you drunk?" Leona asked. "As small as Volkswagens are–"

"I know, I know. Look, I'm serious. There were apologies and things like that which is why I got the car. He felt bad for nearly killing me and wrecking my apartment."

Leona searched for follow-up questions like a reporter speaking to a politician, but nothing came to mind. *Why don't I buy it? His blank stare, the way he looks around to avoid my eyes; he only does that when he's lying. Let's test it.* "Did you ever have sex with Noelle?"

"What?!" Mateo' immediate face of angry stone gave Leona speaker's block. Much like writer's block, words were impossible.

The car was now parked on the side of the road smack in front of an ice cream shop and cell phone store.

"Why the fuck would you ask me that?"

Why the fuck is he so angry, it was a joke. Leona's leg shook, up and down it went almost lifting her foot from the floor of the car. "It was a joke, Noelle had told me that she fucked

Trevor and took his virginity. That was my way of jokingly bringing it up, I'm sorry." She said her words so fast that they could have been mistaken for gibberish.

"Don't say shit like that."

Why's he getting so defensive?

"I don't want to think about that fuckin skank, I hate her fuckin guts."

"Whoa, Mateo relax."

"You fuckin relax! I hate her with all the problems she's caused between us and with you. Fuck her."

"Mateo, enough."

Silence. Then he pulled the car from the curb and they drove. A few yards down, while stopped at a red, Leona grabbed some extra fabric from her seatbelt and leaned over to nibble on Mateo' neck. Although he wanted to fight it, she could sense his body leaning over.

"Now's the time for dirty." Leona said.

"Why because I snapped at you?"

"Because you took my mind off things and hated on another girl."

"All great reasons." His sarcasm nearly fogged up the windshield. "I love you more than you know Leona."

Her mouth fell limp. "I love you too." She gave him one last peck on the neck as he pressed the gas. "You've been such a mush lately. I love it."

"For everything I've done, I just don't want you to think I take you for granted. I don't and I'd do anything for you."

So much, so great, so lovely; his words had never been so beautiful and she had never been at such a loss for her own, even compared to a few minutes ago. "Mateo, you're killing me. I love when you're like this. But believe me, I know and I'm not going anywhere."

"Okay."

Mateo turned the key and there they were: inside an apartment that had recently been ambushed by a man who now gifted Mateo with a brand new car. Life didn't make sense, if Leona's were a book she couldn't tell whether she'd stop reading or not.

"You wouldn't even be able to tell people almost died in here." She said, looking around and inspecting the walls.

Mateo shut the door and hung up his keys. When the jingling stopped, Leona grabbed Mateo by his stubbly face and kissed, never giving him the chance to fight back.

Five minutes in, the apartment was back to looking like there had been a brawl inside.

They did it on the counter.

Up against the bathroom wall.

On the couch.

On the floor next to the couch.

Mateo' hands felt illegal. They were aggressive. They were unfiltered. Her breasts were already sore. Her nipples were hard. Her ass was most likely red. There were bite Hectors developing, kisses drying, legs open, and then she screamed. Not because of Mateo but because of what perched itself on the top of his bookshelf.

"IS THAT A FOX!?"

"Yeah," Mateo continued to kiss her neck while putting his manhood back inside her. But she was drying up and getting chills now.

"Whoa, stop…stop…stop! Explain that to me please, I'm scared."

"Now?" He kept going.

"Yes Mateo."

Mateo stopped and sighed while plopping down on his rear-end. "He helped me find Bradley and he also saved me from Swanson's men. I don't have a choice with him following me, so I named him Finder."

"Who are you Jon Snow?"

"I wouldn't be surprised if I stole his idea, but then you'd have to be a redhead."

"Wait, this is vastly illegal Mateo." Leona sat up, grabbing her breasts with a forearm so they didn't jiggle everywhere."

"Henry was grateful so he let me keep him. As long as he stays put of the eyes of the police it's fine. He goes in a litter box and likes staying in. I think he was previously domesticated."

As if Finder had understood Mateo speaking about him, he leapt off the bookcase and landed beside Mateo' naked body, brushing up beside him like a puppy.

"What if he's got a disease?"

"I took him to a vet under a false name, the results came back fine."

"The vet didn't keep him?"

"He's here now isn't he?"

Leona did find the little beast cute, maybe because Mateo was treating him like a baby.

"Pet him," Mateo said, grabbing the little ball of red fur by the forehead.

"Will he bite me?"

"No, or at least I don't think so."

"Comforting," Extending a few fingers, Leona reached out to Finder where he then stuck his chin to the air and pawed his way over to her. His hair was silky soft. Irresistible was finding him cute. Finder closed his with every scratch beneath his furry chin.

"See, he may be a fox but he's harmless."

"He reminds me of the wolf bookend you had." Leona could see that it had been a stupid thing to say, being that the thing broke in the midst of a major fight. But Mateo seemed to careless, watching Leona has she pet his new roommate. "Is there anything you want to get off your chest?"

"No, I just wanted to keep fuckin you."

Is that what his face is about? "I know, but I still feel like there's something you're holding back. I can't tell with you ya'know."

Mateo pulled himself onto the couch, nudging at Leona to do the same. Finder took a spot on the top and quickly curled himself into a ball. "If you could guarantee Remy's finances and protection for her whole life at the cost of your own would you do it?"

"Yeah, without a moment's hesitation, why?"

"What if you got hurt or died, wouldn't that hurt Remy more than anything you can give her?"

"Why are you asking me this?" It was hard to feel fear while spooning, but she had somehow accomplished that.

"No reason….I was just thinking about what it would be like if I joined the military."

Not happening, ever. "That's not happening, ever. You understand me?" She craned her head to meet his eyes, then she pulled down his face by the chin so that he couldn't look away. "Understood?"

"Yes Leona. Can I ask why? Just for kicks."

"Because, I would never get to see you, and I'd be constantly worrying about you dying."

"What if the military were in Nome and the chance of dying were slim."

"That would mean you were a cop. I could somewhat deal with that. It'd be hot. You in a uniform."

"But the getting killed aspect, what if I was locked away for years for accidently killing someone?"

"I'd wait for you to come out, as long as it was an accident."

"You wouldn't be able to hold off on sex."

"I held off while you disappeared…aside from fucking Noelle."

"What?"

Leona couldn't help but laugh. "I just wanted to see your reaction. It wasn't as angry as the first time I brought her up." She bit into the side of his arm after gentling kissing it.

"It would be fuckin sexy, I'm not gonna lie."

"Moving on," She bit him again, and before she knew it, they were back at it, this time without Finder to surprise her.

Leona walked with Remy down a green mossy street. The trees were gigantic thick monsters where if they could talk, they would have the deepest voices known to man. Peaceful, comforting, relaxing, all feelings that the empty street lined with white and blue houses exuded.

"Is mom going to wear a dress?" Remy asked.

"I hope so, dad deserves that."

The sky went dark, then black. The trees distorted and Leona found herself in a dank and equally dark house where the staircase held cracks and dripped water while somehow being encased in vines. Remy sat in the corner holding her knees with no eyes.

"Mom?!" Leona screamed. "Remy can't see me scared. You have to come back, I can't be strong anymore."

"Where is she?" Remy asked in a whisper.

"She's here I promise, just hold on Remy."

"She's late to renew her vowels big sister, dad's going to be mad."

"I know, it'll be okay though I promise."

"I hate you." A voice from everywhere echoed. "I hate you both."

"Does she mean that?" Remy asked.

"Stop, please! Don't do this Leona screamed. Running into what looked to be an old living room. Everything was grey and black, rusted and covered in dust. It was her living room she realized. *Am I in the future?*

"I hate you both." The voice was feet away, and when Leona lifted her head from the floor, there was her mother. In a white-grey dress that covered everything but her arms and face, she stood like a ghost: a keeling over body holding a spirit. The dress looked like it was holding her all together.

"Mom, you can't let Remy hear that. You can't let her see you like this."

"Stop hiding the truth from your little sister, we raised you better than that." Without taking one step, Liz Price floated across the room which now was missing the dining table. Her hand shot across Leona's face, creating nothing but a cracking sound.

"You deserve that." Remy said.

Leona graced her eyes on the eleven year-old. She stood in the doorway wearing the same dress as her mother except hers was covered in blood. "Remy, I'm sorry."

"You should be. You're the reason mom left. This is all your fault."

Leona went to seek the forgiveness of Liz Price, but whatever her body was had been gone now, along with the hideous dress she wore.

"I'm truly sorry Remy, please forgive me. I can't have you mad at me. You're the one person I can't have—"

Without any warning, the tip of Remy's shoe kicked Leona across the face. Blood sprinkled across the musty floor giving it it's only color.

I deserved that.

Again, her shoe kicked, this time against the side of Leona's cranium. Her long curly brown hair fell into the blood. "I'm sorry, please Remy."

"Wake, hey, Leona baby."

The ceiling was the ugliest grey Leona had ever laid eyes on, luckily it was doused by the jaw bone and ruffled hair of Mateo Colon. She grabbed him immediately, wrapping both arms around him like he had dropped down out of a helicopter.

"It's okay, you were crying in your sleep."

She dabbed the moisture from her cheeks. "I'm sorry."

"What are you apologizing for?"

"I'm sorry, I'm so so sorry." She cried.

"Leona you're scaring me."

"To Remy, I'm sorry that I pushed our mom away."

"Hey no," Mateo said, lifting her wet face from his fuzzy chest. "Don't blame yourself for that. Is that what you dreamt about?"

"Yeah, I'm not going to be able to find her Mateo. I don't even know where to start."

"It's okay, shhh. You don't have to figure this out now."

"I do though. Every time I see Remy I know that's on her mind, I know she's wondering how I'll do it. I know she's wondering where she is, and I definitely know that if I'm blaming myself—so is she."

He took no time for his next words. "Okay but Leona, none of this is your fault. Not in any way, shape or form."

"Maybe it's not my fault but it's my responsibility and I gave her my word. I just feel lost."

Finder pounced onto the bed, his small size didn't do so much as to un-crease the blanket. Mateo stared at the ball of fur, who acted as if it were play-time. Next Mateo scooped him up with both hands and held him in the air like he were Simba from the Lion King.

"Are you listening?" Leona asked.

"Yeah, and there's a reason he's called Finder."

Workplace Guarantee

If working full-time at Waymart was to be Leona Price's future she couldn't argue the idea of finishing college. Cashier audits, till reports, lottery data, bottle redemption amounts; all was her life for eight hours, five days a week in a small room with a peach wall and shoebox sized window. It did allow her to day dream about Mateo. Sometimes when there was no work to do she'd imagine their naughty times together. Tempted to touch herself in the confines of her little box. Luckily the camera up ahead was there to thwart that temptation.

And now there was another reason to keep herself from day dreaming—Emma. Aunt Betty and her ideas sprouted one which lead to Emma's first day at Waymart; to get her out of the house, give her something to put her mind to and more importantly, it was an attempt to shake her from a dreary outlook.

Aunt Betty had been concealing something which Emma probably didn't care to hide that Remy found herself confiding in Leona: Emma doesn't want to go home when the Summer comes to a close and Aunt Betty along with Uncle Charlie is more than happy to accept her. The deal being she gets a part time job to cover her extra expenses. God only knows her makeup budget.

"Navy blue is the brightest color I've ever seen you wore." Leona said as Emma stood waiting with slumped shoulders by the cashier manager's podium.

"It sickens me."

"Adult life isn't going to grant you the option to wear black everyday Emma, you're going to have to get used to this if you want a real job."

"Who said I did? Funeral home owners are scarce to come by in this city. It would go well with our families cemetery theme."

Dignifying a response would only draw more idiotic statements like that, so Leona refrained. Perfect timing accompanied their manager Mike, who even with new people held little to know eye contact and always seemed to be in his mind thinking of his next seven sentences.

"Nice to meet you Emma," Mike said followed by a forced and awkward interaction between the two. For the first time ever Leona found a cuteness in her little cousin; witnessing her attempts at being normal humanized her a bit. Unfortunately it was wasted on a human who considered corn chips a meal. "You can hop on register five, your cousin will train you."

At first Leona hadn't wished that. Emma and herself had never spent pro-long periods of time together, but the more Leona observed the what was under the dreadful wardrobe, she could spot why Remy gravitated towards her.

"Hit enter, your employee number and then enter again. That's how you sign on." Leona said, pointing to the register pad loaded with colorful, faded buttons.

"Exciting."

"Work isn't supposed to be.. or at least not this job."

"I gathered that the second I saw the pharmacy technician yell at an old lady."

"Yeah, don't speak to Rufus. He hates his life."

Their conversation was interrupted by a short and stocky customer with shoulders that could hold two obese eagles. Surprisingly Emma held her own on the customer service end of the spectrum.

"Yeah, the weather is miserable I'm surprised so many people came shopping today." Emma said to the man who gingerly placed his eggs in his own bag.

"Hey, sometimes you have to brave the ugly to feed your face."

When the interaction ended Leona didn't know whether to applaud or remain standing in awe. "Where did that come from?"

"What?"

"The courtesy, the smile, the bubble of glee and small talk that I thought would cause you to burst into flames by attempting."

"It's not hard to be fake, your boyfriend does it all the time."

If words were comets, one just landed. "I just paid you a compliment, why must you come back with…"—*shit*.

"What? The truth? Sorry, it was the first thing that came to mind. Something about your boyfriend rubs me the wrong way—like he's constantly not being himself. He reminds me of every lead male character from a Nick Sparks novel."

"What would you know about Nick Sparks?"

"I know whoever is in charge of your life up there watched one too many of his movies."

"You're say God is a –"

"Gods a strong word. Hi how are you today?" Emma switched her attention to an elderly lady customer who took her time placing her items on the belt. Leaving Leona to silently sizzle over the comments made over Mateo.

There's not one person that doesn't have something nasty to say about him. I don't get it, he's changed so much. They still don't see what I see. Emma's only meant him fucking once what does she know? I'm tired of the same discussion—being the villain for liking who I like.

"Mateo isn't perfect but that's why I like him." Leona said once the lady had slowly waddled off.

"I didn't mean for my words to burn. But no offence, maybe he should show everyone his imperfections and not just you."

Leona couldn't disagree but her leg shook more than she could produce a rational comeback.

"I'm never going to hold back with you. I'm not Remy."

"Believe me I know you're not Remy."

And after that the girls kept to themselves, only breaking the awkward with Emma asking questions about the job and Leona feeding her answers. As Emma scanned and interacted with strangers in a form rarely seen, Leona surveyed. She watched her mannerisms, the way she fell into her own thoughts during idle periods. Her smile would instantly fade once the customer had been on their way. It was then that Leona sympathized, realizing that underneath the dark makeup, the dreary outlook, the monotone voice and abundance of silver jewelry—Emma was as wounded as her favorite songs.

"I'm sorry that I'm a bitch to you." Leona said.

Emma never changed body language, leaning up against the small desk which held the receipt printer and item display screen. "It's okay. I'm used to defensive nature in people. I'm sixteen remember?"

"You're sixteen but still have a creepy doll collection…are you bringing them to Aunt Betty's?"

Emma shifted in place, lending a stare to the floor and the side of her thumb to her teeth. "My mother is shipping them yes."

Leona left the topic there, leaving Emma to fair on her own for a bit while she worked on a cart full of returns.

Waymart never changed, except during holidays, but even then it was the exact replica from the previous year. There rarely was more than a hundred people in the store lined with twenty-three aisles. Sesame Street was how Leona imagined it. The store was an un-changing little world with the same characters day after day, year after year. Michael still pushed his shopping carts, Phil still stocked his shelves and the customers never failed to stick to their mini routines of small talk and pain-staking slow shopping.

How long will I have to work here? It's going to be tough full-time when I start school. Amongst her mood's lull she remembered all the time she spent on the colorful sales floor with Mateo Colon. Memories can make something old feel new, she realized.

"Yo,"

Leona's feet stopped like a car who was about to rear-end another. Michael hadn't spoken to her in months. When she tried to remember the last time, it might have even been when Mateo broke his nose.

"You gonna turn around or just ignore me?" Michael muttered.

Leona spun around with most of the weight on her bad leg—it sent a searing pain right up to her knee. But there stood Michael, leaned over a shopping cart with his dirty blond hair over his eyes and the striped collar of his polo shirt budding out from the top of his smock.

"What do you want?" She said in a softer tone than desired.

"I don't know, I just missed talking to you."

"No sluts to keep you occupied?" Being defensive kept her from being anything else.

"No. Yo, what I did to you happened mad long ago can't we just be friends? I did try and save your ass that one time and got a broken nose in return."

"Karma."

"Doesn't that make it close to even?"

Leona took a moment. She was in no mood to bicker. "Maybe."

The slightest of smiles grew on Michael's face. "I was an idiot for cheating on you."

"I'm aware of that."

"Do you forgive me?"

Leona's father, the cemetery, Noelle Santiago, Remy pissed off, the car accident, Mateo disappearing, Mateo being withdrawn, Mateo, Mateo, Mateo, Mateo; it all flashed across her psyche and went into her clenched fists.

"After everything I've been through in my life you think I have the heart space for someone who cheated on me?"

"Leona,"

"No, my father taught me better than that. That's my limit, that's where I draw the fucking line." Her fingernails dug into her palm.

"Why are you getting so mad? It was just a question yo."

Gasoline on the fire. "Because to have the audacity to even ask that, you don't know how much that fucking hurt me. You don't know the self-esteem issues that followed. You just think that it was meaningless physical contact, but like, you were my fucking boy, I fucking loved you and to turn around and abuse my trust.

"Turn around…" Michael mumbled.

And that she did, to see Mateo Colon standing at his straightest with an unreadable mask above that rock solid stubbly jaw bone.

"Mateo...I didn't..." Leona spoke but couldn't think.

"It's okay," Mateo said, looking passed Leona to the boy who once held her heart the same. "Michael,"

"Sup,"

Mateo nodded, and for a second Leona watched her boyfriend speed down a highway called the highroad.

"What are you doing here? I thought you were taking Finder to look for my mom?" she listened as the wheels to Michael's cart creaked their way to a fainter sound.

"I had just wanted to see you before I left...I don't know how long this will take or how far he'll take me if this even works."

Leona left her shopping cart in exchange for a stance on her tippy-toes to lend Mateo a long aggressive kiss. "Thank you for not being him."

Mateo' lips laid idle, like he were in a hypnotized trance. "I have to go now."

"Are you okay? You seem...different."

"Just thinking about finding your mom."

"Alright."

Without a kiss goodbye, Mateo was gone. The ripples in his back made like strong waves wrapped in a black tee. After that Leona continued on with her cart, pondering about her interaction with Michael and if Mateo' little new pal could actually find her mother. When she rounded aisle twenty-three and made for the registers, she spied Emma with a customer. The head was cut off by a candy rack, but the chest seemed familiar. Too familiar. Leona's feet acted before her brain could send them signals, and then, in ten steps she saw her. The evil smile. That fake glint in her eyes. The lustful aura which shrouded her every move. Noelle Santiago picked up what looked to be a candy bar from Emma's bag carousal and said but three words. Her eyes met Leona's, and there crept her infamous smirk followed by nothing more but the back of her head. Something was amiss, something was odd, something was too coincidental. So Leona booked it to Emma.

"The hell was that about? Why was she here? Did she see Mateo?"

"She was buying an energy bar."

"She can buy that anywhere." Leona's heart skipped rope. "Yep."

"Why are you so quiet? What did she say?"

"Nothing. Nothing important."

"You're not looking at me, you're hiding something."

"Please drop it, if there was something you needed to know, I'd tell you."

"That means there's something." Leona's eyes caught her cousin's shoulders tense in the slightest of ways. They looked to be rock solid. "You're getting tense Emma, spill it—"

Emma spun around in the quickest time Leona's ever seen the girl move. Her black painted fingernails were the only things visible, darting up like jet planes soaring through the air. The unmoving metal of the register behind Leona was now digging into her back and the ceiling was before her. Emma held her down by the shoulders.

"You're getting on my nerves," Emma grunted. "When I don't want to talk about something that's your queue to leave it alone, understood?"

Why is her voice trembling?

"You think I don't care about—" Emma let go, looking up and leading Leona to peer behind herself. Mike was at the podium, gazing with his mouth open.

"We're just playing around." Leona yelled.

Emma released her grip, and the girl awkwardly returned to where they had been before Leona moved off with her cart.

"She said something to you....that I should know."

Emma never turned to face her. "That's where you're wrong."

"You're protecting me." Leona's eyes went blurry with moisture.

And Emma's voice revealed the same. "No I'm not, I just don't like when you talk about my dolls. I still remember Ursula, God rest her porcelain soul."

The arms wrapped around Emma's waist for the first time. The warmth of her body, her thin frame and the softness to her shirt underneath her smock revealed she was human after all.

"I did not give you permission to hug me." Emma reverted back to the monotone.

"I didn't give you permission to almost break my back, but you almost did that."

"Whatever."

"You're going to tell me what she said."

And there was silence.

The Foxy Road Ahead

Finder kept antsy in his cage, secured in the back of Mateo Colon's Mercedes. The small tracking device flashed a red light every second on the little fox's collar. He was ready to search, with a few of Liz Price's belongings in a shopping bag next to him. A shirt, a brush, and against Mateo' will but under Leona's insistence, a pair of her unwashed underwear. Leona had been adamant with her demands, sure- tongued in her plan. Mateo could only keep quiet and follow orders, not sure what he would find at the other end of this very weird search. But it would have to wait.

The phone call was cryptic, and followed an even more eerie voicemail.

"It's Swanson, call me back immediately." His voice was mellow yet it held a withdrawn fire. Three seconds was how long it took for Mateo to redial after listening. Four seconds was the conversation between the two. "Get to the farm. Come Alone. Eyes on the rearview." Something was amiss, something had changed, and fear was all Mateo knew in the moment.

The engine only stirred the contents of his chest. Dizziness followed his short breaths as he listened to Finder rattle along in the back. *I don't want anything to happen to him, if something happens to me.* Mateo watched the tall green trees breeze by in his peripherals as he used every ounce of self-control not to speed to the farm which had once promised to change him and only exchanged him more problems.

He didn't want to arrive quickly, for then he would have to face whatever it was that he was summoned for. *Is he mad because I turned him down? Is it the car? Does he want the car back?* But that wish was unfounded. Distance and time flew by much like the trees outside the car window. And before he knew it, he was there, pulling up onto the dusty brown dirt where the creepiest of calms cast itself over the barn, the house, the fence and everything around it.

Mateo brought himself up the dusty trail, through the rickety fence and up the freshly swept steps that put a little ease into Mateo' chest. *If she had time to sweep, Anne's not wounded or dead. Things may be okay. Why am I scared?*

Knock Knock his knuckles went.

There was no answer.

Knock knock they went again.

Still nothing.

And then, the door slowly opened. The forehead of Swanson peered out holding atop its golden slicked hair. Then his eyes revealed themselves. Somber they were, cold and merciless they rested.

"Mateo, Mateo Colon please. C'mon on in." Swanson's tone was laced with so much sincerity that it led Mateo to believe it to be a trick. There would be a bullet in the back of his head once the door closed, he was positive.

Mateo' feet took their time through the door. Even when they landed they still felt as though they were in mid step. The blood seemed non-existent in his legs. From there, he spotted Anne sitting at the table, her head in her hands. Sniffling was the only sound that filled the house until Swanson opened his mouth again.

"The kitchen Mateo, please, have a seat."

The entire time Mateo took to place his ass in the chair he kept his senses on high alert. It was only until Swanson sat down across from them both that he let his posture melt in the chair, letting out a deep exhale.

"They killed Bradley." Swanson said. "The State."

Dead, as in not alive. Bradley's dead. Not breathing. He's no longer alive. Mateo said to himself, not quite sure how to fathom the words. He pictured him in twenty different situations and couldn't believe his ears. Nor could he understand what to feel. "He's dead...?"

"I'm afraid so. It was a drive by. Here on the farm."

"When did this happen?"

"Yesterday." Every word from Swanson's mouth was a poor attempt at keeping his composure. The man was hurting. Mateo didn't know what was harder to believe, that Bradley was dead or that the man he once considered heartless was holding back tears.

Mateo clenched his fists, bit his lower lip a few times and then shut his eyes out of reflex. When they opened they were stinging with moisture.

"You're allowed to cry. I understand that you got close with him." Swanson said. The second his words finished Anne let out a hushed whimper. She fell deeper into her hands and Mateo couldn't help but to rub her back. "I know this doesn't change anything, but you're the only one my head keeps going back to."

"Back to what?" Mateo finally said.

"To succeed me."

"I already told you,"

"I know you did...but that was before you had even more of a reason to fight on my team...and frankly..."

"What?"

"I don't know."

"He's broken." Anne said through tears. "He needs an assistant, an ear, young blood to run this family."

"This is crazy, okay." Mateo stood. "I cared about Bradley, but just because I took down two assassins doesn't mean I'm fit for a life of crime or that I'm fit to run an organization."

"Mateo everything you've been—"

"You don't know my life!" Mateo yelled at Swanson. "I'm sorry. But the answer is no."

"And what about your girlfriend? The ones you care about. Including Bradley? Don't you think you owe them the sacrifice, the guaranteed financial stability? You say crime, I say doing what you need to do to make things right, to make sure the one's we care about are well taken care of long after we're dead. I'm talking protection, wealth, anything you can dream of under the sun. People who fuck with—"

"None of that could save Bradley." Mateo said to a now also standing Swanson.

"None of it could, because I'm not who I used to be. I need the legs to carry out my voice, my power. The one's I have peddling, aren't cutting it. And now, my son is dead because of the people who almost killed you…and your girlfriend."

"What do you mean my girlfriend?"

"She was next."

Now Mateo was angry. "I'm leaving. I'm sorry about Bradley. It's not that I'm not upset, or want them dead, I'm just not as strong or reckless as you think I am." Mateo turned to the doorway and made his exit.

"You are. And you'll be back. And when you do come back I need only death from you, and you're in for life."

"What do you mean?" Mateo asked to the door in front of him.

"An initiation kill. It's collateral in case you turn against the family. But, I like to think of it as a nice little perk. You can eliminate anyone you'd like, that boss who was a dick, that pesky ex, the teacher who fucked up your grades. Can't say it's not tempting."

Noelle. Mateo thought. "Goodbye Swanson."

Parked on the side of the road, by giant trees that concealed its contents, Mateo sauntered around the car and surveyed the highway before him. *I hope this works.* Mateo thought to himself. Before he went for the driver's door he checked his cellphone to see how Finder's GPS signal held. There was zilch. *What the fuck?*

Mateo sat himself in the back next to Finder's cage. "I'm going to open this, and you have to promise to behave." After five seconds of hesitation, Mateo unlocked the cage's shiny silver cage door and slowly out came Finder. The light on his collar was dark and it wasn't turning on. *Fuck.*

At Thew Pawns the old maroon awning read above the petite pawn shop Leona seemed to fancy. Inside was the owner, no one else.

"Mateo, I barely recognized you without your other half."

"Yeah, for a love story we haven't spent that much time together as of late." His sarcasm was unintentional.

"What can I do for you?"

"I need a reliable GPS tracking system, something better than what the stores are selling."

The man's face morphed into Christmas lights. He hobbled over to a pile of what looked like parts to a crashed airplane. From the rubble he yanked a square black foot long box, brought it before Mateo and dissembled a little chip from the side. "This shall do, just put the other chip inside your phone's SD slot."

"How much?"

"It's on me," The man turned his back and struggled in his legs to walk back to whatever he was doing.

"How long did it take you to perfect the American accent and that bullshit walk?" Mateo said, letting his arms hang with his new toy.

"Pardon?"

"I won't pardon a father who abandoned his family." Mateo' nose stung as if he inhaled soda that also traveled beneath his eyes. But crying wasn't allowed right now.

The man stood up straight and turned himself to Mateo. "You got me kiddo, Leona told you?" Mathew Colon now spoke with a tinge of a Spanish accent.

Leona Knows?! "No, I just knew. I did snooping. Why did you leave us? Why did you fake your death?"

"Mateo," Mathew's eyes welled. "Sometimes it's best to remove yourself to prevent the ones you care about from getting hurt."

"What are you talking about?" Mateo took some steps forward as his father locked the pawn shop door.

"Coincidence is strange. I worked for Swanson when he was a little older than you. And, that life is only good if you don't value your own. But it's why you've been able to live without worrying about finances."

"And here I was thinking God was just bad at spotting his own plot holes. Mom killed herself because you left."

"Your mother killed herself because of me, yes. I wasn't there for her. Instead I was a husband to my career. Or whatever you want to call it."

The tears were still waiting to jump from the bench but Mateo hid them by sending his attention away from his father and into his gadgets. "You said coincidence, so you know about Swanson's offer?"

"Yes, and the fact that they found you of all people. Anne's farm isn't the easiest places to wind up."

"I'm debating on doing it. They killed a kid who was like a brother to me."

"Vengeance isn't a reason to do that, I didn't give up my life and your mother's so that you could do the same."

Mateo' hands fell limp, nearly dropping his GPS to the dirty rugged floor below. "What do you mean?"

"You know what I mean."

Turning to face his father, the man's eyes were dark steel, his back as straight as a vertical arrow.

"You killed mom?"

"An initiation kill can be postponed."

Mateo took but three steps forward and lunged at Mathew Colon and as soon as his hands tickled his flesh they were seized. Mateo was now face down on the floor with a knee to his back. How he got there he couldn't recall.

"Relax yourself, your mother needed to be put out of her misery, better yet, your misery. All the hateful words she spewed your way, the times she left you with addicts and street scum. You can't tell me that the person who died and changed your life wasn't a blessing for dying and changing your life." Mathew let go and stood over Mateo who rubbed his wrists. "Be mad, but she wasn't a mother. Your Aunt Rosa was."

There was no argument there. Too many questions, way more comments. Mateo had an overloaded mind. Helped to his feet by his father, the two held eye contact and Mateo, despite the murder of his mother, the absence of a father growing up and lies on top of lies, he extended his dad a hug.

"I didn't think you'd forgive me." His father said.

"You're a liar and a murderer."

"Exactly."

"I don't know if I do. I have more questions and the better sense to turn you in." He watched his father's smile melt off.

"But?"

"I'm not sure." Mateo walked to the door and unlocked it. "Depends on if I take Swanson's offer or not."

"I'd rather serve life than see you do that."

"You won't have to see it, because you'll be my kill."

The door shut.

Sick Tapes

It amazed Leona how not a line of makeup or a piece of jewelry was out of place on Emma even after waking up from ten hours sleep. Walking down the stairs to a breakfast of scrambled eggs, bacon and pancakes, the morning smell must have acted as her alarm clock.

"You really bring a whole new meaning to the phrase *I woke up like this*." Leona said to her sleepy eyed cousin.

"It's a blessing a curse."

"Sit, while it's hot."

Emma followed, extending Leona a weird feeling; seeing her in a more submissive light was alien.

MERF PARK, NORTH SIDE OF NOME CITY; DAYS BEFORE

Noelle Santiago sat herself down next to Leona Price's unsightly cousin. She had been the darkest yet palest one amongst the spiky sea of green in the sun covered park.

"Doesn't one wonder where their niece had disappeared to?" Noelle asked, throwing her curly black locks over her shoulders.

"I said I was going for walk. Sadly my aunt doesn't notice when her vehicle is gone."

"Cut to the chase please, I get that you're in my way with things, how do I get you out of it?"

"I hope Remy's doctor appointment goes well today, Aunt Betty was vague about it." Leona scooped up a pile of scrambled eggs, the steam circled its way around the giant spoon and onto her plate. The glistening greasy juices from the bacon nearly drew her hand to start sending food to her mouth before sitting down.

"She told you about that?" Emma lifted her raccoon eyes from her plate.

"Um, yeah why wouldn't she?"

"There is no *out of your way*, you've lost. I know that Mateo cheated on Leona. I'm a modern day Sherlock Holmes. Whatever plans you had are done. But if you want what I have on you to stay in the dark then you'll do me a favor."

Just before Leona could swallow the fluffy eggs bouncing around in her mouth, the doorbell rang.

"Were you expecting a delivery?" Emma asked.

"No," Leona let the fork clatter against the plate and scooched her chair to make an even uglier sound. When she opened the door there was not a soul to be seen. The house to her left still seemed to be holding the sleeping, same went for across the street, and the road to her right occupied no tires. But below, down by her pink-fluffy slipper worn feet laid a disc which read *watch this Leona* written in marker.

"And what about the tape?" Noelle asked.

"You'll do the right thing and give it to Leona, because if it comes from anyone else she'll resent you for hiding it further. If you truly do give a damn about her. And of course, if you want me out of your hair."

"Who the fuck are you?" Noelle's tone did a 360.

This can't be good. Leona's heart said. *Maybe it's something from mom....or Swanson...Noelle?* A shaking hand dug its fingernails beneath the discs side, scraping against the concrete slab holding it.

"What's that?" Emma asked as Leona marched to the living room where the DVD player called. "An answer is usually what humans give following a question, but I've been molested by the sun for sixteen years, what do I know?"

"Emma, if I knew what it was I wouldn't be frantically putting it into the darn DVD player."

"You're allowed to curse, I'm not eight."

Leona shot on the television and after a jumpy few screens, there came on what Leona couldn't fathom. Emma shielded her eyes, leaving the room in a dark blur. And there before Leona's was Mateo—mounting Noelle like she were his horse; that he loved, that he lusted after.

The tape was edited to show only the most graphic scenes, the most ear murdering of shrieks. Everything tossing around in Leona's sternum screamed to stop watching, to shut it off and cry like a lost toddler. But instead she braved each and every kiss, bite, grab, pull, smack, grunt, thrust, lick and hold. Twenty minutes passed and Leona remained motionless, standing in place like an English soldier serving his Queen. And then the screen went black. Whatever Leona had been feeling dissolved, an emptiness filled.

It was Emma's sensitive touch upon her shoulder that yanked her back into reality. "Sit, while you're still hot." Emma said.

Without question, Leona parked her rear-end on the couch, losing the ability to form speech.

"Whatever that was, she's just trying to hurt you. But she also did it to help. At Waymart she had told me what she discovered at the hospital. Something Aunt Betty had been hiding with Remy from the both of us and Noelle didn't need to do me the favor in telling me. But, I guess it was part of her closure."

A fire, one laced with explosives ignited in Leona's chest and behind her eyes. Her gaze alone was enough to get Emma to say whatever it was.

"Remy has been hiding a tumor."

When they dance with no inhibition, they swallow their watchers.

For they must always have eyes on them.

Eyes open and eyes closed, their burn never fails to scorn.

Their nature whether good with intention can never be without fault.

When believed they are flawless.

When they are exposed they are,

Lies or humans?

Leona held her headache riddled head in her hands supported by elbows that grimaced with pain against Aunt Betty's table. The conversation had started, few words resonated with her ears and between Emma and Betty's awkward fidgeting amongst the silence; Leona could have ripped her own brain out.

"Slower," Leona said.

"It's called a Wilmer's tumor. It's at stage one, very easy to take care of." Her aunt spoke like a hostage negotiator. "There's a ninety-nine percent chance that it can be removed without issue."

Between Emma's stoic out of place standing and Betty's nervous fidgeting, Leona was attacked by a fog of tension, adding onto her already heavily pissed off disposition. "An what happens if that one percent trumps? What would have happened if I woke up one day and my sister was dead? Not even knowing that she was undergoing surgery."

"I wouldn't have hid this if I wasn't sure that it would turn out okay."

Leona lifted her steamy forehead from her sweating palms. "And are you sure? I mean, are you 100%?"

Emma broke her staring contest with the floor to observe her aunt's answer.

"No," Betty forced out.

Leona hadn't been hoping to be right, she had been hoping for her aunt to be sure, for Remy to come out okay. "So why the fuck keep it from me? You don't think I've been through enough?"

"That's exactly why I kept it from you." Her aunt's voice came with tremors, "I couldn't serve you anymore pain."

A long sigh escaped from Leona, her rear-end couldn't bare another antsy moment in her seat. "Where is Remy?"

"Taking a nap, I'd much prefer you to not berate her with this. Half of it was her idea to keep this under wraps."

She doesn't know when she's making it worse, like this is some surprise party I'm ticked off about. "How long have you known about this?"

Of course, the answer that was about to come out was prefaced with a face that could have lead one to believe Betty had shit herself. "Since your mother left."

"Why did you keep it from me?" Emma finally asked.

"Because…Remy didn't want you treating her differently."

Leona had never seen anger upon Emma's face. Her blackened lips and raccoon eyes always held a stoned mystery, but this time, her eyes twisted to strained portals to her soul.

"I may only be sixteen but since when do you take orders from an eleven- year- old?"

"This hasn't been the easiest of situations for me, especially with uncle Charlie away on business. I apologize." The defeat dripped off Betty like blood off a flesh wound.

She doesn't deserve any of this. The burden that mom left on her shoulders, it's selfish and thoughtless. And then it dawned on Leona. "Did my mother know about this?"

No matter what the circumstance, Aunt Betty never failed to keep it chipper. The time Leona broke her leg when she was little, Betty was the second one to her father to say 'bones heal, don't worry.' Even at Patrick Price's funeral where dry eyes were scarce and Leona could no longer keep a stable vocal cord, Betty knew how to control a conversation into being less dreary.

"Your father would have loathed this." Betty said, removing a dyed black rose from her hair."

"He never liked funerals to begin with." Leona swallowed a gulp of saliva when finishing her sentence.

Aunt Betty smiled but still spoke in a whisper. The family, along with friends, men dressed in their police uniforms, military men decked out in their camos, all formed a hectic solemn line to drop their roses on Patrick Prices' coffin. "I remember one time. It was Margaret Penson's funeral, God rest her soul. Your father snuck into the Janitor's closet and had put on one of Margaret's dresses. Lord knows how he got his hands on the flowery thing but when he came out—the laughs."

In turn Betty had done the impossible: making a girl smile on the day of her father's funeral. Things like that were unforgettable, even under circumstances which proved life changing.

"Yes dear, I found out through her by a text. It was the day after she left that my phone lit up with her name. God forgive me, I wish it had been anything else."

"Why God forgive you? You're not saying anything wrong. My mother did a fucked up thing, to all of us."

Emma left the room on that note. But there was enough tension to replace her void.

"I wish you had told me." Leona's hands went back to her forehead as she then went to fridge. The orange juice was just as cold as the situation, she thought. If not less.

"In a way, I wish I had too. But again—"

"I know, I know. You didn't want to hurt me." Fleeting was the anger towards Betty. Flourishing was the anger towards her mother. "How could she leave knowing that about Remy?" Leona sat and her aunt's warm hand fell upon her shoulder.

"Perhaps,"

"Don't."

"Perhaps it was one of the reasons she removed herself. Not to take any blame off of her," It took a second for Leona to even realize that Betty had sat down and taken both her hands in her own. "Your mother was a pessimist, always seeking the worst case scenario. When that scenario came to fruition—it was the end of the world."

"I know my mother." Leona took her hands back. "And as bad as she was with dealing with drama, she shouldn't have done this."

"I know dear." That very same tension had seemingly evaporated into the dust of the room, illuminated by white sun rays lasering through the kitchen window curtains. "What's going through your mind? You can talk to me about this stuff. I won't piece together any opinions to try and argue your feelings. It's a bad habit of mine."

Leona pondered, unleashing the tears and the occupants up in her crazy head would be a relief and less baggage for Mateo to carry when he comes back. "I don't even know where to begin."

"There's no starting point, just begin with your first thought."

Just then Emma burst into the room. It had been the quickest Leona had ever seen the girl move. "Remy's gone."

When the Mother Plays

The Mercedes had vanished by now, shrouded by a field of brown topped off with bright and dark green leaves. Unlike the last time Mateo Colon had been brought into a forest for a search, he brought two bottles of water and a few energy bars. *The nutrition of homeless man,* he thought.

Finder kept good on living up to his name so far. He was at least looking, something Mateo feared he may not have been able to do a second time around. Mateo didn't keep track of miles, but he did keep track of time—two hours. Without stopping every couple exits to find Finder and check on him, it might have been an hour and a half. Mateo did the best check-ups he could without knowing much about foxes. If the little ball of fur felt hot, they rested. If his attention span wandered, he fed him carrots. For some reason he loved carrots. But overall Finder was taking the search in stride. Somehow he understood the task before him and motivation never dwindled. But then things changed. For Mateo at least.

First it was Finder's little furry head that lifted like his ears told him to. And then it was the rustling of leaves and branches behind them both that sung their song.

What is it? Mateo meant to say allowed. But his body froze, unlike Finder who spun in place and let out his little screech.

But Finder never moved forward and never moved back. He simply stood in place, waiting for whatever it was to make the first move. Mateo followed his lead. It was until Finder let his back loosen that Mateo turned to face the unknown.

Remy Price.

"What are you doing here?" Mateo asked knowingly that he didn't have to.

"You're on the search for my mom, no?"

"You don't get to ask questions until you've answered mine."

Remy looked about as if she were on a hiking trip. "I wanted to see what you turned up."

I can't get angry with her. "You should not have come. Where were you, my trunk?"

"Yeah, I broke the lock."

"You could have flung out!" His tone took control while Finder laid down on a fluffy pile of leaves.

"I stayed to the corner where some of the roof—"

"It doesn't matter, if anything were to happen to you because of me, I'd never forgive myself."

"It would have been on me."

Mateo ran his fingers through his haircut that sprouted droplet after droplet of sweat. "I'm bringing you home."

"I won't go."

"You're going to be difficult?"

"Yes." The auburn hair and stubbornness did nothing but remind him Leona.

"Why? There's no reason to do this."

"Because I need to see what you find with my own eyes. If it turns out bad, then I'd never find out."

Mateo couldn't argue that, but he could still lie. "That's not true."

"Yes it is."

"I don't have time to argue with you. I want to find your mother and be done with this. I'm taking you back."

"I'll run."

Fuck. "And I'll catch you."

"You could try, or you could just let me go with you. I don't see the harm in it, and it'll save you some sweat. I had a nice nap here. I promise you, you won't catch me."

Mateo wiped the sweat with a small towel from his back pocket, guzzling down half a bottle of water to bide himself some thought time. "Fine, but there's no guarantee that we'll even find anything, and you're to call Leona and let her know what you did."

After Remy's posture sunk, Mateo extended her his phone.

At least Finder isn't taking any breaks. Mateo thought, observing the second water bottle that he relinquished to Remy in an attempt to keep her body hydrated. There was a quarter left of the clear time reminder swishing around in the bottle. Remy didn't pay any mind to the heat though, instead she her focus on Finder. Focus it was. She was determined, despite the no breaks, despite the sun that reminded warm even during it's sunset and despite the fact that they may just end up at the end of a forest with nothing to show for it.

"If you start getting too tired I'll carry you on my back." Mateo finally said.

"I'm okay." The rubber of her soles marched through the grass and leaves in a war serenade of perseverance. She wasn't going to give up anytime soon he realized.

It was such on the contrary to the way Leona had viewed the situation. Yet both Price sisters' displayed an equal amount of hard-headedness.

The only reason I'm here is because of this girl. And now she's by my side with this. "You're a lot like Leona." Mateo said to the back of the four and a half foot tall Remy."

"I'm less whiny."

Mateo laughed. "You also really want to find your mother."

"She doesn't."

"I know. That wasn't what I was going to say next."

"You were going to ask me why I want to find her so bad?"

"Yeah."

"Because I'm her daughter and I love my mom. That's it. There's nothing else more to it. But I wanted to make sure that I see this myself."

Mateo nearly tripped over a fallen branch trying to keep up with Remy's lightning legs. Finder wasn't making it any easier. "You're mature for eleven."

"Unfortunately."

"Why do you say that?"

"Because If I was immature I'd be home playing with my Barbies." Remy jumped over a moderately sized rocked, one which Mateo took his time stepping over. "You're not as terrible as you seem from far away."

"What do you mean?"

Just then Finder stopped. He sniffed at the ground and then let out three screeches. Remy spun around to give Mateo concern. When going to touch Finder he jumped from Mateo' hand, taking steps back and lapsing into a familiar stance. It was the same one he took right before ending the hitmen back at home.

Without warning, Finder leapt into the air, over Remy's head, causing her to tumble to the ground. Mateo sent his body to shield hers, the sounds behind him where enough to embrace that instinct.

"What's happening?" Mateo asked in a push-up stance.

"I don't I can't see. I think my leg is bleeding."

From the pain on Remy's face, Mateo didn't doubt it. When jolted his head down there where blood soaked leaves next to her torn pant leg. "Crap."

That's when the sounds behind him stopped, and Finder sauntered his way back into Mateo' field of vision. His chin matched her leg.

When Mateo made it to his feet, the bloody jagged rock was what he noticed first and then a dead crow behind him.

"A crow? That's what you stopped for?!" Mateo said to the jittery ball of fur.

"He is a fox after all." Remy sat upright, giving her leg a disappointed scowl.

"We have to get that tied up or it's going to get infected."

Finder started to walk, sniffing the ground as he went.

"Quickly. He's beginning to search again." Remy said, bringing herself to her feet.

"I think it's best we turn back."

Remy salvaged the ground, picking through little shrubs and moving braches and dusting off bark. When she was done she ended up with a giant leaf. Removing a shoelace and dousing her leg in her remaining water, she firmly tied the bright green piece of nature around her wound and ripped off the dangling hunk of fabric which used to be the lower half of her jeans. "We're pushing forward."

"Where did you learn how to make a tourniquet?"

"My dad. Let's go."

The end of the forest, better yet the end of Finder's search wasn't as close as Mateo had hoped. Twenty minutes had gone by. That had been the last time he checked the time. Since then Remy was on his back, thin, peach fuzz covered arms wrapped around his neck. For whatever reason, it made him miss Leona and made him feel closer to her at the same time.

"You alright?" He asked.

"Yup."

"I'm sorry that your life's been rough." The exhaustion tickled his emotions.

"You don't know the half of it." Remy joked. "When you used to fight, didn't you ever worry about dying?"

Mateo paused and hoisted Remy further up on his back. "Not when I was younger no."

"Why?"

"I don't know. I guess when you feel like there's nothing at the end of the story you don't want to read it." Leona popped into his head after that; her unapologetic smile partnered with those long curls. It was enough to give him a second wind.

"I see."

"Why do you ask?"

"I don't know."

It almost felt like a mirage seeing the dense forest disappear before his eyes.

"Houses!" Remy yelled. "Why couldn't you just drive around the forest?"

"Because I didn't know if there was a cabin or something in the middle. Not like I expected you to be on my back."

Remy took the hint and jumped off, not even making a slight grunt at the mercy of her scabbed leg. Finder's legs were working just as well because at the sight of the neat row of houses, Finder jetted off, zoomed across the street, skipped four of them and perched himself on the stoop of a bricked two story family home.

"You think that's it?" Remy asked.

"I don't see any reason why it would be unless Finder has nice taste in real estate."

When they made it down the hill and across the street like Finder, the little red fox waited as they took their time passing houses. Mateo stopped. Two steps later Remy stopped as well.

"What is it?" She asked.

"If your mother is in there, we don't have a game plan here, we're just going in blind."

"So?"

"So, I haven't thought about what to do if we find her."

Remy tightened her pony-tail. "I guess we wait to see what she says first."

She's eleven, she doesn't get how weird this is. "Your mom may not want to be found."

If sarcasm had a face, Remy was wearing it. "Ya think? That's why we're here." Turning around with no remorse, Remy brought herself to the stoop where Finder sat so quickly that Mateo had to shuffle his way over.

Remy knocked.

There was nothing.

Remy glanced at Mateo.

Mateo knocked.

There was nothing.

Mateo knocked again,

There was the faintest of sounds beyond the door; footsteps, or things being moved. Without a doubt, there was life inside. Mateo nudged Remy behind himself, there were footsteps, they got closer and heavier to the door by the second. When the oak rectangle finally swung open, Mateo had wished it never had, for he knew exactly what he had found.

There will be no hiding this with Remy here, this will be handled today and it's going to fall on my shoulders. Mateo took a long blink and then opened them back up to the wild hair, the five-o'clock shadow and the beer belly—Hank Robinson. *Say something to this fucker.*

"Where's Liz?"

Hank's face scrunched like old leather with eyes that fell past Mateo and straight to Remy. "You're an idiot for bringing her here…but not more of an idiot than someone else I know."

And there she was in the room behind him, with the straightest red hair Mateo had ever known along with those bitter looking reading glasses that he grew to loathe. Liz Price was the woman who filled Leona's ears monster stories about Mateo. And Hank, Hank was the monster. The monster who took advantage of a widow and then beat the living snot out of her when she came to her senses.

"You see this?!" Hank yelled. "They found you just like I said they would."

"Mom." Remy said while inching closer.

"You ain't coming into my house. Your mother don't want you."

Remy halted.

"Ay watch it man, you don't have to talk to her like that."

"Go away. Please." Liz's voice could have been a ghosts' shocking in its existence.

Mateo knew he could hide his own shock, the unexpected situation had made his face butter and now there was his girl-friends' sister that he had to somehow sugar coat for. *She had to have heard that.* "How can you just leave your daughters like this?"

The door shut.

And then locked.

And then locked again.

Behind Mateo stood someone he had no explanation for, and no way to make it better. *What would Aunt Rosa say?*

Remy had her back turned, an arm clearly was wiping away what she wanted to conceal from her face.

"Hey, it's not your fault." Mateo wanted to cry himself.

"I know," She said with a little blubber.

"No I mean it—"

When Remy turned around, she was ice. Not a drop of a tear resided on the eleven year-old. Not a whimper of the lips or quiver of her cheekbones. Before Mateo could make a move she was knocking on the door again.

Fork in the Road

It wasn't in the car. It wasn't anywhere on the floor. It wasn't in her bag, or underneath the napkins on the coffee table or in the bathroom.

"I've never lost my phone. I've already lost a sister now my fucking phone. What else?! What else is going to happen to me? Are you going to vanish too?" Leona was first talking to the air with her hands like it were a Broadway play, she had finished on Aunt Betty.

"The police should be here any minute dear, we can report your phone missing."

That was stupid Leona knew, her aunt wasn't in the right frame of mind. *She lost Remy, I'd be a fucking wreck too. I can't deal with this.* "She's not the type to run away, I had my phone on the way here." *I'm not making sense.*

Cold thin hands enlightened Leona's sweaty clammy ones. "I know this is all scary, but God will figure this out I promise. You need to relax. It'll all be okay."

The word God was like a bumble bee stinging her ear. The sentiment was nice but Leona was nowhere near relaxing. To rid herself of Betty's piety she excused herself into the living room where Emma sat all too quietly.

"Why are you so calm?"

"Because I found your phone." Emma held the thing out but when Leona went to grab it she snatched her hand away. "Remy went with Mateo. She snuck into his trunk. I called off the police."

"What? Give me my phone."

"No, you have to promise not to call Remy back and to leave them on their journey."

"Who are you an old Pokémon master? I'll do whatever I want. Why did you let me fucking bug out, why did you let aunt Betty call the police? What the fuck is wrong with you?!"

"I had to bide time, Mateo wanted to bring Remy back."

"He should have."

"Why? So there's no witness to what Mateo finds? I wouldn't trust that, no offense, especially after what you saw."

"Excuse me? Leona took two steps forward.

"Um, so I didn't lose Remy?" Aunt Betty interjected.

"No." Both girls said simultaneously.

That's when Leona took a deep breath. *I don't know who to be mad at. Emma's right, it's not Noelle's fault, I kissed Trevor. It's like, both Mateo and I are wrong.*

"What?" Emma asked.

"Yeah sweetheart, what is it?"

"I don't know what to feel, somehow I feel like this is all my fault, everything."

"No dear,"

"Yeah, if anything, life just shows that everyone's a little wrong."

"My boyfriend cheated on me." Leona lifted her head to an already overwhelmed and spaced out Betty.

"Oh dear." She shut her eyes, resting her head on the door-frame. And then, she was on the floor.

Emma beat Leona to her spaghetti-like body as it laid motionless between rooms.

"Oh my god," Emma cried, her head like a squirrel.

"Fuck fuck fuck fuck, wake up please," Leona crouched before her feeling her pulse. "Call 911 back immediately."

"They won't get here in time you can drive faster." Emma's heavy black makeup streamed down her face as Leona hoisted Betty over her4 shoulder.

The car blew red after red, nearly clipped several cars and spared civilians who could have lost their lives if Leona hadn't been a better driver.

"Keep an eye out for ambulances." Leona said.

"What if we should have called 911?"

"We should have, but I'm quicker. Is she still breathing?"

"Yeah," Emma was still crying.

Three cars ahead at the light, Leona spotted the red and white square savior sitting at the light. Without hesitation she jumped the sidewalk divider and drove atop the narrow strip of pavement, running over small trees and bushes to get ahead of traffic. Finally, the blue and reds were in her rear-view, two of them. By the time the squad cars were feet away, Leona was already knocking on the window of the ambulance.

Emma opened both passenger seat doors and stepped out, the police had their guns drawn, the paramedics ran to the back of the car. Leona never shifted her attention from Betty, who now had a stranger ripping open her shirt and pounding away at her chest. Emma screamed as the handcuffs went around her own wrists. But it wasn't because of those, it was seeing the sight of Betty's bare breasted chest extend into the air as two electrolyzed pads pressed down.

The concrete was cold and warm against Leona's face and the jagged edges scrapped against her face shutting one eye. But she never stopped watching her aunt. *Please be okay.*

She thought, as the cold steel of the handcuffs slapped down against her wrists.

Inside the jail cell Leona and Emma sat on the unforgiving wooden bench together. Nothing but a sink and toilet presented them company. Emma was an empty vessel, never showing any sign that she was locked away in a cell, as if the whole thing had been the mundane part of her day. Leona surveyed the ugly stone box, there was nothing else to do. It had been maybe twenty minutes, and occasionally she would send her cousin a glance just to see what facial expression she wore. Beyond neutral it was, even worse that her daily mug.

"She's going to be okay, people faint sometimes…she's under a lot of pressure."

"People who faint don't often need CPR or medical equipment like that, that was cardiac arrest. I'm not stupid."

Leona bit her lip. "You don't know that, I never said you were stupid."

"Okay."

A page out of Mateo' book: the unemotional one-word answer. Leona's leg shook like a martini mixer. Patience had already been non-existent, but somehow the leg stopped and empathy walked in.

"It's easy to think negatively when you're in a jail cell."

"Why am I in here when you were the one speeding?"

"I don't know, that's not the point. Listen to what I'm saying, this will all blow over. Aunt Betty is probably awake right now pissed off that her nieces are in jail. I don't want you upset."

Emma moved not an eyelash. "How is it that your sister has cancer, your aunt could be dead, you're in jail and your boyfriend cheated on you but you're helping me right now?"

"Maybe I'm not as shallow and stupid as everyone thinks."

Silence.

"What are you going to do about Mateo?"

"It never happened."

"You and him?" Emma finally cocked her head.

"No, Noelle and him. I don't want to think about it. We all fuck up."

Trevor.

"You didn't have sex with Trevor, if you're thinking that you two are even or something—you're not."

"I don't think we are, maybe a little. I don't know…I can't be mad at him. I just know him. I know it's not him."

"You're lying to yourself. I don't necessarily want to see you bottle this up."

"Is that your way of saying you care?"

"No chick-flick moments please. This isn't a romance novel."

"I just can't." Leona brought herself to the bars, squeezing the cold steel, feeling the little prickles on the surface. "No matter what, something doesn't let me free from his grasp. No matter how bad he is—I love him."

"But just like I'm in here with you for something you did, love affects the ones around you. And when he hurts you, he'll hurt them. I'm never wrong."

"I can't see that happening, this is my relationship."

"They don't call it a ship because it can only carry two people."

Leona squeezed once more, with both hands. The thoughts of Mateo and Noelle together haunted, they screamed in her mental face. Over and over again, his hands once reserved for her own, ran all over that girl's body. The moans, the grunts, the nails in his back. *Why did I watch it?*

"When do you think we'll be out of here?" Emma asked.

"I don't know. I honestly didn't think we'd be in here this long."

"Don't we get one phone call?"

Leona faced her cousin like her idea had telekinesis. "Did you bring your phone?"

"Even if I had they would have confiscated it. They felt my nipples."

"I know, they felt mine too and for a woman, chick had some fuckin calices on her hands."

"So we don't have any phone numbers?"

"I have one memorized." Leona then called an officer over.

The officer who allowed the phone call had been the good cop it seemed because the crew-cut sporting flat-top of an ex-soldier who couldn't let go of his past explained things to them both like an asshole.

"What do you mean Monday?" Leona snapped.

"Monday, it follows Sunday; the start of the five-day work week."

Leona pictured a dash, an underscore and another dash; the text response she'd send to Mateo when he was being too sarcastic. "But it's Friday, we're not staying here a whole weekend."

"Nome city law doesn't like reckless driving. Up to forty-five years for under the influence, Sara's law: up to life for manslaughter while on the phone. In your case, reckless driving with no variable, that's under judge's opinion."

How long is he going to lecture me? "So there's seriously no wriggle room to be out today?"

"It's not looking like that ma'am. Hands off the bars please."

Leona's heart sunk deep. Three days in a cell for reckless driving had to be unconstitutional, she hoped. The wheels spun in her head for anyway to not endure such a punishment but the mask she wore for Emma was far more confident in that idea that what laid under it.

"Can I at least call the hospital to check on my aunt?" Leona asked the robot raised cop.

"You should have thought about that before you went joy-riding."

"Sit down Emma," she said after hearing fabric move too quickly behind her. "I wouldn't have been *joy-riding* if it hadn't been for my dying aunt in the back."

"If I was your aunt and had to deal with your aunt I'd be dying too." The officer's mouth was as straight as his name plate. *Pantaleo* it read.

"Excuse me?"

"You heard me."

"Fuck you,"

Pantaleo without warning, began to bang against the bars and yell "Sit down and shut up." Leona's heart rose back to where it belonged and did more jumping-jacks she had ever done in her entire life.

"Hey! What in the holy hell are you doing to my girls?" A voice echoed throughout the precinct and into the cell. For the briefest of moments Leona had thought it was her father. "Put that damn cock-replacement away and shut your mouth." The tall-caramel skinned Mr. Torres strutted to the officer wrapped tightly in a dark-blue suit followed by his daughter Lauren.

"D.A Torres I beg your—"

"Oh shut up," Torres smiled at Leona and shot Emma a look, jolting his head back in slight terror. "What happened to Remy?!"

The three girl's entered Nome University hospital thanks to five-hundred dollars and a very lenient impound lot supervisor. Leona's car had minor dents to the front and way too many leaves stuck to the windshield, but it was her aunt that concerned her.

"I'm here to see Lucile Becks, she was just admitted a few hours ago."

"And who are you?" The desk clerk asked, glued to a computer.

"Her niece, this is her other niece and my friend."

"The friend will have to stay down here, you two are welcome to go up. Just sign in here and give me your IDs."

To the girls' surprise, sitting straight up in her bed, with skin glowing as if she had just come from a spa was Betty, nibbling away on a Pricewich. Bright were here eyes, wide was her smile.

"You guys are late." Betty said, pumpernickel bread filling her cheeks. "I thought maybe you had forgot I was here."

Leona's mouth had begun to go dry with how long it fell open. Luckily Emma was there to be her voice.

But Emma had nothing either. It was all too shocking.

"Okay, I understand you girls are shaken. But I don't want you to be, I'm fine."

"We just saw your heart stop." Emma said.

"You were unconscious with para—"

"Shhhhhhhh, must we always live in the past." Sipping from a little plastic cup, Betty shut her eyes while gulping down whatever it was inside of it. After the bottom clapped the table she continued. "Instead of surprise, just be happy."

"We are." Leona said. "Just didn't expect you to be so lively."

"Well I am."

"What happened?" Leona took a seat aside her bed, her legs could handle no more. Emma followed.

"A mini stroke. I'm fine."

"Um, no…that's—"

"Leona, I'm alive. Which means I'm fine. If you're alive you're fine."

She's grateful. Maybe a little scare. "Okay well if you want to talk about it Emma and I are here."

"I've spoken enough about it with the doctor's and your uncle Charlie I'd rather help you with what you're feeling."

Emma was as clueless as Leona on what she meant, lifting one of those perfectly done up brows of hers.

"I don't follow."

"Mateo. What he did to you."

"Oh that, yeah this isn't the time or place for that." Leona went to the window, down below there were three people smoking by a gate across from a falafel truck.

"You haven't built that place yet, nor are you going to sweetheart."

"I tried to tell her that." Emma injected.

"Both of you stop, what ever happened to forgive and forget? Love over all. I know him and I just know him. I shouldn't even be having this discussion when my aunt is hold up in a hospital bed. You don't see the ridiculousness to that?"

"I don't because you're my niece and I love you and it takes my mind off the fact that I just had a stroke. How many times are you going to use that excuse—I know him?"

"Enough!"

If they were all unaware of birds being outside the window, they were aware now because all that filled the room was chirping. And then the blood in Leona's vessels thickened.

"What do you have over Noelle that she gave you that tape? That she went out of her fucking way to find out that my sister has cancer?"

"Are you talking to me?" Emma asked with words that weighed a feather.

"Yes."

"What is this about? Whose Noelle?" Betty shifted in her bed.

"I'll explain that later, what I want right now is to know how my little cousin who only met a girl once was able to blackmail her and rid her from my life."

"Maybe you should be thanking me instead of badgering me."

"Girls please."

"Let's step out for a minute Emma."

And that they did, against Betty's wishes and to the melody of Emma's black boots. The hospital hallway had been too crowded, so they went outside to the crisp and dry summer humidity.

"You're going to answer me Emma, you owe me that much."

"I don't owe you anything. Hell, I've given you more than you should have had. You already live in a fantasy world. I should have just let you stay in an even stupider one."

Leona grinded her teeth. "Excuse me?"

"You heard me, and frankly, the girl is gone from your life. Leave it that way, I made a vow to keep her stuff in the dark. I don't go back on my word."

"I'm your cousin, she doesn't deserve to have privacy after everything she's put me through."

Emma giftwrapped Leona an astonished head-shake. "Finding out that your little sister has cancer, fessing up that Mateo cheated on you, doing her best to be your friend. She's not the villain, if anyone is—"

"Don't say it. This conversation is over then. Keep it to yourself I guess."

"You're angry, and that's okay. But it's hard for me to be sympathetic with you. You make such stupid decisions."

Is she provoking me? "I said this conversation is over."

"Mateo cheated on you with another girl, your mom left you, your aunt had a stroke because of Mateo. Doesn't it all bother you?"

"Shut up Emma," Leona began to walk away.

"It's depressing to think that all the love you shared with Mateo goes down the drain or more importantly into another girl's vagina. All the stuff you thought was special—"

"Stop it..." There were the tears.

"His hands all over her body,"

"Emma, please..." She would not turn to face her.

"How can you cuddle with someone when you know they're cuddle with anyone. Who are you going to really turn to at night when thinking about how your little sister has cancer."

Like a bullet Leona spun around and ran at Emma, the moisture flying from her face, her feet beating the pavement as hard as she wanted to beat her cousin.

"Hit me!"

Leona continued to run, and then she was on the ground, arm scraped heavily to the point where she could immediately sense the blood. On top of her with earrings that glistened in the sun was Lauren, pissed off beyond belief. When their eyes met, Leona began to ball.

"He cheated on me," She cried. "He cheated...." And that continued even when Lauren held her head in her against her chest, lapsing into cries about Remy and her mother–it all came out."

"It's okay, we're here." Lauren whispered as Emma kneeled down beside them.

"I'm sorry," Leona said. "I'm sorry for everything."

"Prove it." Lauren said.

"How?"

"Leave Mateo."

The Mother Who Wasn't

They faced each other like cowboy's in the old west. The tall mother was looking at a miniature version of herself, except this version was pure. The only movement around the tense motionless standoff was Hank, who rubbed his fat hands one too many times over his balding scalp.

"Enough! What're we gonna stand here all day like idiots? These people shouldn't even be in my house."

"Shut up Hank. I want to hear what my daughter has to say."

"You left."

"I did."

"Why?"

That's when Liz Price broke her stillness and walked away.

"She wanted me, that's why. I made her happy. You people think I was the problem." Hank moved like he was performing an act on Broadway. Mateo wondered what drugs were in his system.

"That's not true." Liz said.

"What?" Hank Ceased his theatrics. "You wanna run that by me again?"

"I needed to get away, I couldn't—"

Before the sentence finished Hank had smacker clean across the face. Without hesitation Remy ducked behind Mateo who had been sitting down but now was running around the dining room table.

"Disrespect me again!" Hank yelled. Mateo wasn't having it. Or at least his fists weren't having it.

"Mateo!" Remy Screamed.

Something in Remy's voice had sent Leona's into his ears. His hands red as red wine cracked against nose, cracked against cheek-bone and cracked against skull. Hank was not the fight that he had ever anticipated, it was one-sided.

But then, the wild car struck against Mateo' spine. It was a tall skyscraper that had collapsed against his back, or at least that's what it felt like. When his eyes left the six-foot tall tub of bloody fat it caught the tail end of a baseball bat cracking against his forearm which, was now surely broken.

"I knew you were a piece of shit," Liz said clear enough that Mateo' ears continued to replay her words.

The one sight Mateo prayed he would not have to see was Remy in-between the melee. That happened. With his good and a little help from his bad, Mateo shoved Remy into the corner of the room. She might have flown about four feet and hit her shoulder, but she was away from where the real danger was happening.

I have to get a hold on this situation. A straight back was all Mateo could muster at the moment. Liz Price's was straight, her forehead had not a drip of sweat.

"Leave him alone!" Remy yelled.

The bat swung anyway, missing the top of Mateo' ducking head by a few inches. Behind himself was an unknown. The whereabouts of Hank Robinson was also an unknown. Those two variables put a pit in his stomach.

The cocking of a gun was all the answers he needed, ignoring the bat before him and bolting to the man wielding the nine-millimeter behind him.

One shot.

Missed.

The second never happened because now Mateo was wrestling the bear-like man for the weapon. Against his ribs the bat struck, enough times where Mateo finally felt fear. Those stopped, and then it was that bear-grip of an obstacle—getting the gun from Hank's hands.

Why did the bat stop? Mateo wondered.

Pinning Hank's gun arm against the wall, Mateo cocked his head around to a purple faced Remy on the floor. Around her neck was her mother's hands, drenched in falling tears.

"NOO!" Mateo screamed, the gun popped, the purple went to red and then to pink. *Witness,* flashed across Mateo' mind. And then the gun popped again. Hank hit the floor. Blood spatter into Mateo' eye's. Remy sat up against the wall and Finder ran into the house.

The blood was warm, sprinkling Mateo' forehead in what felt like hugging a corpse. Behind him was a dead man. In front of him was a fox and a young girl holding her dead mother. There were no tears on her face and no expression. There were just caMichaelrous eyes.

"She was going to kill you." Mateo said.

"I know."

Drooping the gun, he wiped the blood from his face and sat in front of them both. The slightest of quivers moved Remy's lips and Mateo fell to his rear end, leaning up against the wall. Remy pushed her mother to the floor gently, placing her on her back to probably cover the bullet hole. The woman's dead eyes were worse though. The guilt, the horror and the shame swam through Mateo' veins. It all dried up when Remy curled herself on his lap, hugging him like Leona would on most nights. As much pain as his arm dished out, he wrapped both of them around her and pulled her in closer.

"I lost a mom,"

"I'm sorry, I really am."

"But gained a big brother."

The Devil's Little Secret

The call was brief but enough to let Leona know her little sister and Mateo had turned up nothing. It didn't surprise Leona one bit: a wild goose chase lead by a tiny fox leading to a dead end. At least Remy had gotten a sense of exploration. And Mateo, well he wasn't coming back to roses.

Before facing two of the most important people in her life, her mentally drained body cast a shadow over a headstone. The cold slab of rock, emotionless yet emotion provoking never failed to send her warmth. Patrick Price still did his duty after death, holding the rank as first important in his daughter's life.

The solace was welcoming. The peace was euphoric. The now charred white house up on the hill caught her attention and cloaked itself over her in mimicry. She could relate to it. Wounded, beat-up, but still standing, it was the only change in the cemetery. Like a mirror almost. Closed doors, windows that revealed nothing, the white paint so pretty yet damaged.

I'm fucking relating myself to a house.

"Dad, I'm sorry." Blank space was what filled her head, emotions are what filled her chest. "I don't even know what I'm apologizing for, but I feel like I've fucked up. If you're looking down on me, you can't be proud. I've been a mess for so long. I've accomplished nothing and I'm sorry. I'm trying to be the hero in this story, but it's all too much. I'm selfish, weak minded, reckless, I don't know how you can be proud of that. I'm just sorry."

Resting against his headstone now was a red rose, released from Leona's cold fingers. Her back was straighter than it's vine, her chin to the sky, a dark and gloomy space ready to cry at any moment.

"I can't come here anymore dad. Not until I feel like I deserve to see you. I can't keep facing you when my life continues to be nothing but bad decision after bad decision. Fuck up after fuck up, I can't. You deserve53 a better daughter. And I'm not saying all this to get down myself, I'll be better. I promise. But until then, I'm sorry."

Walls of peeling paint, staircase bannisters held together with cheap glue; Leona's feet watched where they fell. If the step wasn't covered in gum, cigarette butts rested. Out the second floor stairwell window the parking lot down below was depressing. Faded concrete with barbed wire separating it from the neighborhood, the land had no trouble pushing away eyes.

When Leona reached the door there were still fourth of July decorations clinging on for dear life with scotch tape, which made knocking a gingerly event.

Noelle wasn't at all happy to see her.

"Don't close the door." Leona said as the door almost shut. "We need to talk."

"There's nothing to talk about, your cousin got her way, saved the day. I forfeit." The door swung again and Leona's size eight jumped in between.

"Just listen…please."

Noelle's apartment was seemingly the nicest most well put together spot in the entire building. It was far contrast from what

Leona had expected; dank, clothes everywhere, condoms on the floor. Instead there laid luggage, two purses and a duffle bag.

"Taking a trip?" Leona asked.

"I'm moving in with my dad over in Nugent."

"That's at the bottom of Sugenta."

"Yeah, I need to get away from here." Noelle said, folding one of her giant bras and neatly placing it atop an already stuffed bag.

"Why such a drastic move? What is it that my cousin had over you?"

"Nothing, it doesn't matter. If I wanted to talk about it I wouldn't be packing."

"Okay, then tell me about when Mateo cheated."

"How are you not punching me in the face for that?" Noelle stopped packing.

"I can't blame you for wanting him. I mean, I could but he's the real shit head in the situation."

"I'm surprised you see it that way."

"So tell, when did it happen?"

"After his suicide attempt. He hated himself, I guess he felt ashamed to release everything on you so the sex was his way of getting it out."

"I'm sorry he used you."

"It's not using if the user is under the impression that the used is okay with it. It wasn't until after that I got emotional."

The thought of it all sickened Leona, her breakfast was aching to come back up. "Was it an ongoing thing?"

"It happened three times after the attempt, but every time I knew it wasn't really him. But I hoped it would break you two up."

Ignoring Mateo' actions, Leona pounced on that statement. "So you admit, this whole time you've been trying to break us up?"

"I wouldn't call it that, I'd call it expediting the inevitable." She went back to packing, shamelessly holding her thongs up to fold.

"What you call the inevitable, isn't reality."

"So you're staying with him despite the cheating?"

"I don't know, that's not what I came here for."

"Let me give you a piece of advice." Zipping the square bag all around and straightening her back, Noelle said, "When it comes to dating you have to pretend your life is a romance novel. You can either be the dumb, selfish girl who needs bathes in what's bad for her; ignoring the one's around her to sate her own guilty pleasures. Or you can be the self-reliant woman who gets her shit together and waits until good guys don't bore her. You're not going to change Mateo and it'll only get worse for you. Believe me."

"Then why do you want him so bad?"

"I don't." It almost tripped coming from the girl's mouth. Her hand nearly covered it like she had burped.

"You're not making sense."

"I wanted you." Their eyes met, but Leona's fell to the floor and back.

"What?"

"That's what your cousin had over me. She figured it out and I couldn't deny it." Now Noelle was the bashful one, folding a shirt that had already been folded.

"All this time...you wanted me?"

"You don't have to make me spell it out."

"Why didn't you just tell me?"

"Fear of losing you. But I did that anyway."

The reel started rolling in Leona's mind. "The naked pictures with Michael...."

"Make sure you never got back with him."

"Trevor?"

"That was mainly all you."

"My friendship with Lauren?"

"Jealousy."

"Fucking Mateo….were you even attracted?"

"I'm Bi, so yeah." She laughed. "Sorry."

"You did all this shit, just to be with me?" As crazy as it was, there was enough sentiment to make Leona feel loved. *Is this what Stockholm syndrome feels like?*

"Yeah, believe it or not. I'm not the villain in your romance novel."

"Then who is?"

"You don't want me to answer that."

And she didn't. One too many people considered Mateo to be trash, hearing it now from the one girl who had been known to obsess over him for the past year was way too ridiculous. "I guess this is goodbye then."

"Yes, I do feel better that you know. Can I ask you something?" There was a playfulness to her tone, a different posture that eliminated tension but also served it.

"Yeah sure."

"Since I'm like…leaving forever…can I like kiss you once?"

It was how humble, innocent and honest Noelle Santiago was which made Leona consider it. "For what? To appease the male audience of my novel who want to see us shipped?" Leona laughed.

"No, so that I have something to remember you by other than this entire shitty conversation."

"I've never kissed a girl before,"

"Now you're making it sound like a porno," Noelle took two steps to Leona and grabbed her by the back of her head. She could feel her fingers swim through her curls. And then her lips touched down, soft, aggressive and direct. It was when her tongue came into play that Leona gave it two seconds and pulled off. Once it was over Noelle went back to packing. "You're free to go now."

"Thanks for being honest with me." Leona made for the door.

"Of course, good luck with everything and remember what I said."

"I will."

"Was it as bad as you thought it would be?"

It took Leona a second to figure out what she meant, "No, I get why guys want to fuck us."

"Does that mean you'd fuck me?"

"I'd fuck Lauren first." She laughed and stuck her tongue out.

Later that night, after seeing an overly quiet Remy, scraped and bruised from a fall she played off like it were nothing, Leona chose to save the cancer talk for another day. Today she argued and won; instead of relaxing at Mateo' they spent the darkest part of the night in the back of his Mercedes on the same street where they first kissed. Mateo had wanted to lounge on his couch with the television as a silence filler.

"We haven't been here in like a year, after everything that's happened, it's cute." Leona said, snuggled atop his chest.

"It's unnecessary, my arm hurts."

But Leona held no empathy, falling in a forest right after Remy was his own doing. "Toughen up, you sound worse than me."

"You're avoiding everything."

He knows me like no one else. "Because, getting my mother's ashes isn't the happiest thing to think about."

"You haven't fuckin' asked me why, you ignored Remy… doesn't it matter at all? We busted our asses."

"You said Hank killed her." There wasn't an ounce of emotion behind her words.

"You're acting like a psychopath." Nudging her head from the open part of his button down, he sat himself up in the seat and sent his face to the window.

"I'm scared." Leona said.

"Scared of what?"

"To know the truth."

"You need the truth, it's the only thing that separates me anymore from good and bad."

"What do you mean?" *Is he actually going to tell me?*

"Leona, after my suicide attempt…I cheated on you with Noelle. I was weak," His words sped up, his eyes met hers like magnets. "I was stupid. I hated myself, I felt like I didn't deserve to be with you. I'm sorry I—"

The only sound filling the car now were their lips. Her hand sled down his stubbly cheek, grabbing his ear and going again. But pushed off.

"How can you forgive that?" He asked.

"I don't know, because I love you." She kissed him again, doing her best to keep her cheeks from touching his—they were running with tears.

"What is it?" He asked, never lifting his lips from hers.

"Nothing," Saying it only made it more emotional for herself. And then, her face was in his chest, an ear-piercing melody of screams and cries. Her only thought was her dead mother. Never getting to say goodbye, holding the urn with her ashes. She understood why Mateo wouldn't tell her over the phone.

"Why was she there in the first place?" She asked after a minute of tiring herself out.

"Hank kidnapped her. When Finder lead me to his house—"

"I don't want to know…what I do want to know is…" She took one last sniffle.

"How you got away with his murder?"

Without even looking at him, she knew his exact face. Like surprised stone. "How did you know I killed him?"

"Because knowing you, someone kills my mother you're killing them."

"Wait, before I tell something I need to know you're not hurt by me cheating that you know—it wasn't me being myself and I'd never do anything to hurt you like that. I mean it."

"The fact that you told me helps. I'm still upset, but I love you. Is that why you vanished?"

"Yes, I went to Anne's farm to run and try to change who I was, which only developed more problems."

"What do you mean?" She could feel herself falling asleep on his chest.

"Swanson turned out to be the head of the Nome City Family. After enemies killed his son, he asked me to join."

"What?" She was awake now.

"And I declined."

"And?"

"When you join you get to kill. You need one initiation kill to join. I didn't plan on killing Hank, but it was the only way to sweep it under the rug."

Grief. Fear. Sorrow. Fear. Fear. Fear for Mateo' life. "So… you're in?"

"That's why I bring it up, aside from being honest.…I made a mistake. And I don't know how to fix it."

And neither did she. But every second of not giving him an answer gave her guilt. "We'll figure it out. I'm sure there's a way out."

"When I was on Anne's farm, away from you, I missed you more than anything. I grew to appreciate you, and now I don't want to die or risk my life and all that. The NCF will kill me if I refuse them especially after they covered up my murders."

"Murders?"

"Murder. On the plus side, they promised to pay for your school, a house for us—"

"Stop, no. We'll figure this out. We're not building a life around mafia money. We've overcome everything else, we can overcome this."

"I don't want you involved or getting hurt."

"It's too late for that, they don't call it a ship because it only holds one person."

"I'm scared."

The words were alien coming from his powerful lips. He was a man, but also a boy. A boy who needed to be taken care of. Full of mistakes, flaws, uncontrolled emotions yet when she looked into his eyes with them looking back at hers, she saw love. Never in her life even on her father had she seen someone look at her like she were their oxygen. And it went both ways.

"I kissed Trevor."

"What?"

"Before we go against the mafia, you know to know that. We kissed one night. I don't remember where you were but yeah. I pushed him off."

"Okay." Angry stone this time.

"At least we didn't fuck and I didn't hide it from you for a…ye…while."

"I said okay, drop it."

Leona smacked him across the face. And then again. She stopped at a third time.

"What the fuck!" He said, clutching the swelling skin.

"Don't ever fucking cheat on me again and stop fucking making decisions without me. No more secrets you understand?"

"You're bi-polar."

"No, I just needed to get that out. I kinda let you get off too easy. I hate secrets."

"You won't have to deal with them anymore, I promise."

"No, I still have one more to deal with."

The Strongest Price

Two days had passed since Mateo wore his emotions on his sleeve, and still there was no answer swimming around in Leona's mind for him—the pool was empty. But the more important, pressing issue at hand was that of Remy's cancer, something as minor as aunt Betty made it out to be, yet it still felt like a ticking time bomb. *If only I knew where to begin. If only there weren't a million different things happening at once.* Leona thought, taking herself down the long narrow hallway on the second floor of aunt Betty's. The room ended the hall, previously a guest room, now occupied by Remy and Emma.

The door held a novelty sign *Mafia Parking*. Any other day it would have been cute, maybe even a little funny. Today, all it did was remind her that her boyfriend's life now belonged to a bunch of heartless men. There was light in between the door and the door frame, and Leona made sure to say hey on the way in, to not startle her little sister, who played tossed actions figures around for a change.

"Dad would be proud of you playing with boy toys." Leona said.

"That's sexist."

"My whole life is sexist, feminists hate me. Can I talk to you?"

Remy kept to tossing around the figures but found the time to utter "Yeah."

"Can you stop playing for a bit, please?"

It was quite a slam, but the eleven-year-old definitely appeared inconvenienced by her request. "What? Would it kill you to talk for a second?"

"Yeah because you never start a sentence off with asking can we speak unless it's something serious and dramatic. That's like the way you know the conversation is going to suck."

Leona couldn't argue that. "Okay, but it—*does sugar coat—she's right—whatever.* I just didn't want to jump right in is all." She sat down on the bed, much more comfortable than her own. With the headache stirring, she was tempted to lay down.

"What, about mom?"

Leona had forgot or at least put that in the back of her head. "Sure, we can talk about mom."

"That's not what you were going to talk about?"

"No,"

"Aunt Betty doesn't buy that it was a murder-suicide."

The two words were should have never had to come from her sister's mouth. "Did you see Mateo kill Hank?"

"Yeah. It was self-defense. He came at him."

Remy avoided looking at Leona when saying that. *She's lying.* "What really happened?"

"What did you originally want to speak to me about, I don't want to think about mom."

"Fine, I know you have a tumor. And I know you've been seeing doctors and I know aunt Betty has been hiding it, better yet—you've been hiding it."

Remy left the bed and threw one of the toys against the wall, smashing and knocking down a shelf on the wall which

held trophies and family pictures. Leona had expected something audible from Remy but she sat down the floor instead.

"You're allowed to talk about it, I'm your sister."

"I know."

"So…are you like scared?"

Nothing.

"What are you feeling?" Leona sat beside Remy, looking
for tears. Her face remained dry.

"I'm not going to die."

"I know you're not."

"No, I mean it. I won't die."

She copes like mom and dad combined. "But why you talk
about what's going on inside your head?"

"Because I don't want you worrying."

"It's already passed that—"

"Shhhhh, the one that needs talking to is Emma."

And then, like a lightbulb going off that also called her stupid,
the realization hit her full force. "Are you going to be okay?"

"I told you, I'm going to be fine."

"Okay." And she left her little sister to continue on playing
until the doorway surrounded.

"Leona,"

"Yeah Remy?"

"I'm scared."

Outside on aunt Betty's stoop, Emma poked at the steps
with a finger, the weather or the fact that overtime Leona had
seen a softer side of her cousin made her seem less dark sitting
under the summer sun.

"What are you doing?"

"Teasing the ants. They can lift ten times their weight, I
wonder if that applies to their stress too."

"I don't know." Leona sat next to her, wondering how she can still wear heavy black clothing despite the eighty-degree weather. "You don't ever mention your little sister."

Emma poked her finger a little harder. "I knew this would eventually come up." She rose and flatted out her pants. Leona grabbed her by the wrist and pulled here back down.

"Sit. Remy has the same thing your sister had doesn't she?"

"Similar."

"It's not the same, and Remy will pull through."

"I'm fine, I don't know why you're out here making this a thing."

"Because I know how close you've gotten with Remy, she's the reason you didn't want to go back."

"Shut up shut up shut up!" Emma screamed, jumping to her feet and doing her best to contain her flailing arms. How quick her makeup ran had to be a world-wide record. How quick Leona jumped up to give her a hug had to be another.

"Relax, relax," Leona said over cries. *I didn't think she'd budge that quickly.* "It's okay, she's going to be alright. I'm glad you're not bottling it up."

"I don't want to lose her,"

"Neither do I."

"Is everything okay?" Aunt Betty said, peering out from the doorway. "Why is she crying."

"Aunt Betty you should be resting." Leona said.

"Yeah I'm fine." Emma wiped the blackness from her cheeks.

"Is this about your mother?"

"No, about Remy."

"Oh," Betty stood in silence for a few seconds way to long where her eyes gave away all her cards.

Her sister is dead. Oh my god. I didn't even think of that. "A

"Are you alright?" Leona asked, giving Emma a glance. She caught on to it as well.

"Your mother always did the double-sniffle when she cried. Your grandfather's knee would always buckle at that, no matter how bad she was." Betty's voice grew more unstable at the end of her sentence. "I wish your uncle Charlie were back,"

Leona walked up the steps and wrapped her arms around Betty. The sniffles weren't late to arrive and the crying lasted a few good minutes.

"I could have helped her...if I had known what was going on...I would have drove there myself." Betty said.

"We all could have helped her, it's not your fault."

"She was a good mother, I always told her that."

Remy was now in the doorway. Without a word she joined in on the hugging, not long after did Emma join as well. And the four of them held each other, sharing tears and sharing a loss of blood.

"You're going to be okay Remy, you have us." Betty said.

"I know."

"We have each other, and that's all that matters." Leona added. "As long as we stick together, we'll be fine."

Sauntering by like someone who had spotted a live news broadcast was an old man who stopped dead in his tracks to gawk.

"Keep it moving grandpa." Leona said.

"I'd like a hug too." He said back, garbled and slurry.

"Okay I think hug time is over." Betty cleared her moisture with the back of her hand.

We'll all be okay. Leona thought. *Remy will be okay.*

Later that night Mateo smacked, he grabbed, he bit, he pulled, he made Leona swim in her own ego. Whether or not he had sex with Noelle, there was no question where his passion laid. There could be no denying it. The way he pulls her hair and says her name; even aside from sex, he was different with Leona Price. And she knew that.

He loves me,

The thought blared through her mind, briefer than a second,

He's misunderstood,

In and out he thrusted with her name mixed in with grunts and moans. Pulling out and turning her over he kissed, and then he was back inside. "I love you," He grunted. "I love you more than anything."

All she could do was kiss back, running her fingers through his hair, so soft, so stubbly. Her hands fell to his thick shoulders, bulging against every second he held himself up. His smell was what made her nails enter his back. His manhood was what made her scream his name.

And then, maybe twenty minutes later Mateo' eyes shut closed, his mouth fell open and his arms gave out. "Fuck Leona, fuck," Was what filled the room, along with her smile. It got her every time.

Mateo' chiseled arm and thick leg draped over her and the blanket draped over them both. He laid there a grown man in age but a boy at heart. Or at least with her he was, and that she didn't mind. To have the mafia after you and be as relaxed as a baby, Leona Price took the credit. Rubbing his head gently, running her fingernails up and down his back, there was a sense of fulfillment in his comfort. And that was enough to say nothing; enough to just lay there and feel as one.

"I love you." He mumbled out.

"Remember when I had to pry it out if you to say it first?"

"I was fuckin stupid."

"I'll agree with you on that one." She laughed and he craned his head to kiss her.

"I really am sorry for everything I've put you through."

Leona snuggled further down to meet him face to face, laying another kiss on him and then leaving her hand upon his chest."Shhh, I don't want to hear it. I'm happy because I have you."

"For now."

She could have smacked him. "Excuse me?"

"When I tell Swanson I don't want to work for him while I still owe him shit—he's not going to be happy."
"Remember when I was against you fighting and all that?"
"Yeah?"
"Well, you're going to fight. And you're going to win." Before he could say another word her lips were back on his, tongue in mouth. "Now fuck me again."

About the Author

A graduate of The New School's writing program in New York, Joseph Reilly was born in Brooklyn, and now considers himself a Staten Island transplant. He writes to bring his readers into relationships that some may relate to while others may not understand.

"It's easy to not understand why people stay in 'crazy' relationships. But everyone sees their partner through a different lens and if I can put that lens in front of my readers and help them to either understand better or create an empathy for characters then I feel like I did my part."

Writing superhero short stories for his little sister, Joseph loved reading and writing at an early age. But once Joseph, his sister and their grandmother got evicted from their Flatbush Brooklyn apartment, Joseph took a break from writing.

With life presenting a field of uncertainty, Joseph pursued uncertain careers to spite it, trying his hand at professional wrestling, stand-up comedy, and nearly joining the military. It was the death of a loved one, a bout of alcoholism, and an immense feeling of hopelessness that lead Joseph to penn his first piece of writing in nearly ten years, leading him to get a degree in the field. The rest is history.

Today, when Joseph isn't writing happy and sad love stories he's with his wife and two cats, probably reading a book or playing Nintendo.